The English Soil Society

TimN 12/05

The English Soil Society

stories

Tim Nickels

LASTIC
PRESS

ISBN number: 0-9548812-4-9

Printed by Blitzprint (www.blitzprint.com)
Cover photograph © Uncle Snuggles circa 1969
Cover Design by Dean Harkness
Typeset by Marie O'Regan

Published by:
Elastic Press
85 Gertrude Road
Norwich
UK

ElasticPress@elasticpress.com
www.elasticpress.com

For Charlotte, Lewis, Thom and Charlotte. And also to the memory of my friend, teacher – and first editor – Tim Wood.

To those writers, readers, family and friends who have helped me along this way of words: thank you.

Basil & Sybil; BBLBx; the late Kenneth Vye Bailey: Grahaeme Barrasford Young; Paul Beardsley; The Sisters Counihan; Andy Cox; Kevin Cullen; The Delayed Theatre Company; Trevor Denyer; Francesca, Simon and their 'puter; Philip Sidney Jennings; The Boy Kenworthy; Keith Matthews; Nik Morton; Manda & Chris Tooley Reed; Nick Royle; Salcombe's Pantomime People; The Smell of Wet Umbrellas; Michael Spencer; Anne Stevens; Conrad Williams; Peter Yates; and all Cassandrans everywhere.

And of course my special gratitude goes to Team Elastic: Marie O'Regan,Dean Harkness, Sandie Hook (that's her on the left) and my editor and herbal advisor, the quietly astounding Andrew Hook.

Table of contents

maybe

Carlo Frendly had diplomatic fingernails.

When he pressed the fingertips together – as if in prayer – they never met.

He pronounced the word 'compromise' in a very special way. His accent was flat and vague. "Let's talk," he might murmur down his mobile in a grey restaurant or lay-by. "Let's do lunch, Oscar. We can work out a *cant-promize* on the Latvian deal."

Carlo was heavily into Latvia. And any other -*vias*. And Polands and Ukraines. He had a carpet bag all packed for the Axis of Evil. When hell had frozen over and was safe to drive on, Carlo Frendly would appear in a glistening Humvee with a clutch of ballpens and contracts. The pens and contracts weren't as diplomatic as Carlo's untouching fingers. They touched quite a lot.

Carlo didn't have a wife or girl or boyfriend. His genitalia had shrunken under the trinity of caffeine, low finance and drinking the tap water in Moscow. He was offensive to women, but not gratuitously. A gratuity was a little something extra in Carlo's mind. Offensiveness was as free as sweat. Carlo had buckets. His singlets could re-salinate the North Sea.

In the parlance of popular literature, Carlo had associates not friends. He pronounced them 'asso-shits'. Carlo had a lot of women asso-shits. They didn't say much. He kept them tiny, silent and unclothed among the credit card pockets of his wallet.

The English Soil Society

Wit was as alien to Carlo as the concept of children and strawberry ice-cream: wit dwelt on another planet and the purchase of a telescope would have been *gratuitous*. He smirked at the Argentinean inflation rate; he might titter at the sight of hurricane damage beamed a thousand miles into his wall-hung TV. But wit – wit was a penguin flying through molasses in the mind of Carlo Frendly.

*

And so the letter arrived.

Carlo had returned to his glass studio on the Southbank at 2am after a trip to one of the newer Asiatic republics. The experience had been unusually harrowing: deals had not come easily and involved smuggling missile-ready uranium through Tajikistan. Carlo was in the habit of whiling away airline flights telling dirty jokes to stewardesses. But this time he'd spent most of the trip in the toilet: his hands stuffed into the miniature sucking washbasin, his fluorescently white features snarling at themselves in the mirror.

And here was the letter on the mat as he tumbled in during the tiny hours. Carlo Frendly never had letters sent to his home. His Post Office boxes flourished in such profusion that 1Gb of his electronic organiser was devoted to simply listing them.

He bent and picked the letter up. Buff envelope, rather blotchy typewritten address, postmark... obscured.

Carlo opened the envelope and a Czech beer. Packaged ambience cranked itself up on the CD. The letter was short, the paper one half of a white A4 sheet torn in two:

give your life so a million may live

No punctuation or capital letters, the same worn-out typeface. It might have been a letter from God. It might have been written on God's battered, blotchy, billion year-old typewriter by God Himself.

Carlo turned it over and held it up to the light, checking for celestial watermarks. He noticed that the last two words now spelt *evil yam*. Six months before, Carlo had been smuggling yams from Florida into Ukraine. The taste for yams in Kiev goes unrecorded: Carlo failed in his market research because he was too busy forcing North Miami punks to tunnel out the yams' insides; was too distracted with getting the punks' mothers to stuff up the space with crack cocaine. Carlo Frendly had done well, a glorious middleman bestriding the New and Old Worlds like a sweating colossus.

But Carlo was now experiencing difficulty bestriding the distance between his futon and his fridge.

As he huddled in the reflected light at 5am – the satellite porn wriggling on the wall as he gazed straight through it – Carlo experienced a realisation. He realised that if his diplomatic hands actually *did* come together – the fingers interlocking like pale uncertain worms – he might just be able to stop shaking.

*

give your life so a million may live

The letter still lay on the ebony coffee table as Carlo Frendly spluttered back to life with mid-morning make-over programmes. He pulled up the blinds. The sky was a dazzling beige, an apocalyptic overcast.

Carlo gurgled passion fruit juice and attempted to gather his thoughts for the day ahead. His toes caught an envelope as he padded past the front door.

God had been busy again.

Letter number two said:

really

His consciousness seemed to spiral away and return.

Carlo fell into a shirt, pulled on a trench coat with its weight of pagers and address books. He scrambled the combination of the front door and took the lift to the basement car park.

Carlo Frendly had a very long, very black German sports

saloon. He beeped it open, dis-alarmed the alarm and started the engine. The engine was soundless: a light vibration shivered through the steering wheel.

He sat in his humming universe and watched the digital clock on the dashboard. It was set an hour ahead on European Time. Carlo felt he was watching the future already as it carried on without him.

A gap had appeared in his life. The merest rill perhaps, the slightest stream of doubt. But what ocean lay pounding behind those two sheets of paper? What agency had slid inside Carlo Frendly's studied anonymity?

He looked out at the sign forbidding NAKED FLAMES AND THE FILLING OF PETROL TANKS. The red and yellow letters seemed to dance, change and take on new partners.

give your life
really

Despite his tumbling thoughts, Carlo had isolated the personal pith of the two communications; they hung like jewels when he closed his eyelids. Already *so that a million might live* had been discounted as a redundancy, a matter wholly concerned with others. Other people were *gratuitous* – extras with toes and souls...

His brain blurred, wandered, reconnected at the other end of the equation.

If he gave his life (really) a million *might* live.

Carlo went into spasm, knocking his knees against the steering column. Might... or *may*... Already, the uncertainty implicit in those two words dangled like the damp rope of a lifeboat.

"*May* live! *May* live!" Carlo was out of the car and capering like a waltzing rat.

"May! May! Live! Live!" He rolled about the upward-bound lift hand-jiving.

"Might! May!" His soft Italian pumps tried to tap back down the corridor to his apartment.

Carlo fell in through the doorway, his mind already sweeping away memories of the absurd letters, already planning the lunchtime assignation with Oscar at Butlers Wharf. He felt winded when he contemplated and attempted to analyse his fleeting concern with the unknown million. And Carlo might have been *concerned* for his concern. But in his euphoria he strolled by this bright dilemma, a blindfolded man in sunglasses.

The third letter was leaning against the empty beer bottle. God hadn't bothered with an envelope but He'd discovered punctuation:

two weeks. really

*

Carlo Frendly took to the air like a dark angel.

He soared over England in a Docklands shuttle bound for the West Country. The far-below fields resembled half-sheets of green A4; cattle and farm machinery seemed to form letters and words and threats without punctuation.

Rain lazed off the Channel as he stumbled with one of a dozen passports onto the Plymouth car ferry bound for the Continent.

Would the letters follow him? Like fiendish paper Concordes could they cross oceans? As Carlo looked down from the stern of the big boat at midnight, he imagined the wake as a foam bath of letters: a bath he could throw his sweaty-singleted body into... *so a million might live –*

Carlo snapped back, retching into wakefulness.

A young woman stood alone on the far side of the deck, looking down to where the waters were smoother and darker.

"Do it, darling," he leered over. "Don't *cant-promize*. Those dead sea-men are waiting for you-o-o..."

And as the woman turned away in disgust, Carlo realised that the comment hadn't been made altogether unkindly; that it represented a reaching out to the first in a million.

*

And so he travelled. He pilgrimagéd.

He wandered with his head cocked over his shoulder on

5

constant watch for letters from God.

If he had ever previously considered God it was with a distant disdain; that God's believers were *fools* and *weaklings*, putting their faith in a mystical extension of frail humankind itself.

Foolishly, he went to a hundred churches and lit a thousand candles.

Weakly, he shuffled through Rome on his knees.

He bought munitions factories with promises and poured their bullets into the sea. He chartered dredgers to net those bullets so the fish would not die of lead or cordite poisoning. He pledged millions into fuel research so the diesel of the dredgers would not leak away, covering the waves in deathly rainbows.

two weeks

Carlo Frendly cruised the corridors of Brussels. He dispatched blackmailing regiments of private eyes into the bureaucratic heart of the enemy: the meeting of three *cant-promized* signatures cut global warming legislation by decades. Carlo scaled and liberated food mountains; cast rose petals upon the surface of oil lakes; loosed the corporate dam that withheld antibiotics from the developing world.

He wandered through old Soviet states in trousers rendered kneeless by the Roman shuffle. Carlo smiled and children brought him watery strawberry ice-cream.

two weeks. really

As Carlo walked he also waited, his head always turned towards England. But the letters couldn't fly like Concorde; they remained a memory on an ebony coffee table. And the memory was enough.

The hours and days were disappearing into the past but Carlo didn't realise it. He'd given his Rolex away in Albania, his dearest wish that he might turn back time and liberate pit ponies and toddler chimney sweeps too.

Ten days after leaving London he swayed exhausted in a phone booth at the southern edge of Europe. Carlo inhaled the fine grains of the Sahara as they blew through the door from Africa. He smelt erosion and charnel-stiff ashes; blood dust whipped up from the heart of a place where hearts no longer existed.

And Carlo Frendly picked up the receiver and made two calls. And those calls parented call-babies. And grandchildren followed. And within three hours the telecommunications satellites geostationed above the planet were singing like angels to each other.

And mankind spoke.

And mankind listened to mankind.

Really.

*

Thirteen days after he'd left London, Carlo sat on a rock in the gentle waves of the eastern Mediterranean. He was exhausted but unbroken. His face had taken on the ethereal pallor of a saint or hunger striker.

It was five to midnight.

Across the bay, a city was coming alive. For a generation it had lived in a state of civil war, as street fought street for control of a standpipe or church. Electricity had been restored. The citizens formed a conga line outside the bright cafés along the waterfront. This was Carlo Frendly's gift: every new light bulb in the city owed its existence to him, every friendship restored and new love discovered, every child, every new born baby... A million might come to live and love him.

Carlo dozed. He was naked. He'd given away his last pair of boxer shorts that afternoon.

A ripple smudged the sea and God walked across the waters of the bay with an old Imperial typewriter under one arm. Even without a beard She was very beautiful.

"child. you are tired. come walk with me. i will take you to my garden where you may rest in the bosom of my angels."

Carlo looked up. He clasped his diplomatic hands together in gratuitous prayer. He could barely speak.

"Really?" he rasped.

The bayside lights winked once and God smiled.

7

Airbabies

We've got airbabies.

They live in the hay loft and in the diesel molecules of my Land Rover. I've seen them on August midnight afterglows when the heat of the day radiates into space: I've seen airbabies dance in that radiation. They fly into the upper atmosphere, creating the electrical storms that lace the summer sky. They are bio-conductors: lightning sprites that follow the charge right down into the ground – and bounce away into the smoking cornfields, laughing.

Airbabies. Cutebabies. Muppet-Disneybabies. Corn-bouncing sugarshit babies. Badbabies: gathering under the boughs of apple trees and ambushing sheep. Pissbabies: doing it in milk churns; squealing and scratching into hens' eggs to extract the foetus ghost.

*

I remember the island.

They sterilised the livestock and set the fields afire; doused the kitchen in *HP Sauce*. They made my daughter hide under the bed. Smuts fell down for days like Pompeii. I telephoned the Ministry. They showered us with gelding leaflets. Inspectors watched from the sea through binoculars – checked if we were swigging the sheep dip. Ministry handouts: *Airbabies – Existence and Legality to be Confirmed.* Well. Should they be a country? Might locusts be a nation? May we applaud the infant statehood of Babybubonica?

*

The cutebabies were ripping up the tarmac all along the causeway to the mainland. My wife dragged the coracle from the boatshed, slid it down into the water. Surfbabies joined hands and microwaved the sea with a kissing vibration. They made the sea disappear. Georgina toppled from forty foot onto the naked seabed; lay broken among gasping mackerel: the outboard and coracle like a giant whirring rusk fallen from the new babysky.

*

Sue left me for the city at swealing time.

Grey clouds darkened the stubble fields behind the bus station. Bits fell about us. "Up Pompeii," I said, like an idiot.

The engine of the coach belched itself into stinking life. She reached down from the steps, fluffed up my remaining hair, pecked my forehead.

"Cheers, Dad. Thanks..."

She flicked at something in her cold violet eye. Grunge from the coach perhaps or something off the burning field.

"Thanks for everything..." She kissed me again but the lips didn't quite touch.

She strode up into the body of the bus, pulled out a *Hello!* and I was lost to her. Sue was in the future already.

The vehicle pulled away. The road from the bus station out to the by-pass was clear and straight.

And I could watch for a long time.

*

So I took up the Bluebell Farm offer.

Bluebell was a mixed concern at the head of Bluebell Creek. The creek was barely tidal and seemingly survived for days without seawater. The mud stank and the shingle beaches were littered with dried weed and cuttlefish shells.

The women had often invited me to help out at the farm. There were three of them: former media persons or art gallery supervisors, born to wear bib-fronts and weigh themselves down with past relationships. They'd dropped in from London with a battered copy of *Soil & Sense* and some shabby marijuana plants.

The Bluebell Girls bumped along now, legislation experts as all farmers had to be: a decade on they were legal mistresses of milk quotas and the seasonal workers' scheme. The Bluebells' touch with the nitty-grittys was lighter perhaps: their sheep had the biggest dags in the district.

I arrived in Maytime.

A heat wave hit the country, silent and heavy. Sidney the taxi man wasn't amused as he drove me the four miles out of town to Bluebell Creek. "Bloody drought again, betcher life. Think they'd fix it."

The hedges were a blur of primrose and star of Bethlehem: wild garlic thrust its headiness through the open window of the Ford Mondeo. A stray hop tendril lashed the windscreen.

"Bloody summer..." Sidney grunted.

He had been very kind to Sue and me after Georgina died. He used to run a small B & B by the bus station but divorce and the business rate had forced him to get mobile. He wasn't a summer person. "...But the town needs it: coachloads of pensioners, teenagers getting arseholed. Yah, hurrah, bleeding summer..."

We reached the summit of the final hill before the descent down to the farm. The estuary stretched out in a desert of grey mud. A small stream glinted along the centre of Bluebell Creek.

The stream, the river, the sea... I thought drowsily. The ancient metaphor; the glib pattern of life. I had a brief flash of rushing outgoing tides and dry-drowning fish.

We cruised into the farmyard, pulled up by a heap of sour milk churns. A goose hopped out of a dustbin and honked at us. Sidney stayed behind the wheel resting his legs while airbabies

11

opened the Mondeo's boot from the inside and helped me with the luggage.

*

It was good to be among the women again. It was like an end to anger.

When I'd first met the Bluebells they exuded a bluff petulance; perhaps a fear-reaction to the countryside. They had certainly choked at the nursery name of their new enterprise. Muriel, a no-nonsense New Englander, had scanned parish records in vain for any ancient alternative.

The women were more settled these days. The angry posters were still there but fading now on the door of the outside loo. Commitment to the planet had been commuted to a caring practicality on a much more local level. They smiled quite openly.

I was shoved into the outhouse with a camp bed and the goose for company. The goose farted: it was a revelation.

On the second day, Mo got grumped out with Francie and Muriel and took her fluorescent tent up to Top Field by the main road. We could see the tent from the kitchen table like a bright piece of fruit. Francie sulked as well, making finger patterns in her porridge. Muriel gave me small (but open) smiles. "It's all right, Steve, it's all right..."

I hiked up to Mo's tent at lunchtime and asked if there was anything she wanted. She said there wasn't and if there was, her fucking airbabies would do it for her. Mo was in her forties, foul-mouthed but charming. She peered up at me from behind the tent flap on that hot afternoon. Her cropped head was as brown and weathered as a nut. She looked at me very carefully and I knew she was sorry.

I wandered around to the head of the valley before working my way back down along the stream. The trickle was bordered by beautiful cherry blossom, pink and cream escapees from some lost mansion house. An airbaby watched me from a topmost bough. It was young, gilled and semi-sighted. I almost

12

caught a smile before the baby zimmered into invisibility: perhaps re-locating to the autumn when the cherries would be ripe.

Francie had the tractor out by the time I got back. It had an air of *Dig for Victory* and land girls about it: there were even blackout slits on the headlamps.

"Yo Silve-e-er..." yodelled Francie to the tractor, attempting to fire the old Perkins back into life. There was a brief stirring of far-within mechanics.

Francie used to run an art gallery. She wore her prized Balinese wicker hat and earrings that clung to her like Technicolour crustacea. "I'm sorry, Steven. About Mo, I mean." She clenched her small face, letting the lines squirm out of her with a sort of bitter triumph. "It's a women's thing."

Francie had always been a little more distant to me than the others: Mo or Muriel wouldn't have said anything; wouldn't have needed to. Francie had joined the enterprise last. She was the youngest and – after all these years – still the doubter.

"I saw her. She's fine." I was awkward. It needn't have been like that.

"Well, I'll leave you with old Bessie then. Bessie the Tractor."

If a thing didn't need saying Francie would say it anyway.

*

I waved Muriel and Francie goodbye as they cycled up the lane into town.

I was lucky in finding a good load of spares, oily-ragged and waiting under my bed in the outhouse. The points weren't too bad but the clutch cylinders needed some work and the rear tyres were mosaicked like a dried-up reservoir.

As I worked, I became aware of a constant peripheral presence; distant bees or far off hills, heat-hazed.

They were watching me.

Airbabies were watching me. They were all around. Just waiting for me to call on them: bright flyers, smug helpers.

A low hum: imagination or sugarbabies? Very darkly downpitched, crawling out of the creeks and sky like honey. The sound touched the window of the farmhouse, buzzing the panes and exciting their molecules.

Seagulls seemed to drop like slow heavy paper and the creek loosed up its mud and water to meet them. A coracle sliced through the thickness like a flying saucer, a rusk thrown from a high chair...

"Steady, chum."

It was nothing. The babies had been playing: teasing me for working all afternoon and not allowing them to help. The seagulls rushed away from the mudflats with sharp cries.

"Steady, chum..."

The man had my arm, pulling me up from the ground.

"Slingsby. Max Slingsby's the name." He pronounced it 'Mex' like the Mex in Mexico.

He seemed embarrassed by physical contact and once he'd helped, retreated to the other side of the tractor.

He was a slight figure, somewhere in the fifties, wiry like Fred Astaire. A fussily waxed moustache below hawkish features; clear blue eyes nestling like unhappy rock pools. His appearance was quite singular, timeless even.

"You had a bit of a turn, old man. Fancy a gasper? I get Waverley in Oxford Street to make these up for me."

He leaned over the top of the tractor with a silver case. Astoundingly, each cigarette was monogrammed *Waverley & Son, London*. I shook my head and he returned the case to a blazer pocket, carefully brushing back the tie of some long-disbanded regiment.

I sat on the tool box, talked up to him. "Steven Trefula. Steve. Thanks. It must be the heat... You know..."

"Yes," he said.

Max turned and moved abruptly through the broken fencing onto the beach: I got up and followed him down to the shoreline. A couple of herons were poking around in the barely moist mud. Their movements, elegant and deliberate, were not unlike those of Max Slingsby.

"Came down on the off-chance, Trefula. Knew the girls from way back. Well, Maureen actually.

"Mo, you mean?"

"Mo, Maureen, Mrs Slingsby – take your pick." His reply was

14

light enough – but not so light as to encourage further investigation.

The herons, suddenly nervous, stretched their wings and disappeared into the buzzing trees.

"Know anything about tractors, Max?"

"A touch, I fancy. I learnt quite a lot in the Corps."

He pronounced the word like a dead body.

*

If engineers had oily thumbs then Max Slingsby had a whole handful.

"Call me Doctor Max," he murmured, inserting his frighteningly thin arms into the engine compartment. He urged me to assume the nurse's role, selecting tools and widgets – even wiping his brow with a dishcloth in the latter stages.

Max was a good team player: he needn't have involved me. He gave little grunts and all the while soothed the tractor: "There, there, old girl – we'll soon have you better..." as if the machine were an ailing child. Yet Slingsby's cooing held not a scrap of patronisation: it was as if it were the meeting of two equals – one of whom, quite by chance, possessed the screwdriver.

I surveyed the countryside and creek. All was quiet now. Far out I could see a tide of sorts inching across the mud. But the airbabies had retreated, gone amongst their secret places where men and women never went.

"Right, old man, give the girl a wind-up."

Bessie – charmingly – had a manual crank handle beneath her slitted headlamps. I took up position while Slingsby jumped onto the driving seat.

"Slowly, Trefula. Gently now..."

I rocked the handle to and fro as he tried to find neutral. The crank suddenly swung more easily and Slingsby gave a snort of triumph. "That's the lad! Thirty years in reverse gear can't have done the poor love any good. Right. Welly time!" He stuck his arm into the air and whirled it like a helicopter blade.

I corresponded with a 360-degree crank. Bessie gave a sort of stammer.

"Welly, boy," Slingsby almost whispered with a sly smile.

I started to turn the handle. The tractor suddenly caught with a roar. My shoulder wrenched and I found myself being flung across the farmyard.

Slingsby whooped like a dog and chucked in a gear that took the cracked rear wheels six inches off the ground. The tractor lurched forward and disappeared up the lane. I could just make out the overgrown hedgerows swaying on the hill, marking the tractor's progress: but Bessie's coughs and Slingsby's whoops would have been sufficient.

My shoulder had been dislocated.

I managed to stand up without fainting. It had happened before; I felt quite calm. Last time around a burly rugby referee had put things to rights with a startling half-time counter-wrench. But now I was alone. Muriel and Francie were in town; Mo sat glaring out of her tent in Top Field.

I wandered about, beginning to sob a bit and feeling that lazy bile-rush in the lower throat. I was hardly close to death but it hurt like bloody hell.

The dustbin clattered: I wasn't alone after all. The goose honked away into the cowshed.

An airbaby peeped out at me from the bin. The jelly-fin arms were moving about above its head as if they were courting each other. The airbaby rose out a little further, revealing its slow grin of smuggery.

My shoulder buzzed.

The airbaby smiled.

I came closer.

*

"So sorry, old chum. I *do* feel like a complete arse. I really had no idea." Slingsby favoured me with a brief show of teeth between moustache and brandy glass. "Leaving a feller like that... But, I say, we got the old girl up and running didn't we..."

"I think you're great – the Goddamn pair of you." Muriel stood up and cleared the supper things. "I'll leave the crap here on the draining board. You can wash-up now or in the morning. No big deal for The Fabulous Furry Tractor Brothers." Muriel gave me a kindly wink and disappeared upstairs.

Francie followed Muriel. "Well done, Steve," she murmured, brushing past me. She almost didn't walk too slowly.

Slingsby made to move. "Well, time I turned in. What about you, Mrs S?"

Mo had a sleeping bag stuffed under her chair – all ready for a return to the tent if need be. She looked at him through half-closed lids. "Turned into what, Max? A nine bob note? I'm going to check out the cowshed."

The Fabulous Furry Tractor Brothers were suddenly alone.

"They fixed your shoulder then."

"Yes. It's pretty good. Aches a bit. Like it did when I buggered it up before."

"Rugger player?"

"Mmm..."

"Prop forward, of course."

I smiled.

Muriel and Francie could be heard overhead, the old timbers sighing to their footsteps, the ancient air carrying muffled voices debating the latest demand from the Min of Ag.

"You're an airbaby aren't you, Max."

Max examined the brandy bottle. A full moon had risen over Top Field. Small shapes flew across the face of her.

"Maybe. We don't always know." He looked right at me then, his blue rock pools suddenly de-colourising, his face seeming to fade away into a dim vibrating light...

He said: "How do you know you're a human being?"

I grunted, refusing again one of his cigarettes.

"Look." He thrust the silver case back into his blazer, slipped the blazer off, tossed it over a chair, began to unbutton his trousers.

He stood before me in the moonlight, a pair of comically baggy Y-fronts hanging from a torture-thin body. He glowed quietly like a night storage heater; like something that had found its ambience, its desires – and desired no more.

Tears were pouring down his face as I helped him back into

17

his clothes and tied his shoelaces. And he tried to help *me*: unbuttoning and rebuttoning my shirt, brushing my hair with his fingers. Trying to be like one of them. He was a great fussy bird. I managed to settle him into a chair with the brandy.

I turned at the door and he raised his glass.

"Thanks, old chum," he said.

*

Muriel was standing in the darkened hallway.

"Hi, honey – just checking I turned the light off."

"The light's off, Muriel."

She was a paleness peering at the wall. "Just checking the switch. No good looking at the light. You've got to look at the switch as well..."

*

The cowshed was warm and rustling, a stink that stung the nostrils and sweetened the heart. Mo sat at the far end in the near-darkness. The only light came from the dozen or so airbabies that floated about the cattle like large lambent snowflakes: they purred and worked the hairy heads into cowlicks.

An airbaby lay in Mo's lap, warbling to her, rubbing her face gently with its gelatinous fingerlets. Mo looked up at me like a child:

"He's not Max. Is he."

I leaned down and kissed her forehead. The airbaby brushed me with its glowing stubs, the warmth rising up my arm to soothe my aching shoulder.

*

The herons were calling as I tripped across the farmyard.

My wife came to me as I lay on the bed in the outhouse. In the moonlight, I saw Georgina wearing the blue overalls that she always wore; that she had worn on the last day of her life. She came close, her dark hair falling in a smother across my nostrils. It smelt of

18

seawater. It smelt greasy; it smelt like faintly burnt hair. I couldn't quite see her eyes: memory told me they were there. "Don't worry," she said. "Keep trying the Coastguard. Is there enough oil in the fuel tank?" Sand jammed her fingernails: "How do you know you're a human being?" She grew a seaweed moustache like Max Slingsby: it scratched my cheek, trying to burrow into my body. And I realised that it was bloody Francie, rasping me with her earrings, rubbing her small hairless night-storage body all over me.

The vibration from the window panes drowned out the herons.

*

I rose early – earlier than farmyard early – and dressed quickly in the greyness. I foraged around for my things, plunged them into supermarket bags, maybe crunched an earring underfoot.

*

I spent some time in London. I sought out Sue, trying not to embarrass her with her college friends. I stayed at the YMCA with my plastic bags; spent days in the launderette and library, nights in pub corners.

Some evenings I managed to spend with my daughter: cinemas, Italian restaurants... She had a boyfriend called Wedge who was a government clerk and could make slippers out of paper napkins. I told Wedge about the airbabies but he didn't believe me. He was a funny man, a good sort of man. Officially they didn't exist, he said. Barely anyone in the capital had heard of them. Some sub-committee at the Ministry of Agriculture was looking into it, like they had sub-committees looking into slurry pollution and the Colorado beetle. He gave me some telephone numbers, a couple of names. He apologised that he couldn't do more. He bought me another drink and talked about football.

*

I tried a number. It seemed vaguely familiar: maybe I'd tried it before from the island. I got through quite easily to someone senior who didn't even pretend to make a secret non-song and dance about it. I was the bearer of unspectacular news that they were already aware of. I received the small child treatment. "...Yes, we're looking into it, Mr Trefula. But you hear a lot about these sorts of things at this time of year. Parliament's out... You know, crop circles and all that..."

Sue and Wedge went to Greece for a fortnight and I did some flat-sitting for them. I got into the habit of scanning all the news media; papers from cover to cover; Ceefax and Google to their remotest page numbers. Airbabies were not news. They were nothing. I imagined the Airbaby Sub-Committee wrestling with their bottled water and blank sheets of paper.

I left before the kids came back, depositing the key with a neighbour. I took the train, peering out into the unknown countryside. It was raining. An August rain that smudged the carriage windows with warm brown water. The train passed over Salisbury Plain with its chalk brush strokes. We went through tunnels burrowed into red-rust soil: emerged behind a shingle beach, a seaside station whirring by. A signal clanked up as we sped on. The sun shone off the water. An airbaby with floppy ears swung from the signal box and waved at me.

*

The taxi didn't take me to the farm. I asked Sidney to drive to the cliffs; up amongst the weather stations and gorse bushes.

The rain had stopped, or had never started here. The day was bright. Down below, beach-crashed by breakers, was the old village with its scatter of cottages and barns. I strode to the rocky edge, leaving Sidney in the National Trust car park.

Across the wide shimmering expanse of bay was the island. Barely discernible, the broken causeway umbilicaled itself into the mainland. I knew there were lights at night now – and only some had been placed by Trinity House.

I tried to make out my old farm but the ruin was lost in the smudge of distance.

Memory told me it was there.

Sidney was snoring loudly in the back seat when I returned to the car. I sat in front and waited as Sidney's airbabies slipped from their quiet places into the engine and transmission systems. The taxi sparked into life. We bowled down the lanes. An airbaby danced about on the wheel, steering with its feet.

I closed my eyes.

Memory told me it was there.

*

I was roused by the gorgeous stink of wild garlic. We were still in the lanes – our progress halted by a herd of sheep. They milled about, savaging the hedgerows, regarding us with their sham group telepathy. The airbabies chortled quietly, floating about the herd like benign and bloated ticks. I slipped out of the Mondeo, wandered back up the lane.

I found a gate and clambered over it, close to the hinges. I was in Top Field. Mo's tent lay a few yards to my right; Bluebell Valley sailed away to turn into the yard and house and mud.

I could see movement down at the farm. A slow and graceful waltz. It was like the farm was preparing to leave the planet. Bits had left already.

I peered into Mo's tent. She was in there. Airbabies were helping her out of her body.

I rushed down the valley, falling and slipping.

The airbabies were de-building the farmhouse. Worn and ancient slates were left carefully on one side: the roof timbers had been stacked neater than a lumber yard; bricks of dressed stone lay about in orderly piles. Demolition-babies were presently engaged on the internal walls. Muriel and Francie sat in a kitchen awash with vertical sunshine. They looked like something from a silent film, renowned as silent films were for outdoor-indoor sets.

Muriel looked up from toast and marmalade.

"Late breakfast, honey. We saved you some. Come and sit down – there's still a seat left. Have a good trip?"

I entered through the wall. I looked at Francie. "Is Max about?"

She gave one of her tiny reluctant grins. Even in the brightness of day I could see her teeth glowing. "On the beach, Steve. Steve..."

I walked around the building. The air was full of whispered laughterings. I passed through the broken fencing onto the shingle. The goose was wandering about, coughing on cuttlefish shells. The tide was in and the inlet stank. Max Slingsby sat on a pyjama-striped deckchair, his shoes mere inches from the foetid water.

"Hello, old man." He half-raised his panama. "I've missed you."

An airbaby – a sort of crocodile cherub – soared down and took the hat from him, giggling off beyond the trees.

It stayed there and watched us. Waiting.

Max laughed. "They've got to learn, you know. They've got to find out about *everything*."

Pieces of motorcar began to explode into the water fifty yards offshore; the front bumper fell out of a clear sky and caught on a mud spit. The familiar TAXI sign came last, rippling like a sycamore seed-pod.

"Looks like rain, chum." He flourished the silver case. "It's easy you know, easier than you think."

I remembered him standing in the kitchen, scared and glowing.

Surprising myself, I took one of Max Slingsby's cigarettes, thrust my face towards his lighter.

"Good lad."

I inhaled deeply. I abruptly sat on the beach, feeling faint and realising that I'd probably last had a fag when I was ten years old.

The airbaby hung above me like a soft chandelier in a panama hat. I thought about Muriel and the light: the difference between seeing and knowing...

The airbaby was waiting. It was waiting to dive down my throat: to follow the smoke into my lungs, divulging itself to all the tiny blood vessels. I would never see it again but memory would tell me it was there.

I lay on the beach with my mouth open.

Colder Still

The world was white.

In these higher latitudes Winter came easily. Winter came like an old friend. Blizzards rushed across the earth like frenzied polar bears scattering their pure white fragments. The earth was frozen to a point twenty metres below its surface: the surface sang and vibrated when spades tried to break into it.

The mountain-man came down to the village in the whiteness. He slunk naked among the houses in the pallid dawn-light. His body was ice-bitten and as hard as the singing earth. His entire being spoke of brutishness.

The beast skulked on the outskirts for two days; his speech gibberish, his movements pathetic. Folk threw cauliflower cores and doused the already stinking hide of the creature with sour beer. He tried to perform handstands but collapsed in the gutter. Schoolboys running home paused to kick the mountain-man, egged on by obnoxious younger sisters.

On the evening of the second day, he found Moraya's hayloft. The creature lay among the warm animal smells and slept at last.

There was a terrific snowstorm that night. On the third morning the ground glistened under a metre of snow. Low clouds lit up from the glare of the land beneath them.

*

Moraya forced the backdoor open and slipped on her snowshoes. Her two sisters slept in the kitchen behind her: they were both eighty-three years old and too ill to make the stairs anymore. Moraya turned and smiled at them through the sleeping fug. The smell of fresh bread and oregano pervaded the house.

She struck out across the snow-drifted farmyard, slitting her eyes in the sub-zero air. Her goat was with kid and the time was very soon. She checked twice daily, cooing to her beast and washing its flanks with straw. It was Moraya's goat: it was Moraya's hayloft; no one else went there.

She unbolted the door and fell inside on a rush of snow.

The mountain-man was awake. He crouched in the corner and gave off a melodious humming groan. Moraya's nanny had given birth during the night's blizzard and licked and chewed the caul of her new kid. The baby leant against the mountain-man, its chin nestled happily over the massive thigh.

*

The two sisters were awake when Moraya returned. They fussed around the stove together like an old marriage. They gabbled in the old language of the district: the tongue used before the pan-edict issued by the Central Committee.

They all sat down at the big kitchen table, prayed and broke bread into the goat's milk that Moraya had taken from her loft. Moraya studied her two sisters as she did every morning: as she had done every morning for seventy-five years. They were called Romanz and Konstantina. Age had turned them into huddled, shrunken men.

The goat and its kid were discussed. There was a brief mention of star positions and the possibility of selling the kid to the local necromancer. Moraya did not mention the mountain-man. Why should she? Such things did not exist.

She had heard reports of a creature entering the village a couple of days previously but had discounted them. She rarely went beyond her own farmyard these days, relying on Demitri and the others for local news. The reports had told of the boys and their kicking. When she was a child, such an event had been greeted with tears of joy.

The priest would have broken bread and ikons paraded in their glass cabinets. A week of festivities. But of course there were no such things. Why, hadn't the Central Committee denied the existence of the mountain-men? Weren't they just the decadent whimsy of a former regime?

She cleared the breakfast things then settled Romanz down in the front room and helped Konstantina into her dark little cubbyhole where she kept her loom. Moraya fretted for half an hour among her sisters, pretending to do little housebound things. Then she threw on her snowshoes and stamped out to the hayloft.

Snippets of snow-light filtered through chinks into the interior. Tiny husk fragments floated in and out of the light shafts. The mountain-man stood in a corner, his body tall and reeking. His eyes were closed but the throat vibrated and hummed rhythmically like a sawing heartbeat. The goat and her kid lay contentedly at the creature's feet. Moraya stepped forward, trying not to make her snowshoes slap too loudly on the flagstones. There was something else in the shadows; another creature that nuzzled at the mountain-man's legs.

Another kid...

It peered up at her and bleated before going back to sleep, snug in the hairy feet.

Two kids at one birth was an occurrence unknown in the village for many years. Goats had been specially bred along lines laid down by the Agricultural Sub-Committee. One kid per birth was deemed sufficient. This was good policy: a policy directly relative to the decreased human population and the systematic defoliation of grazing land.

Moraya stared down at the baby goat. Why had she not noticed before? It looked perfectly normal. She loved new life, perhaps because circumstances had denied her the chance to bring forth children herself. The years had charged by her like a mountain river at Springtime. Years of drought and occupation: of loneliness and scorched earth.

She left the hayloft quickly.

*

The vestry smelt of old wood and honey. Wall hooks held a row of dark musty gowns.

"Do you love Crystos? He who died for you. Do you love Him?"

The priest leaned close to Moraya, his comfortable breath brushing her cheek: "My child, life is strange by its very nature. Every day is a miracle. A discovery. Our lives are short, our flesh is so weak."

He gestured to the entrance of the Mayor's family crypt in a far corner. The bright Byzantine colours etched out a death's head above the litter of crosses.

"But, my Father – I cannot keep this thing to myself. It is a miracle. In my childhood – oh, you are so much younger than me... You will never know."

The priest stood up and smiled. He was a kind man caught between sides.

"There is something we all must know, Moraya. Love God and keep our mouths shut."

*

The mountain-man had gone when she came back. Huge untidy footprints curved off across the deeper snow and down the cart track that led to the village.

There were two Trenake trees by her farm gate. They both grew slender dripping icicles that flashed in the warming air of mid-morning. Moraya touched the trees with only mild surprise, then rolled her arms around one fully. The sap poured across her face, diluting the tears.

"You will never know, my father," she whispered. "You will never know."

She hugged the new tree tighter.

*

She met Demitri coming up the cart track, clearing it as he went. The old man had seen army service on the Crimson Lakes but the only decoration he had received was an ugly blanche down one side of his face. He grinned and the deformity rose up like a nightmare.

"Seen Dolly gal?" He spoke in the old dialect and jerked a thumb down the track behind him. Dolly was Demitri's pride and hope in his old age: a beautiful Arabian mare. He kept her on a piece of waste ground by his shack on the banks of the river: Demitri netted there for Winter sturgeon and hung them on lines to smoke. Dolly was Demitri's foible, a ridiculous dream: a miracle in itself. Dolly trotted up the track now.

Two Dollys.

One followed the other, each careful of its footing on the treacherous surface.

"Did y'see the mountain-man, Moraya? Did y'see him? Ha, beautiful. It was a beautiful thing. He touched her. He just touched her. And just look at Dolly..."

Moraya broke into a giddy half-run, passing by the old man and his two horses.

History was happening. Not just a re-occurrence of events or legends past: but a history all of its own. Folk would talk about this. The Father's flesh and that of his flock would wither: the Committee would fade away; and yet the story of this day would be etched into the memory of mankind like the glacier scouring the mountain.

*

The village square was crowded. The snow was brown and scummy. It was market day and farmers from the surrounding countryside lurched about and shouted at each other. They were hideous men: their hearts as frozen as the land in Winter. Their faces were raw and red and they might have bartered their wives and children away if need be.

The mountain-man stood in a flood of white cockerels. Five women had fainted and lay sprawled in the slush. The birds pecked at their headscarves with curiosity. Schoolboys, let out for the day, laughed and pointed. They were doubtlessly the beast's former tormentors but had turned with the fickleness of childhood.

The mountain-man stroked and hummed at a cockerel and from beneath his great smelly paw another would float out – an exact, noisy, pecking duplicate. Birds were everywhere. Old men chased after them crazily. The Mayor crawled laughingly among them, his robes streaked with excrement and dirty snow.

"Herculo! Herculo!" they cried, plucking a hero's name from legend and bestowing it upon the mountain-man.

The mountain-man began to laugh too. He roared. His chest rose up and down and his bellows echoed across the village and up into the ranges beyond.

It had come like a miracle and Moraya's tears kept flooding across her cheeks, spilling onto her smock, soaking through onto the old skin beneath.

But her heart was dry and her heart was warm. And she believed.

*

Spring: and the land was loud with the rushing of water. High in the mountains, tiny blue flowers peppered the receding snowline. The valley was full of birds.

Manolis was the first to ride in with news of the War. He was a cousin of Demitri and kept sheep on a low range of hills ten kilometres away. A band of Romanes had camped next to him and had whispered of border incursions; of treaties made and broken.

The news was taken by the village with an air of resignation: an acceptance born out of experience. The mountains marked the natural border between their own country and its neighbour and the land had changed hands a dozen times in as many decades. Some prepared half-heartedly for departure: others, even more half-heartedly, checked antique flintlocks before continuing on their daily round.

Travellers passed by but could say no more than Manolis. Soldiers of their own country rode through with heavy horses trailing small field-pieces. The soldiers didn't even stop long enough to steal their food; to whisper to women of the glorious battle to come.

Perhaps the village would be lucky this time.

*

Herculo the mountain-man continued to live in Moraya's hayloft. He had been persuaded to bathe in the river next to Demitri's smoking shack. He wore a linen nappy during daylight hours but removed it at night in a curiously human gesture. Moraya often had to chase away young girls from the chinks in her loft.

There were twice as many piglets that spring. Twin lambs gambolled in their dry-stone corrals. Life glowed everywhere. Herculo lumbered with an odd grace through a light mist of mayflies and the mist became a dense fog.

"Herculo, why can't you talk?" asked Moraya to her creature. They sat by the river one fine Spring afternoon.

The creature just looked at her with his yellow eyes. The shaggy brows wrinkled, almost in thought – almost as if he was seriously pondering the question.

Herculo reached out and touched her. The huge fingernail traced the line of her seamed old mouth; touched both of her lips.

"Two," he said.

*

A week later they came for Sticks the necromancer.

It had emerged that the field-gun detachment that had ridden so hurriedly through the village had been brutally ambushed in a nearby mountain pass. The work of a fifth column had been intimated: no one knew why the necromancer was suspected of spying.

Three military policemen cantered up the valley with a warrant for his arrest bearing the seal of the Defence Sub-Committee. They carried flintlock carbines and the eldest of them was nineteen-years old.

Everyone was frightened of Sticks. Even the priest kept his distance. The necromancer lived mysteriously in a nearby copse, discovering portents in shallow pools and copulating with the daughters of terrified farmers. The necromancer would scowl and cackle; leer and display himself.

Sticks leered and cackled now as the policemen helped him up onto a fourth horse. He was a small man like a monkey and he smirked at the gathering crowd through painted green teeth.

A heavy silence fell across the square. A solitary stork rose up from a nearby chimney pot and flew away to the East. The necromancer glanced up and giggled and slit the throat of his youngest captor.

He withdrew a long poisoned fingernail from the youth's neck and was off the horse before his victim's head hit the cobblestones. Sticks shrieked wildly and was on the other two before they had time to prime their carbines.

There were screams and movement in the crowd. The necromancer would slay them all! Would kill every father and son; would rip and darken every maidenhead with his shadow...

A precise movement slipped through the panic and a huge hairiness whipped out at Sticks. Again the paw of Herculo the mountain-man shot out. Again and again.

And with every brush of Herculo's paw, the fingers of the necromancer gained a poisoned nail. Sticks' hand flailed out like a broken fan, trying to shake the death away. But the nails grew and curled, dripping a black alkali venom. In his madness, the necromancer's hand clenched in anger and a spasm sliced through the wrinkled simian body. He cried out: crawled on the ground; threw himself at the crowd. Blood and poison flowed from him. He wrenched an axe from a speechless woodsman and clumsily tried to amputate the poisoned hand. But like a scorpion in a ring of fire, Sticks was too late and he collapsed onto the cobbles, his back arching in a final dreadful rictus.

The crowd gasped. They turned as one but Herculo had gone.

*

She asked: "Why do you kill?"

Moraya and Herculo sat together in the kitchen. The two sisters snored in their separate corners.

The mountain-man spoke in an odd fashion: the words were thick and deliberate.

"He was dead in heart."

"The necromancer was a hated man. The people love you for what you did."

Herculo was silent, looking out into the night.

She continued: "They want to see you. They want to be with you. You have touched people's lives: do you know how many lives you have touched?"

The creature gave a grunting sigh. He took her hand and pressed it against his barrel-hollow chest: he placed his own paw, gently and without embarrassment, against her slumped unsuckled breast.

"Two."

*

Summer tempered Spring's rush of water: it stilled the torrent to a trickle among the roasting stones of the riverbed. The late-flowering Trenakes brought forth a creamy-yellow blossom that rose and fell on swaying boughs: rose then blew away like thick sweet rain.

News of the War was sparse. Three month-old Committee broadsheets were circulated, vigorously defending the nation's stance as protectors of Civilisation. Victories had been glorious and the few defeats had been orchestrated by traitors and mental patients. The broadsheet exhorted the nation to seek out its turncoats and punish them in the traditional way. The article was graphically illustrated for the benefit of the country's illiterate majority.

The mountain-man continued to be popular in the village. The church was able to step up its re-building plan: Herculo could carry the riverbed stones unaided and rigged the wooden scaffolding with ease. He laid out a new dry-stone wall for the cemetery at the highest point in the village: the nearest point to God. Children ran around him, laughing as he worked. Herculo looked at the graves: some of them had portraits of their occupants hung over the crosses, rendered by paint or the new photographic process. The faces were solemn, yet held an inner joyous glow.

The mountain-man touched the pictures but nothing happened. The faces were those of the dead.

*

The English Soil Society

The Trenakes had lost their blossom and their leaves lay thick when Romanz died.

The funeral processed around the square and along the main street that led to the cemetery. It passed through a gap in the new wall: the air was heavy with the scent of herbs warmed by departing Summer. There were many tears for Romanz: she had been one of the oldest people in the village and a Godmother to most of the mourners. But their tears were of joy for a life well-spent, for a death that came quietly and with dignity.

Herculo stood a little to one side of the coffin, its open half-lid revealing the still sleeping face, the coin-covered eyes. He came closer, gently shouldering away the weeping mourners. Herculo held out his paw and lowered it towards Romanz's blue lips.

"No."

The young priest looked at the creature without moving.

"No," he repeated. "Her time has come, my friend. She has been called." He motioned to the new wall. "You have built well. Be content."

Herculo left the group, passed through his new gateway and strode slowly down to the river. Moraya watched the creature go but presently turned back and whispered to her sleeping sister.

*

Manolis collapsed in the new snow. The flakes caught on his hair and froze. He had run all night and had left his flock in a cave hidden deep in the mountains. He lay now on the wasteground outside Demitri's hut, surrounded by concerned villagers.

"The War," he gasped. "The War is coming – "

They helped him into the hut where Demitri rubbed his nephew with rags and poured hot lard down his throat. Manolis had met his Romanes on the mountainside but they had been in disarray. Their traditional Summer grazing grounds had been overrun by enemy troopers possessing breach-loading carbines with paper cartridges. Their rate of fire made the weapons formidable. The broadsheets provided by the Central Committee had made no mention of this development – perhaps because its own army had mutinied in the shortening days of Summer: or so the Romanes said. However exaggerated the reports, it was obvious that the enemy had the upper hand. And the village lay at the bottom of the pass that had provided the easiest invasion route for many centuries.

There were contemptuous and familiar grunts from many. Hadn't the village lived through invasion before? Let the enemy come. They would bend with the winds of change as they had always done. But others were not so sure. The advent of this new unknown technology might change everything. There was something diabolical in this strange harbouring of wind and fire. Words were whispered: there were many who began to think that the Dark One led the enemy army.

Brave souls journeyed up the mountain with bags of rock salt to scatter around the lonely grave of Sticks the necromancer: to stop his heretic's ghost from rising in the hours of night to aid the invaders.

*

Winter.

The old friend. The freezer of the earth. The bright one that killed the young and unwary. It was not a season that engendered hope: before the warmth returned, the world would become colder still.

Moraya stood in the dark kitchen looking out at the night. Konstantina sat upright in a chair dozing: her breathing was rapid and shallow. Moraya watched her surviving sister in the reflection of the dark window. Konstantina looked like a ghost.

No one had seen Herculo since the funeral. There was little concern: folk seemed to be too caught up in their own serious or semi-serious attempts at stemming off enemy invaders. Details regarding the enemy's position differed: various sources reported that disaster lay hours, days or weeks away. No matter: the crisis would come.

Moraya stared hard out into the night, trying to focus on the reflections beyond the dark glass. Perhaps she could just see a whisper of a Trenake tree. Herculo's Trenake tree.

The snow was falling thickly, muffling the farmyard and turning sharp outlines into vague white impressions. Sounds petered through the gloom, lilting on the borders of perception. A crowded hiss of voices: the priest was leading a midnight mass in the church a little lower down the hill. His beautiful warbling voice came more clearly now, answered by a hushed *kyrie eleison.*

The voices filled the air, becoming thicker than the snow. She tried to peer even further into the darkness but the land had become invisible.

*

The invaders came during the night.

The snowfall ceased just before dawn and long shadows moved across the rooftops. Soldiers flitted between the mountain ramparts above the village, circling down the icy stream beds that led to the cobbled outskirts. People came drowsily from their houses: many had slept in the church. The Mayor tried to fasten his collar in the reflection of a frozen gutter but with little success.

The first troopers crept into the village even though they knew their presence had been detected. There were only perhaps a score of them: lean weather-beaten men with bad teeth. They took it in turns to break down doors and loot food whilst their fellows kept guard around them. They slipped from house to house like nervous birds.

Yet they were not alone: these first soldiers were merely the pathfinders, the harbingers. More silhouettes appeared on the skyline; and more still as the valley began to echo with cries and the jangle of equipment.

Presently, an impossible sea began to slip down the mountainside: a murmuring human ocean of green and mauve. Horses, carts and howitzer carriages followed. Wooden wheels groaned and split on the frozen trails; gaunt women scampered after wagons festooned with pots and pickled animal carcasses. A squadron of their priests rode on the backs of camels, reciting diabolical liturgies from beneath their orange cowls. The army was massive, like some mobile piece of epic landscape. A vacuum seemed to linger in its wake as if a million pairs of lungs, human and animal, had breathed in as one.

34

The ocean reached the village outskirts and halted.

Rumour had scurried ahead of the army. It said that this was the greatest force ever assembled. Mercenaries from a dozen countries had rallied to its banner. Reports told of distant great powers using the War as an opportunity to test their experimental weapons for more serious conflicts to come. The scene was redolent of destiny; of a powerful memory blasted backwards from the future.

A small man detached himself from a rear column and calmly wheeled a small cart into the village. He stopped near the square, adjusted his rakish blue beret and began to set up a bulky box camera in the snow. Village boys came forward warily – and then more confidently as the photographer beckoned them on with enthusiasm. More soldiers approached, slinging their infamous new carbines. They smiled, fumbling for sweets in their tunic pockets. Hands were shaken and toffees distributed. Soldiers hitched young children up onto their shoulders and grinned oafishly at the unlying camera.

Older villagers held back. The smiling soldiers did not concur with their past experience. Most of the civilians remained huddled in the square. Moraya looked at the young priest. His mouth was set, his eyes darting as if trying to look into the soul of every single soldier in the valley.

The photographer finished his work, putting the used plates into a black hatbox. Helped by the sweet-giving soldiers, he steered his little cart back the way it had come. He turned once to smile and wave to the children.

The Mayor was still wrestling with his collar when the first bullet hit him. His knees folded and he fell almost to attention. A cage of chickens exploded. A trooper lobbed another smoking grenade and the old war memorial fragmented: chunks of masonry blew out like horizontal grey rain. There were more gunshots. Manolis grasped his arm, swore, and staggered towards the great army yelling incoherently: a burst of fire left him in pieces.

The air was full of screams and the smell of gunpowder. The civilians had unconsciously been corralled into their own village square. Soldiers were on all sides, their ugly faces pale against the smoke. Mothers fell onto their children. Grandmothers tried to shield them all with their black skirts of mourning.

Moraya crawled to the Mayor and tried to turn his head around. He was quite dead. The priest was there too. His formerly darting eyes darted still – yet the reason seemed to have left them. He was saying something and Moraya strained to hear above the chaos.

A grenade full of grapeshot blew off the church door and she covered her face, curling up into a ball. The cobbles were covered in blood and snow and chicken feathers.

There was a sudden clatter and an unshod horse's hoof brushed her ear painfully. It was Demitri's prize Arab, Dolly. She galloped around the square, eyes wide and bellowing like a human being. She ran like a beast from Hell. Her twin – Herculo's gift – cantered behind. Moraya watched the progress of the two horses as they left the massacre in the village square and galloped on up the track that led to the hilltop cemetery.

Moraya rose to her knees and looked up at the hill. A huge figure cavorted among the crypts and gravestones.

A massive weight slammed against her shoulder. She gasped, trying to breathe air back into her body. Her lungs seemed to have shrunk and they didn't work properly: her mouth was full of a sudden sweet warmth.

She forced her eyelids open. The horses had reached the cemetery now and stood panting by the wall. Herculo leaned over and nuzzled them. Moraya tried hard to think what he might be saying but the effort was too great. The mountain-man turned away from the animals and continued with his work. Even from this distance, Moraya could see that Herculo was passing among the graves, touching and humming as he did so.

The world clouded: a very light snow began to fall like little pieces of Heaven.

She felt her whole body shudder and realised that death was only moments away. And not only her own. Moraya realised with a gasp that she had barely survived to see a day that she had never thought possible. For Herculo was the bringer of life: the bright cutter of darkness. The invaders would never take the village now. They had come by night but would never live to see another.

Herculo danced through the graveyard. And where he danced the army of the dead rose up.

Hearing Colour

So we passed from the rowdy bar into the singing rain. Tiny symphony drops: splashy figures for the tired time of evening. The spaces between them were a blessed silence.

So out into the singing rain came Winifred and me; the party girl and her pooper. Agents of chaos or maybe not. We could have been rebellious weekenders: maybe she would have been better off with one of her proper boyfriends. Left alone we might have worked our mystery but it was not to be:

The monsoon had come early that year. The streets sighed with the sweat of rockers and shopgirls and reeling farmers: public flogging had been abolished the previous week and a party mood lingered, hoping for a revival. A crowd shimmied its way past us, hands on ears. "Singin' in the rain," they crooned, unfurling umbrellas and turning them into coracles. Singin' in or out of it – something was happening at Rainbow's End Junction that night, and the world's puddlesters were there to hear it.

A generator whined its way over from the railway station. A dozen gas lamps on Rossetti Avenue sent up their tiny glow, spat and nearly died under loathsome precipitation.

*

It was the night of hearing colour and some heard it not.

Colour blind from birth, many jogged the town's outskirts to plunge their heads into the wintry rushing river; to drive fingers into stubborn ears. Monochrome monitors had been stationed at every street corner. No expense was spared to broadcast sympathy to the misguided and mishearing. Council workmen sluiced the monsoon gutters. Their day-glo waistcoats screamed like cornered weasels: their thermos flasks – bedecked by a graver colour – hummed in the manner of distant breakers.

Winifred ran through the storm to the railway station, clutching her weekend ticket and plastic bag. The transparency of water fooled the ear: a constant shimmering in and out of high and middle octaves.

"I'm an artist! Let me pass!" wailed a small man as he tried to beat us to the barricade. Soldiers milled uncertainly around the stationmaster. The old man nodded wearily and the troops lifted the barrier to let the simpering aesthete through.

Down by the cinders, humans put their heads to the silvery rails. The rails were like solid tubular rain disappearing into darkness: a thousand ears leant against the metal and tried to go there. All the bohemian idlers had gathered. A vague notion to travel the district in search of new sounds had circulated.

I knew one of the railcrawlers. "Arnold," I called as we passed through the barrier onto the platform. Arnold looked up. He was a telegraph engineer and a member of the Rainbow's End artists' enclave – a good enough fellow. He seemed keen to hire one of the new snowmobiles to take his ears – and anyone else's – up to the Steerforth Glacier. The endless echo of ice crystals; the simple sound of shadows. I admired Arnold's presence of vision in extraordinary times.

An armoured personnel carrier pulled up on the far side of the tracks. Folk had become used to the dull lumpy strains of khaki. Several civilians emerged from the rear of the vehicle, among them a woman with the inevitable gash of deafening lipstick. Tape recorders were produced; fabulous dishes were erected on top of the potting sheds that ran parallel with the railway lines. The devices were multi-coloured and the scientists worked with admirable concentration: they crawled between their equipment like millipedes traversing an orchestra pit during a thunderous Wagnerian denouement.

*

"What colour am I, Win?" We sat now in the muted tones of the stationmaster's office at five in the morning. The train had never come: its shrill silver livery had caused an avalanche up at Steerforth: rumours of deafness and derailment were rife. A small fire crackled merrily in the corner, its colour a wavering tone of primeval beauty. The stationmaster dozed with his feet in the grate.

"Win – what colour am I?" I repeated.

Winifred sat for a while and fidgeted with her sighing earrings. Outside, I could hear the shrieks as dawn sliced its way through the rainclouds like a meteor. It made the floorboards hum.

"Pardon?" she said.

A Million Toledo Blades

Spins: the world spins. Rain spins off it as we race across the sea in a storm. A headland looms. We rise up over it. A building lies ahead. It's the Heights Hotel closed for the Winter. We wheel like the gulls and disappear down a chimney pot. Tunnelled darkness and we're out and into the lounge bar. He's there. The Barman. He takes a corner table in the empty room. A fly, sleepy with February, softly butts the windowpane. The Barman shakes like a wild animal. His agitation is utter. This is his story. Let him speak:

> *In the corner of the old look-out (next to gun slits and stinking lavs) I crouched in a tremble terrific. Terrific: it held my heart, the pumps throwing blood around my body in time with the midnight surf far below. Terrific: my brain tingled with that strange 5am awareness and I smiled in recognition.*

The Barman pulls out a journal from the shrunken folds of his monkey jacket. The book's outlines have been softened by wear. The air of the planet lies heavy upon it.

    The Barman reads:

High above
the river-encircled city (with the warm plain
winds and Spring's hint of rain crawling across my cheek) I lay,
boulder-stretched. I had pulled off the winding hill road long enough

for the cold stone to go right to my head.
A hawk arched over on invisible rails. Down in Toledo,
a million blades were out and shining. I could see them
behind the flesh-dry, sun-coloured walls. The blades were candles
Little flames, little souls pacing down the alleyway streets. Slinking
incense caressed my nostrils. Its delicacy impressed me. It impressed
me as much as those solid walls, those Christian guardians –

*

Judy is suddenly with him like a ghost of Summer. Chambermaid, waitress, beetle-ess, botanist. She *cannot* be with him and, indeed, she is speaking five months earlier. Judy takes a spare stool and pulls it up at the Barman's table. Her eyes glint with lost sunlight. She speaks:

"Our walk back across the cliffs was delightful. The birds were awake, of course – and the dawn glided up the grass slope, dewy with the cobwebs of tiny spiders. The morning was tied up with sea breezes and the distance to the sky.

"You were jaunty – as worrying sleep fell from you, as gorse snarled at your unheeding legs. You exhilarated at this exploration of a new planet. The heat came out of your armpits and spread across your body.

"Eyes puckered into the wind, we descended through the bracken and came across the tree trunk. Wood fibre had been blown and eaten into tall piles like freakish rocky outcrops. No trees grew here. No trees had grown here for ten thousand years: the sea lay before us now, but once we could have rushed down onto a plain and rejoiced and hunted wolves..."

Judy, an uncomplicated girl, becomes mysterious.

"Brown fern-shrouded... the tree trunk lurked, declaring to be turned. You reached down and pushed the unembalmed tree away – sent it flying into gulls' nests or the sea. Its whirling form looked like a spinning Toledo. Your dream. Now you would never forget it.

"In the blackened space that had homed a stump, five horrid lives lay. They curled up in protection. White – grown man's thumb-sized – the tails of their wood-gorged bodies now curving to touch the clutching orange snouts that open-closed, in-out, eating nothing but air, fresh air. Clustered three-pair legs trying to walk: but they never had; they never had walked in their woody womb, their darkness snapped by you – the Barman Uncreator. Some weird kid who slept the Winters through outside, ready to de-hibernate into Summer's affable cocktail-maker. And Summer would soon be here and the grin would return and the world would be repeated..."

*

Judy has vanished. Her ghost has gone. The stool has replaced itself at a neighbouring table. Disgusted, the Barman rises and leaves the lounge bar. He prowls the deserted, rain-lashed building. The weather is at war with the world's hotels. He thinks about the five worms, the five larval stag beetles. The five brothers – or sisters – zipping up their shiny sable suits all ready for their big roles.

He strolls through the games room with its scattering of cracked ping-pong balls. He sees himself and Judy lying together beneath the billiard table:

Barman: I'm glad we never talk much.
Judy: Yes.

Pause

Judy: You dreamed of Toledo.
Barman: No. That was last night. After we saw those bugs on the clifftop.
Judy: Babies, not bugs – Nature's wonder nasties. You've no respect for Nature, have you? You *were* dreaming about Toledo. Something something Toledo something...
Barman: Spanish?
Judy: No. Not Spanish. Odd. UnEuropean.
Barman: UnChristian?
Judy: (*giggles*) You looked like one of those stag bugs when you said it.

The English Soil Society

Barman: Ah, of course: I am the human harbinger of the insect revolution. Lay me an egg, Judy.
Judy: Hmm!
Barman: Hmm?
Judy: It's me – trying to fly away.
Barman: Flap...
Judy: ...Flap...

The space beneath the billiard table takes on its true and empty reality. The Barman clears a chair of eggshell ping-pong balls, pulls out the journal. A pen is brandished. This is his story. Let him write, let him speak:

> *I sat in the empty lounge bar at a corner table. It was early afternoon and the rain battered the window, bouncing and streaking to the foot of the pane. I thought about the ghosts and the memory of glasses in salutation. And there I was behind the bar: mixing, shaking and changing the muzak; thinking about myself thinking about them and there. The wallpaper could do with a change: embossed herons and unidentified river grasses. And then, without warning –*

*

And then, without warning, he's back up in the cab of the truck as it thunders south out of Vittoria:

> *The stinking interior – air-rippling hills – hunting butterflies many many miles from the truck-laden eucalyptus.*

A 'plane has lost its undercart in Burgos (or not far away) as we thunder south on church-peaked roads.

> *Silly dreams of a million Toledo blades: the feeling of the iron-worked cat sores; all those spitting alleys leading to the salt-buttressed sea cathedral.*

44

*Silly dreams of strange late sunsets and canals like on that Losey film,
stalking around palm trees – following in footsteps and only half
suspecting it.*

*And then back to the bars and altars and the beautiful blue
of Galician girls and rain...*

*

The Barman leans back in the chair in the games room, pondering
these last lines: the clouds that you get up in the north of the country
and the extraordinary attraction of the night of Palm Sunday when
the communion is over... the pungency of chorizo and one of the
cheaper Riojas, the perfume of the mussel beds and the Latin
lovers...

He is glad that he can still remember it all. The multi-layered
throbbing reality. In his self-appointed role as compère to the beetle
revolution, good memory retention is vital. His antennae glow
happily in time with the storm outside.

*

The Barman passes through the games room door and makes his way
to the staff quarters behind the kitchen. He ferrets out a volume from
beneath the bed in his tiny box room. He locates the relevant page:

GRECO PAINTS TOLEDO AS IF DURING AN APOCALYPTIC
CATASTROPHE (PLATE 259); ON ITS ACID GREEN HILL THE
CITY SHAKENLY ASSERTS ITSELF WHILE THE SKY IS
RIVEN BY THUNDER CLOUDS.

*

The service bell rings. Unlikely. It rings again. Impossible. The
Barman tosses away the book, thrusts his journal deep into his own
clothing. He enters the staff common room, leans through the
window, peers around the side of the building to the front door.

The English Soil Society

The Advertiser is here. Cub reporter little Lindy Adams in her '88 Citroen. TransAtlantic Essex accent. Grasps her mini-cassette, throws out questions, asks about the dying... but the Barman is ahead of himself. He sneaks out to reception, snaps his elasticated bow-tie. A mass of deadbolts and the front door is open.

Lindy: (*displays press card, consults notes*) Ah, the Barman. Yes. I'm from *The Advertiser*. You might remember me. May I come in?
Barman: Lindy Adams. Of course.
Lindy: Quite a day.
Barman: Yes.
Lindy: They say the rain's settled in for the rest of the bloody week. Can I come in?
Barman: I guess. How can I help you, miss?

They stand dripping by the reception desk...

Lindy: Well, it's about this mystery girl –
Barman: Judy. From Spain. From Toledo. Where they make the swords.
Lindy: Yes! The Toledo blades, no less. They never found out what *really* happened, did they? It's six months since she died and it's still a bit of a mystery, you know? (*More consultations with notes*) She was found at the foot of the cliff, right? What a bloody shame. But it happens a lot, you know: all around the coast. Foreign girlies come over to party and learn the bloody stupid language and do a bit of work maybe. August is a bad month for this kind of thing – it gets wild. That's what my special's about. I'm doing a special, you see: far from home, parents' angle, coroner's report, awful bloody British Customs acting like shits, you know?
Barman: Suicide, of course.
Lindy: Hmm?
Barman: Suicide most like. I mean, I didn't know her really. A student like most of them. She was some kind of biologist, I think. Pretty good on insects. Beetles especially: *escarabajo* she called them. She had some striking theories. In Visigoth Spain – after the Romans – there was a belief that stag beetles would foretell the

46

Millennium; that their bodies would spell out the Final Word of God on the parched hillsides. You know, Judy told me once –

Lindy: Not that you knew her, right?

Barman: No, not that I really knew her. No. No. I really didn't know her at all –

Lindy: As you told the police, of course. Have you ever been to Spain?

Barman: What? Yes. No. No. Never. I've never been there. I didn't know Judy really, not at all. She was very quiet. She got upset when Tom Luscombe went crop spraying though...

Lindy: I know – in that bloody gyrocopter thing, right?

Barman: Right. Tom took off from the old MoD strip near the bunker where Thatcher was going to hide when the war came. Judy thought he was just practising with his lawn mower, before it shot up into the air and looped over the farmhouse to disappear inland. They use it for crop spraying. Do they still use DDT? They're intelligent, you know: these beetles have abstract thinking. You can just imagine those little stag buggers going berserk with their titchy little nervous systems all ablaze, their lung slits working nineteen to the dozen to counteract the fall of the Devil's rain.

Lindy is out of tape and desperately tries to re-spool...

Barman: (*now seemingly unaware of Lindy's presence*) And down there, at the foot of the cliff, lies the last of Judy: watch the crabs get excited, watch the white mean tide voles twitch whisker at the nearness of her. And as the moon shifts and sends the oceans running back to the land, Judy floats out to sea only to be hauled in by a Spanish trawler fresh out of the Devonport Fisheries Holding. They're storming back across the Bay with a clutch of coggies (sold the legs to the Froggies) and they, the good men of Santander, lay her out in a cedar coffin and fly her back to where she had floated from.

*

Lindy has gone. The Citroen has disappeared, you know? The

The English Soil Society

Barman senses a warmer air coming. He steps back in through the front door, checks the CLOSED sign and throws the bolts.

Objects hurl themselves at him as he jogs the corridors. A clutch of three-year old brochures catch at his speeding ankles. In the box room, a volume dances up from under the bed. Words swing and turn grey:

DURING THE CIVIL WAR, TOLEDO HELD OUT FOR THIRTY-NINE DAYS. AT A CERTAIN POINT DURING THE SIEGE, THE CITY'S COMMANDER RECEIVED A TELEPHONE CALL IN HIS OFFICE IN THE ALCAZAR. THE VOICE AT THE OTHER END – HISTORY DOES NOT RECORD ITS OWNER – DEMANDED THAT TOLEDO SHOULD SURRENDER WITHIN THE HOUR OR THE COMMANDER WOULD WITNESS THE EXECUTION OF HIS SON CAPTURED ON THE PREVIOUS EVENING.

*

This is the Barman's story. Let him write, let him speak, let him remember:

>There's a hostel just beyond the city walls, beyond the
>River Tegus. Sunday lunchtime and they're all falling over
>themselves: kids screaming, the beautiful surveyor's
>wives cut loose for the grand occasion, 15,000 bottles
>on tiny tables: waiters running up two steps
>at a time from the steaming kitchen with
>lizards on the roof (we looked afterwards warmed
>by Ponche): and the plastic cloths are ripped off
>and wiped and we all get hablo-ing and the con gas
>comes and the salad comes and we're scared about the
>olive oil death scandal so we stick to vinegar and then the
>chicken in garlic comes and then cordero asada for yours
>truly and boy! those bones just float off and the air becomes
>heavier and heavier and the box behind the bar's showing
>"Sanders of the River" and it's 5 o'clock and there are people

still piling in, the bonnets of their Seats rippling in the heat
of the plains, knackered from being parked up to
Plateresque archways and getting tickets from
the Guarda who look like bearded commandos escaped
from Cuba ("Well, let's commute the green
stamps to candle-lighting – peseta diez – and I am
blessed... oh, bless me, bless me, Father...")

And at night Judy and I go back down to the city and get lost in its
catacombs roofed with darkened sky before crossing the new bridge
with its striplight walls on the road to bed.

And we lie there thinking of absolutely nothing – a feat of
near impossibility – allowing our bodies to suck in the lack
of light, allowing our bodies to sink into a state very
near to death –

And then morning comes gently in.

And the electricity has gone.

And you put a hand inside and just switch me off –

*

The Solar System swings to green. Planets shine and roll. Reds and pinks and blues caught by the black sun. Snookering. Orbiting. The vacuum of the games room holds nothing: as empty as Judy as she soared up the crematorium chimney.

Winter sunshine turns the Channel into strips of hot lead. The Barman ghosts himself through last summer. Phantom tuxedos stained with forgotten gravy. Glittering wives linger in Habitat corners. Cocktails: White Ladies and the one called Futurity are drunk and absorbed and make their urethral departure. ("What have you done to the weather? There's been so much weather lately...")

*

The English Soil Society

The Barbeetle sees it all in the box room in crawling February:

**Look at them. Drooling baboons. Weighed down with vertebrae.
Harnessed to a brain that weighs a pound too much. They wear
their armour on the inside, and stuff their hairy faces with holes
for ventilation.
They're weak.
They are
unable to
operate
with each
other. They are
individual.
They are
unable
to raise
themselves
above
the weakness
of their
individuality.**

*

The Barmanbeetle lies there, watching his story being spelled out on
the ceiling. The T comes first. Insects scamper around the central
light fitting, spelling out more letters: O and L and E. The tourist
sword from Toledo lies next to him: one of a million Toledo blades.
The rain falls again.
And presently he begins to cut himself out of his old skin.

*

They have won.
Fifty billion stag beetles attack the roots of the Island Albion
with appetites of insanity. It is the Millennium. Those beetle-
buggers are like living chainsaws slicing through the schist:

50

gobbling, processing, turning themselves into huge black cockroach olives.

The air over Europe explodes with the flying carapaces of *escarabajos*. The atmosphere gives out and the continent sinks, taking half of Asia with her. A three-mile high tidal wave hits the Pacific Slope and Gondwanaland re-appears for a split-century before being lost forever.

Spanish ceases to be the planet's most spoken language and is replaced by the sonar of cetaceans:

And so it spins: the world spins. It throws off water and plasma. All remaining life forms are hurled out into the void. They are instantly frozen and shoot like upward hailstones through a night in Winter.

The bricks and blades of Toledo are scattered and must build and defend a citadel to a more alien heart. An unknown army will gather on a strange hillside. Their armour might be glorious, their weapons extraordinary. And they will barely be aware that they speak the speech of angels –

S

There was once a country where everyone wore two hats.

The country itself had some moderate hills, pretty average woodland and the sort of wildlife that could be found just about anywhere else. Neither warm nor freezing, it was regarded as something of a meteorological disappointment. If *disappointment* were not too strong a word: for neighbours rarely considered the country much – what with its modesty of area and capital income; its ceremonially-sized army and benign anonymity.

Anonymous, that is, save for a millinery tradition of seemingly significant if baffling singularity. The citizens had taken to the habit of wearing two hats. Together. At the same time. Simultaneously.

Observers conjectured on the curiosity of the two hats. Anthropology students had scraped through degrees on ideas half-baked in an oven of feverless debate. Was there some primeval motive? Were the two hats adopted in some quaint throwback to heady chivalry? Had past burgomasters – recognising their country's complete lack of individual character – decreed that two hats be worn to ward off ribald ruderies from more fascinating neighbours?

There were two hats on the Twohattan national flag. The flag – an otherwise averagely stirring gold and navy blue – sported a brace of bowlers in the top right-hand corner. The national army – as mentioned, a token force – affected national bowlers on (occasional) active duty; and at other times assumed all manner of coupled headgear when mucking around in village squares or marriage parlours as soldiers are wont to do.

*

So life slipped along smoothly for the citizens of Twohatta. They continued to quietly thrive in their nondescript climate, whittling away at double-hatted woodcarvings for passing foreign tourists.

Yet their whittling days were numbered. For through some bureaucratic what-have-you, the World Olympic Committee had shortlisted Twohatta's second biggest city for the next Games but one; but were then – with some embarrassment – pressured to scrub the idea due to the threat of event tampering by the home team.

The mind may boggle, but the Twohattans were loathe to remove their hats even for the most inappropriate of events: the national 200 metre swimming champion undertook her record-breaking butterfly in double tricorns with connecting tassels. Neighbouring countries became dubious of all this hat business. Yachtsmen had been accused of sporting personal spinnakers and dark rumours told of sprinters in aerodynamic wizardly hats; of relay runners using capacious headgear to store spare batons – or even spare teammates.

Little by little, Twohatta became an outcast in the modern world. What had once seemed charmingly fanciful in old Michelin guides was now looked on with some suspicion. What *were* these Twohattans up to? Holidaymakers took to bypassing the country and made two thousand-mile detours through bug-infested swampland to avoid it. The new monetary mechanism that the continent was trying to unite itself with began to founder – allegedly because of Twohattan intransigence on several key sub-points. Sheep herds – to cater for modest winter linings in mild Twohattan winters – were kidnapped over the border by hatless neighbours.

The international community chose to turn a blind eye while Twohattan students were locked up in world capitals and their headgear impounded. The very few Twohattans claiming asylum from the remarkably tolerant Twohattan political regime were kept waiting in their underpants at foreign airport terminals. Worldwide hat sales plummeted. The spring collections of leading couturiers were utterly *non chapeaux*. Hats were yesterday. Didn't hats contribute to that ozone thing? Hats were *out*.

The Twohattans remained philosophical. Things had been worse, surely – but no one could remember when. Life would get better – but no one knew how. The Twohattans in their modest unspectacular way attempted to keep a low planetary profile. The symbol of the double bowlers was quietly shrunken on the already discreet national postage stamp. They stopped their (token) protest about kidnapped sheep herds. Indeed, they feigned not to notice when national neighbours – proclaiming the logic of aligning political boundaries with natural features – pushed their own borders a further fifty metres into Twohatta.

In fact, one neighbour to the north of Twohatta (with a national predilection for extravagant moustaches) pressed its state line on for a further one hundred kilometres to a natural border bisecting fifteen sitting rooms on a Twohattan housing estate.

To the south of Twohatta lay the country politically opposed to the moustached northerners: this southern state was famous for its fanatical attachment to market gardening. It was unfair, went a Market Gardener press release. Moustachio's formalisation of borders through sitting rooms was a gross act of war. The government of Gardenia intended to free the Twohattans from their hated hairy-lipped oppressor forthwith.

And one and a half minutes later the Gardenian army of liberation marched into the capital of Twohatta three hundred kilometres from the southern border.

A curfew was announced in Twohat City.

Gardenian special commandos (war crimes committees would wrangle for years over the identities of those responsible) dropped killer rats down the previously rather wholesome Twohat City sewer system. Bubonic plague was induced. Thousands of Twohattans died in their capital: three Moustachians perished as a result of fleeing the rats and getting lost in the mountains.

The Moustachians launched avenging air strikes that decimated

Twohattan suburbs while Gardenian armour lurked at a distance in schoolyards covered by camouflage netting. Minefields were laid and their plans tossed away. Special forces from both sides met in media-choreographed exchanges of small arms fire.

Twohatta was a serious news item now. The Twohattans – previously seen as figures of suspicion on the sports pages – were suddenly everyone's friend. Foreigners who went on brief skim-the-surface charity trips to Twohatta were treated like shining heroes when they returned to their own countries. Cameramen received awards for their footage; a reporter who sustained a rat bite won a medal.

An international peacekeeping organisation met every night for three months on the trot. This Twohattan business was at the top of the agenda. Diplomats worked far into the caffeine-fuelled night trying to muddle out a solution. A forgotten member of 80s rock royalty wrote a song and a hat auction in Paris raised millions.

At the end of its three months, the international peacekeeping organisation came to a decision. At the end of a further five years those decisions had been formalised through the usual channels and were ready for the world to know: Twohatta was now off-limits to all international trade (they said). A web of embargo would be spun around the country (they announced). Peace would triumph by a simple implementation of The Do Nothing Principle: the world would look on with a quarter of an eye and it would all go away.

Twohatta dropped off page one. The world became bored. It was Olympic-time again and the smell of cortisone was in the air. Anyone remember that problem just before the last Games? Ah, those Twohattans probably deserved it anyway.

*

In a mountain fastness far above the capital, the pitiful remains of the Twohattan Freedom Force crouched over a spluttering campfire.

The Freedom Fighters had just dispatched a TV reporter back down the rocky pass and were attempting to fry the bubblegum he'd just passed out. The reporter had winked conspiratorially as he dished out the pink gum: "Cost me my job, *hombre*," he rasped, glimmering with the sheer shit-ain't-this-on-the-edge of it all. They could see him now down on the road as he tried to patch into the link from his luxury motorhome. A couple more trucks were parked up to it: four-wheel drive emissaries from different broadcasting organisations. They'd sent their reporters up too. One had left them a portable television with the promise that they might see themselves on The Eleven O'Clock News.

The young leader of the Twohattan Freedom Force left the glow of the campfire, the warmth of her companions, and walked to a precipice a hundred metres further up. It was darker here and the woman was alone with the stars. A slight chill slipped down her back, the modest harbinger of the gentle Twohattan winter. A brief sparkle caught her attention high up in the wonderful night sky – and then it was gone. But then another sparkle. And another. Shooting stars: silent, brief, gone before they were there. Not really mattering, yet so beautiful. So *otherly*. She should share this moment with her friends. The commander looked down at them: the campfire was extinguished now, all attention on the glowing tube hitched up to a car battery.

Scratching her heads, the woman turned away from the stars and scrabbled down into the glimmering arc of the television.

The Dressing Floors

Skin deep, deeper still:

Above the dressing floors the clotheless are nothing. Rumours. Phantoms-in-waiting. But not even *pantomime* wraiths – for ghost sheets are in very short supply.

Above the dressing floors.

*

The dressing floors occupy the first three levels of the house by the reservoir. Rumours abound of a secret cellar and a super-secret tunnel below the lorry park in the basement. And *deeper still* the dark, dark waters that lead to the planet's liquid core: a domain of alien pressures and bathyscaped demons that wait for the first explorer from the light above.

But:

No frogsuits on the dressing floors. Monkey suits perhaps. Donkey jackets almost certainly. Maybe with a *touch* of frogging, the lick of the Crimea and lost dusty empires. Boots worn by Wellington and Bücher. Pixie boots from Whittington to Ultravox.

And Things To Keep Them In:

Vast wardrobes (such wardrobes!) and dressers on the dressing floors. The wardrobes that can clothe countries and harbour their allies. Coathangers are strewn like a restless barbed wire – but those are for the new clothes: a mere century old. On hooks are the crinolines and bum-rolls of an earlier age, stained and charming. They throw skeleton shadows illuminated by dim – always dim but always on – electric candelabras. The electricity is inferior. It's not enough. It comes from too far away. The system has to work hard and sometimes sounds like the distant coughing of failing fridges.

*

In the attic above the dressing floors we remain undressed. It is chilly and bracing. The windows are open and wide. We have a clear view across the reservoir; the surrounding moorland that currently rusts with autumnal bracken. Our nakedness is unembarrassing. We have become accustomed to the comforting North European whiteness of fellow bodies. It is the thought of clothes that is frightening. That elusive sweetness of identity. We don't do a great deal. There are many settees and club armchairs. There's a coffee machine and a ping-pong table and a shower and loo with a lock on the door – for the naked are concerned about such things.

*

Miranda slips through the cat flap into the *attic*.

She returns from a scout of the dressing floors; under the feet of the tailors, fitters and seamstresses – their numbers disappear into infinity on the second level above the wardrobes. The tailors hate windows and electricity and make do with thick yellow candles, sickly with whale fat. The tailors are cross-legged on tables and on the floor facing away from each other; the catchers not of eyes but of stitches.

Miranda has seen a sight today that makes her purr with ear-twitchy pleasure. A young tailor with the head of an egg and purple socks has sewn his own trouser turn-up into the green felt of the table – because he daren't look down on the tailor who squats on the floor beneath him.

Thread slips in-and-out: eyes never touch.

Miranda purrs again in the attic as her memory transfers into instinct as is the way with animals. Animals live in the *now*. She will *now* gain pleasure whenever she's in the presence of needle and thread and heads like an egg.

And purple socks if she had the *eyes* for them.

Miranda slips now about the bare calves of the undressed as they read their Sunday supplements. She locates the comforting friendly foot of Alfredo. Alfredo is very old, perhaps the oldest of the undressed. A white beard foams down his chest – the happy home for many tiny spiders.

Alfredo smiles and lifts the cat onto his fleshless shoulder and takes her to the big window; he quietly avoids the ladies as they knit with Number 14 needles and make-believe wool and discuss beetle drives and the new cooler weather.

There are people with clothes out on the moor.

They appear ponderous and thick. They have trouble standing up in their thick linen shells, their polyester carapaces. One even has boots on, lumberjack boots. The figure is a woman with blond hair tied back with invisible faraway string. Alfredo has seen this woman before. He thinks she works on the reservoir, perhaps lives in one of its two hexagonal towers set at either end of the wall above the vast grey waters. Perhaps the others are her family down from the city.

Perhaps it's Sunday.

Alfredo glances over at Glenadine as she snoozes under several layers of supplements: there have been so many Sundays. Once one could tell quite easily. The bells from the church towers of the city might echo across the woods, ruins and tors of the wild countryside; filter through the incurious windows above the dressing floors. But the bells are a memory. Perhaps the steeples have been pulled down. Maybe the bells are *unclothed*.

Alfredo waves to the reservoir girl. She looks right up at the old man but seems unable to make him out. She seems aware of his presence but uncertain of his nature. Of his origin. The reservoir girl throws her head back and sniffs.

She turns away and looks into the reservoir. She can see her reflection – or thinks she does – and waves to that instead.

*

There's a flap on.

Miranda's familiar heaviness is absent from his knees and Alfredo is immediately awake in the dawn of tomorrow. The others in the attic snore quietly on; an occasional whimper from the rows of tall hospital bedsteads that line the inside of the eaves.

Alfredo shuffles his bare feet across the floorboards, cursing the god of careless nail hammerers. He makes his ears as wide as he can. They are large, transparent pieces of business like the dorsal cooling fins of Palaeozoic dinosaurs.

The air is full of shivers. It hums and the ears of the old man quiver imperceptibly.

The floors below are *dis-dressing.*

The tailors unpick the past week's labours and pile it into the articulated lorries. The building quivers again. Far below, just above the cellar line, lies the underground loading bay where the lorries back in every third Tuesday.

Or sometimes every second.

The truckers jump down from their cabs decorated with Walsall bunting and babe pix from Back Street Heroes. They hitch open the rear trailer doors, empty and waiting for the latest knittings. Three tons of fishbone weave, an acre or two of corduroy (difficult stuff).

The apprentice tailors chuck in the week's makings that they have wheeled from the dressing floors in shopping trolleys. The tailors are pale under the arc lamps that the truckers insist on: these strivers of the whalelight. The tailors might eye the outsiders widely. The outsiders perhaps look around, down, up, muttering "Jesus..." and adjust their fluorescent body warmers.

And when the job is done – when everything from the dressing floors is in the back of the big lorries – the tailorettes scurryingly return to their table tops, while the truckers laugh and roar up the ramps into the sunlight.

Miranda sees it all, curled up in a spare wheel on the docking bay; a tabby going to fat on cold milky Néscafé, the gift of apprentices.

Alfredo folds back his ears with his hands above the dressing floors. He lifts his nose and widens its nostrils. Like the reservoir girl.

Distantly, through the downbelow mist of camphor and dry cleaning bags, he smells today's diesel. The double-glazing shudders very briefly. The passing of the great lorries is invisible as they take the circular underpass that leads out to the motorway.

*

Miranda flops on the crown of Alfredo's head like a humming ginger toupee. The attic letterbox rattles sharply as the slush of newspapers falls through it. Presently, a melodic *clinkety-clank* as milk bottles touch the doorstep.

Alfredo waits the designated fifteen minutes (no watches – but he counts very carefully) and then opens their front door. The corridor ahead is lit with a dullish ambient glow; the walls are adorned with paintings of Neapolitan urchins more usually found in the bedrooms of cheaper airport hotels. Alfredo sniffs once more – but it is the reassuring smog of the dressing floors that touches his nose now: the camphor again; sewing machine oil, sweat and farts from a thousand tailors.

He pulls in the milk and closes the door.

*

Again, the reservoir girl is there. A week has passed. A week perhaps (Alfredo's counting is not trusted by all...)

Alfredo and Glenadine see the girl together. Glenadine puts down her bag of personalised vouchers (*"...IMAGINE, **Ms. G. Gurée**, your name has already been selected for our competition's sensational second round..."* *"...IMAGINE, **Ms. G. Gurée**, a brand new hosiery and life assurance concept for you*

63

and your loved ones...") and places her pretty old nose against the double glazing.

The girl walks from one of the grey reservoir towers with a toolbox. She pauses far below and peers over the wall into the water. She unzips and shrugs off her yellow overalls. Underneath she wears more clothes – blue trousers and a jaunty red-and-orange shirt. She stands and looks at her feet; perhaps wonders whether to remove her lumberjack boots – *all the while* with her hand on her shoulder. Maybe she just worries at a bra strap; or perhaps she simply enjoys the texture of her sunny shirt. And *all the while* she stares across the greyness of the reservoir that sends water into the city.

She looks up at them with a restrained puzzlement. Glenadine waves.

The reservoir girl turns away: the toolbox is in one hand, the overalls over her shoulder; she strides along the wall to the other tower.

And as she strides she looks ever, forever into the water; perhaps wonders if she can wear it. *If she could only quickly zip it on and dry her hands afterwards –*

*

That night:

Glenadine cries for clothes in her sleep. Her hands knit around themselves with the sheet in between. She is twisting the sheet into a blouse or pantaloons. Or perhaps even a handkerchief. (Few noses to wipe above the dressing floors; illnesses are unknown, injuries small – a tongue grazed licking an envelope, wrist-twists after gin rummy).

"Thread, thread..." she whispers as the yellow half-moon glows in through the window. "Come closer now. Come..."

Alfredo pulls the curtain, darkens the room.

Glenadine's eyes are open but Alfredo is unnoticed; as invisible to her as his own nakedness is invisible to himself.

"Come closer and I will *dress* you..." she sighs.

Alfredo crouches at the foot of the old woman's bed for some time. He rises: the crack of his joints make him jump in the still, breathing room.

He goes to the window, drags back the curtain and they are dressed again in moonlight.

*

The plumber comes on the morning of Glenadine's funeral. They watch her coffin as it slips out of the bowels of the building on the back of a pick-up truck and disappears down into the underpass.

The toilet is backed-up. Some desperate soul has stuffed the U-bend with newspapers: water in the bowl is stained a deeper grey than the grey waters of the reservoir.

The plumber has been partially briefed on the situation above the dressing floors. His naked body is pale and pear-shaped. It is unused to being undressed. The plumber – Mr Stanley – carries his plumber's bag at genital level and the heavy tools prod him painfully as he stands on the edge of the loo seat and tries to peer into the ceiling cistern. He rummages around one-handed as the round faces of the attic-dwellers beam up at him. He steps down and surveys the type-print waters of the toilet bowl. He closes the lid and sits on it.

Young Maisie brings milky coffee and Mr Stanley half rises to accept two Garibaldi biscuits from her seventy-year old fingers.

"Well... it's a rum do, folks," says Mr Stanley as he munches and hopes that his crossed legs don't break some attic etiquette. "I'll be needing the electric pump and a towel. And a bucket or three, if you have any – "

"I'll get it, Mr Stanley."

"Oh, I think we'll be needing more than one bucket, sir..."

"I'll get it, Mr Stanley," repeats Alfredo. "I'll get the electric pump. It'll be down in your van, I'll be bound..."

"And you'll be bounding down to get it, old chap? That's good of you but I don't believe that you're allowed..."

"Oh, we are. Within the confines of the building, Mr Stanley – "

None of the attic-dwellers seem to breathe anymore. They stare at Alfredo while desperately... casually... casually... desperately... they attempt to glance in an opposite direction.

"It would save you time, Mr Stanley. Maisie girl could get the kettle going again and you could start rodding and then you'd be that much further ahead when I got back with the pump. It's *allowed*. Within the confines of the building. It's allowed. *Really*."

*

The air is chill down in the basement. Alfredo finds the plumber's small Suzuki van easily enough; and beyond it lies one of the big articulated lorries. The lorry is fully stuffed with knitting – he can see through the still-open rear doors. The loading men and the driver and a couple of uncomfortable-looking under-dressers stand in the Portacabin and watch football on television. The match is going badly and the men are arguing.

A new electrical coolness glides past Alfredo's shin.

"No, Miranda. I'm afraid your old Alfredo is going on a little trip by himself. A little trip to the outside. I need you to keep an eye on those naughty tailors, my sweet..."

He bends down and works the back of her neck with his hand. "A little trip... A little trip..."

A goal has been scored. The Portacabin is in uproar. A glass breaks.

Alfredo rises and shuffles to the open back of the lorry and plunges into the sea of wool; warms his naked feet and stifles a hundred sneezes.

*

The darkness moves:

Alfredo can't know how long he has lain here – his internal clockwork dims in the presence of shadows. His nostrils and eyes are clogged with wool fragments. The lorry is bumping along; the hum of the engine alternates with the hiss/bark of air brakes and gear changes.

Alfredo relaxes into his knitted ocean and dreams of the hours or days ahead, of his journey into a different planet. Or he might dream of the reservoir girl: as she stands on the battlements and looks ever deeper into the waters and wonders what her clothes are for.

*

The lorry stops with a final stagger of its braking system. The sound of the rear doors as they swing open reach through the woolly fug: Alfredo has unknowingly worked his body deeper into the trailer's interior; *deeper still...*

And so light comes back into his world; the unloading of bales and scarves and the looser hanks of wool traitorously reveal his hiding place.

He sees them now.

He sees them...

His revealers:

Muffled with clothes, they hide under their weight, barely able to carry the new deliveries from the lorry. Some limp through the wearing of multi-layers of socks. Jumpers; cardies; waistcoats; greatcoats; shorts over plus-fours over tracksuit bottoms over thick corduroy walking trousers... Bobble hats precarious above bo'sun's caps and balaclavas. Gender is impossible to tell – the bodies have been ballooned into the realms of androgyny.

Only the eyes:

Only the eyes – a flash of some pale male? female? colour: a frowned upon revelation in this overdressed world.

Alfredo tumbles out onto tarmac.

He is outside.

He is outside in some sort of exterior counterpart to the basement lorry park. Low industrial buildings fill three angles; on the fourth, double gates and a Perspex guard hut. The football match proceeds noisily within.

The unloaders – perhaps there are six of them – seem uncertain of this new arrival. Alfredo senses no aggression from them as he rises painfully and hopes a bloodied knee won't collapse under him. Rather, an odd sort of sadness communicates itself by the incline of a head, the limp mittened-hands of some of them. He must seem such a tiny creature: a lower life form surprised during some vital shedding of skins. A forgotten thing: a prehistoric fish long thought lost, netted by accident and held up against the sun, the object of a poignant fascination.

Alfredo clears his throat but can think of no further sound to make. He totters forward on his cramped legs and they allow him through. They keep away (it seems) from his touch.

One gate is open and he pushes through and closes it behind him. Most of the unloaders turn back to their work. One continues to watch him. *Perhaps it's curious*, thinks Alfredo as he rubs his knee. *Perhaps it wants to dress me.* And he remembers Glenadine and her thread of yellow moonlight.

And the colour of moonlight when morning comes.

*

The sun is hot and Alfredo feels his unused shoulders redden.

The streets of the city are awash with walking wardrobes. Pedestrians bustle each other off pavements with the weightiness of their clothing and fight at zebra crossings. One or two fall into the road: they lie helpless inside their bloated garments as the cars bump over them.

There is silence from the people of the city. In the attic – even when the most intense bridge game is in progress, *even* when the Sunday supplements are new – there is always a conversational hum from the undressed. Bickering – petty or otherwise – perhaps; but naked lives are *touched* it seems. By comparison, the city dwellers try to keep as far away as possible from each other: and if by chance they fall into a fellow's path the silence seems to intensify – as if it can cocoon the occurrence more readily than any distant insurance claim for personal injury.

The slap of leather on pavement – or the strangled cough, the barely *breathed* breath. These are the sounds that Alfredo hears.

The clothes seem to walk their inhabitants around. And perhaps some of the clothes are unoccupied.

Alfredo leans on a broken guess-your-weight machine and has a sudden urge to unravel these people, to cast-off their knitted hearts.

*

Before he walks back into the countryside, Alfredo sits on a dustbin behind a restaurant where the orders are telephoned ahead into an answering machine.

He studies his hands. Perhaps his skin has been mistaken for one of the sheerer silks. He glances down at his old body: he could be dressed in a stained pillow leaking white goose feathers of body hair.

A bird pads past his feet and worries at a thrown-out piece of bacon rind. It is not a goose – this would have made a strange day stranger, a strange day *deeper still* – but it is of reasonable size: a pigeon perhaps. It's difficult to tell. Alfredo looks at the bird and the bird looks back – eyes bright in its featherless, free body.

*

The moors are beautiful in the dawn mist. A pinkish glow hangs in the sky as Alfredo glances back at the city. Perhaps it stirs itself awake. He might even hear a church bell – or the embarrassed rush of ten million water closets.

He sits between the two towers on the ramparts of the reservoir. His feet dangle over the water through the metal railing. He fully intends to return to the attic room above the dressing floors – but in a little while perhaps, when he's caught his breath. The seasons are changing: although the day promises to be hot, the passing night has turned his limbs blue and his progress back across the rough ground has been slower than he hoped. Yes. He will rest here for just a little while before he goes back to Miranda and tells her about his strange adventure.

There is a commotion in the waters of the reservoir. Nothing very large. Nothing terribly disturbing. For the first time he notices that the lumberjack boots and jeans and the colourful red-and-orange shirt lie in a heap by one of the towers.

He watches the girl as she surfaces and twists about to descend once more into the wet darkness: in the reservoir there is nothing between her soul and the water but her skin.

She might have surfaced again but it's harder to see her now.

And Alfredo glances up to where he thinks the big attic window might be.

Redapple

This is a story about a place called Redapple and how it ceased to be.

Oh sure. You can go there today. You can cross the city limits coinciding with the railroad track and wander down Redapple's cypress-lined street. Tin cans kick along just as they ever did. You can get that whistling radiator fixed at Geraldo's Garage. And you can watch Geraldo fix it from Gloria's diner over the street – where the coffee is probably almost as good as it ever used to be – and mouth along with Geraldo as he curses you and your mother through Gloria's plate glass.

Let's talk about churches. Churches? Redapple's got three and people to fill them too, throwing up hymns as if there were nothing between heaven and earth but the ozone layer. Not that folk were worried much about the ozone layer back in the old days: they were more mindful of whether Herbert Hoover was a better man in the White House than Mr Coolidge; and if Stacey's Saloon on Orchard Lane could ever quit selling liquor in anything other than teacups.

In many ways the old Redapple was pretty much the same as any small town back then. It had some picturesque industry: barrel-making, rabbit farming and apple growing. The last of these was considered the most biblical and wholesome and so they named the town for it.

But the town *was* different. Travellers passing through were able to comment lightly upon it. They sensed a certain something.

And what those travellers sensed, the residents of Redapple knew.

Redapple was different because it was a town without Pain.

It was a too-good town. Brotherliness and sisterliness flowed freer than the Redapple River gushing down from the Greengage Mountains – the range that rose like a clutch of emerald cities to the east of town.

The togetherness of Redapples – as those residents who thought about it liked to be called – even extended to the name of their harmonious town. Josie and Marie Shortling down at the school were always scolding kids and anyone else within earshot about the shameful grammar of their town's name. Sure, Red Apple would be more aesthetic and pleasingly proper. But no: the citizens felt that the two words as one pretty much summed up things about their fine friendly little town. And they didn't need two school spins – who might be sisters or might be not – telling them about proper nouns and the usage thereof.

But life wasn't completely without worry because Redapple worried about its lack of Pain: a worry in retrospect that brought its own tiny measure of painful thought, and – yes, in retrospect – might have been deemed sufficient and painful enough.

Redapple's wholesome pleasure in friendly helpfulness shackled the town to a lead weight that didn't rise with the heartless tide of the Twentieth Century. Redapples watched the skies for the clouds that carried Pain. But the skies were as clear and as bluely pure as the Redapple River as it passed over the ford by the orchards of the Genesis Brothers to the west of town. Pain lived in another country on a planet that had yet to be born.

Redapple felt that the time for Pain had come.

They fretted about it. They argued (in a friendly fashion) over many a teacup in Stacey's Saloon. Preachers from the three churches were summoned and dispatched again: their knowledge of Pain was exquisite by its absence. The town's oldest citizen – who had hitherto claimed participation in the Civil War as a boy soldier – backed off under gentle interrogation. His knowledge of Pain had been passed on third hand and he'd really spent the War prospecting with his aunt in Mexico.

However, someone – they could never remember exactly who it

was afterwards – said that he or she had heard half a rumour (or a quarter of a myth maybe) about a kind of specialist. He travelled the country with his speciality in a carpet bag. This man was a manufacturer of sorts. He made things people wanted.

He made Pain.

*

And so they called the Painmaker.

The Painmaker wasn't in the book. But Geraldo's brother Joel worked for the 'phone company and he got in touch with a cousin who worked in the Need-To-Know-Telephone-Numbers Section of the State Department.

It all happened rather quickly. Everything was arranged.

The Painmaker would arrive a week next Thursday, stay twenty-four hours and charge a fee of precisely ten dollars.

*

The people of Redapple readied themselves for Pain.

They attempted to beat each other for the two best parking spaces on Main Street; but inevitably one or other driver would give way with good grace. Gloria's award-winning muffins (Greengage Cook-Out Best of Class 1927) went missing from the diner window for a whole fifteen minutes before the thieves relented, returning the pastries with two pies of their own. Geraldo took a shot at over-charging for a replacement alternator, but ended up selling it for half-price and threw five quarts of free gas into the deal.

It was all pretty feeble.

The sisterly brotherly folk of Redapple were hopeless at inflicting Pain on each other.

They were in need of some serious help.

*

Thursday week dawned with a grey sky holding water and thoughts of uncertainty. Two trains a day stopped at Redapple back then. It was the era of the Dust Bowl and the railroad company tried to keep the trains down on account of the hoboes bucking it for free.

Train number one came through at 7.30 in the morning with some auto parts for Geraldo – plus a travelling salesman and two lost sailors five hundred miles from salt water. The sailors hung around the station gambling on a portbound connection while the salesman trotted down to Gloria's for flapjacks.

Train number two came by forty-four minutes later. Three drunks fell out of a freight car and one of them recited Edgar Allan Poe. He was a wild man with a tombstone hat and a necklace of chicken skulls. He rolled in the dirt and howled about unfair tax laws – when he'd done with the ravens and premature burials. Geraldo – who'd only just gotten around to picking up his spares from the first train – leaned down and gently helped the man up. The mechanic peered deep into the wild man's dead red eyes. Could this be him? Pain seemed to sit so well and easily upon the little guy. And he could certainly do with ten dollars.

A yell from Main Street stopped Geraldo's question in his mouth. He lay the boxcar bohemian on the platform bench, the tombstone hat at his shoeless feet.

Gloria was still dancing in front of her diner when Geraldo made it out onto the street. She was dancing around just like she'd done after winning the muffin award in 1927. She waved a white card in her hand like a lotto number.

"It's him, it's him. He's here. It's the travellin' man..."

The card, found floating like a lifeboat in a troubled pool of Gloria's coffee, read:

Professor Joseph Swingler
Painmaker
~ parties catered for ~

And in the bottom right-hand corner of the card was an iddy-biddy little heart.

Shrieks were rising up like startled prairie dogs from other parts of town. Evidently, Professor Swingler had been paper-chasing his

74

way all across Redapple. More dancers appeared with copies of the Painmaker's calling card.

*

They found him in Martha's Hardware & Barber Shop. He was just finishing up a shave and was slipping a white card into Martha's husband's pants pocket. The Painmaker leant back in the chrome and ebony barber's chair and took in a long slow eyeful of Redapple's breathless citizens.

He was a round man. Balding, benign – a favourite uncle perhaps or, at worst, an amiably inept children's conjuror. His voice was soft, husky and not even full of *hidden* honey. His voice was full of up-front concern.

"Good morning," he said, wiping away the remains of shaving cream with a hot towel. He spoke in warm, to-the-point sentences. "You called me and I came. In twenty-four hours you will know Pain and you'll pay me for it. I shall expect payment whether I succeed or fail. But I will not fail. You will come to curse me for it. You will come to hate me almost as much as you will come to hate yourselves. I've left my cards all over town so my name will always be remembered. Cursing my name in future times will be your one release from Pain." He gleamed up at Martha in friendly fashion. "How much for the shave, ma'am?"

*

Joseph Swingler, the Professor of Pain, spent the day in a quiet tour of Redapple. He touched the cypress trees that had been imported and planted on Main Street at the turn of the century. He strolled in the modest but conscientiously-tended municipal park. He entered and re-entered Gloria's diner on three occasions for coffee and pastries. Gloria said she'd call it one coffee plus free refills for the whole day. She twinkled at the Painmaker and the Painmaker twinkled back. He thanked her graciously for her hospitality, remarking on the refreshing quality of her generosity in this increasingly ungenerous world.

Professor Swingler visited Valstoed's cooperage up on Peartree Ridge. The cooperage bestrode the Greengage's rushing waters, a bridge of log cabins engrossed in sweat and industry.

"Mmm, you have a fine way with wood," murmured the visitor to old man Valstoed in the seasoning room. "Just seems a shame to put anything inside them barrels."

The Painmaker took an early lunch at Phil Karrion's rabbit ranch three miles out of town. Phil barbecued three of his lop-eared best with some garlic and tarragon. The Painmaker sucked every bone dry in Phil's guest dining room, the noon sun slitting through the blinds like golden fingers.

"Seems to me the rabbit's been neglected in circles of good eating," remarked the Painmaker, inconsequently.

The Genesis Orchard was the venue for the Painmaker's dessert. The Orchard was the largest on the skirt of knubby ridges that encircled the Greengage Heights. The apple trees were at their reddest, slipping in and out of the mountain folds like confetti on a wedding dress. All three Genesis brothers – Joe, Ray and Aaron – sat in the shade of the family boughs. Joe had run away to a circus once – but had run back faster and now juggled apples for the pleasure of their guest. A small wake of onlookers had taken to following the Painmaker, some making pencilled notes of his utterances.

Professor Swingler bit into a large Russet Mayhew, wiped his mouth with an extravagant handkerchief and said: "Hmm. Good apple."

The sound of scratching pencils almost drowned out the three dull thuds as Joe's charges hit the ground.

By mid-afternoon, the Professor was walking up the path to the Redapple schoolhouse, greeting the old gardener and remarking on the dearth of Pope's lilac that year.

The children had represented the one shadow of doubt in the Redapple's scheme To Know Pain. Had they the right to take their young ones down this road of fearful knowing? But as it turned out, the Painmaker was such a normal kind of fellow. More than that. He just seemed downright wise and wishing to go out of his way to please folks.

The Shortling sisters waited at the schoolhouse door, their small entrustees huddled around their knees with that scaredy-brave look that kids have.

The Painmaker was an immediate hit. He was on his knees entertaining the gathering with the finest animal stories, the tallest tales that were ever told. His kangaroo impression was second to none. He could yodel with the best of them. He could even juggle better than Joe Genesis.

After school the Professor took refreshment with Josie and Marie Shortling on their handkerchief of a ball park and talked about children.

Marie poured more lemonade and said: "Do you think children know Pain, Mr Swingler?"

This was perhaps the most direct question the Painmaker had fielded all day. He closed his eyes and opened them; ran one benignly pudgy finger down the very centre of his amused forehead. "Yes, Miss Marie. Children know the Pain we've forgotten. Your children are safe with me." He smiled shortly. Then smiled a little longer. "When it comes to giving and taking Pain, kids have got me whacked. Now, Miss Josie: your cranberry buckbread is just too delicious. I feel my wife might benefit from the recipe... If I may be so bold?"

*

At nine o'clock, the Painmaker retired to his pre-booked bed at the Redapple rooming house.

Stacey's Saloon didn't turn out till midnight: folk were surprised that their visitor hadn't paid a visit to an establishment that might possibly – even in those days of Prohibition – be the first in line for the new-found Pain of Redapple. At 9.15, Jackson Cordobes Stacey was cleaning sarsaparilla bottles in a bar that had never seen a brawl and had only heard two cuss words since 1903.

Jackson smiled quietly to himself.

Unknown to the rest of the town, the Painmaker had wandered by the saloon front on his way to bed. He'd glanced ever-so briefly in through the window and had winked at Jackson Cordobes Stacey.

Jackson knew what that wink was. He'd had bars in other places besides Redapple. Dark port cities and towns with elevated railroads that terminated in hell. It was the wink of the cheat whose cheating card waited five hands away; of the whore beater who'd be back next week.

Not now, the wink meant. Not now – but *later*...

*

The Painmaker rose at 7.40 the next morning. It was perilously close to the twenty-four hour deadline when he took his flapjacks at the window table of Gloria's diner. He could see Geraldo on the other side of the street: the mechanic was busy throwing in another free battery and oil top-up. The Painmaker splashed on more syrup and twinkled quietly to himself.

Folks were gathering loosely; casually going about their business with an eye and a half on Gloria's plate glass window. Professor Swingler finished up the last of his coffee (graciously accepting some warm biscuits in a napkin for later) and stepped out onto the Main Street of Redapple.

The air was warm, the morning still clutching at a glow of dawn.

The crowd was less self-conscious now. All citizens were present: the great and good of Redapple – and those not so great but still pretty good all the same. Only Jackson Cordobes Stacey remained apart; leaning in the doorway of his saloon, drinking warmed-up last night's coffee and wondering just what in hell was about to happen.

The Painmaker stood on one of Gloria's chairs (carefully covering the cushion with the extravagant handkerchief) and ran the benign finger slowly down his forehead almost to the end of his nose.

"Friends – and I feel I've made some very good friends here, so I hope you'll forgive the impropriety – the time has come for me to leave you. This is in our contract. In my twenty-four hours amongst you I have learnt many things. And you've entertained me like a king.

"I don't mind telling you folks that I had my doubts about

78

Redapple. Never before in all my travels across this great country have I found a town so unready for Pain, so unwilling to take on the ugly world and look it in the eye. I still harbour those doubts, I don't mind telling you..." The crowd murmured in self-appreciation. "...But in the end and whichever way you lay it, in thirty-three years of making Pain I have Never Been Wrong."

The Redapples were quieter now. The Painmaker didn't seem to have changed at all and yet they realised that his voice had taken on an ever-so-slight hardness. He stepped down from his makeshift platform, put his carpet bag on it and pulled out a small padlocked box.

"You've all been very kind to me. You've given without being asked. You've shared with me your wisdom, rabbits and cake recipes. But now I must ask you for something. The something that's written into our contract together."

The Professor glanced over to Stacey's Saloon but its bartender had already ducked inside. He unlocked the box, revealing change and small bills. "I must now ask you for my ten dollars."

The Redapples had pre-arranged their system of paying off Professor Swingler. The fee – symbolically small, even back then – would be shared by the great citizens of the town on behalf of their fellow brothers and sisters for whom life hadn't been quite so easy.

Old Jack Valstoed stepped forward first. He smiled at the Painmaker, pulled a one dollar bill from his pocket and laid it on top of the chair from Gloria's diner. "Thanks, Professor. Come back anytime and we can talk about wood some more." ("Thank you, Jack," said the Painmaker. "But I won't.")

Geraldo sauntered over with one dollar and some axle grease credit vouchers. "If you ever need anything fixed, Professor," he said awkwardly. "Well, you know..." ("I know, Geraldo. But I expect I'll be hokey-doke.")

And so others came forward in similar fashion, exchanging small niceties and handing over their one dollar bills.

Gloria brought one dollar and her brownie recipe. Martha laid a bottle of Extra Special Redapple Hardware & Barber Shop Hair Tonic on top of her bill to stop it blowing away in the dead, windless morning. The Genesis Brothers – as befitted their superior standing in the community – produced one dollar each and a case of the finest, reddest apples. Phil Karrion laid a book on rabbit lore on top of his dollar. "In case you have need of lappish wisdom, Professor..." ("Thanks, Phil, but I don't suppose I will...")

Josie and Marie Shortling, in recognition of their high though semi-pauperish position, contributed fifty cents apiece and hoped the Painmaker wouldn't mind. The Painmaker said he wouldn't mind at all: and how warmly thoughtful they were to come to such a pretty compromise; and how sweet to share the secrets of their peachnut cobbler recipe, even supposing he wouldn't be needing it.

And presently, Jackson Cordobes Stacey came out of his saloon door, dragged – as it seemed at the time and as it would certainly be described many, many years afterwards – by the Painmaker's gaze to lay a till-fresh one dollar bill at the latter's feet.

"Thank you, Mr Stacey," said the Professor, as he bent down to retrieve it. "That seems to be the first job of work I've had to do since I came here. Ouch..." The Painmaker stood straight and rubbed the small of his back.

"If you're ever passing through and could use a beer..." Jackson was already turning away as he spoke, his voice seeming to come from some other place.

"Thank you, Mr Stacey," said the Painmaker. "You never know. If I *am* ever passing through..." He shut the box, turned the key in the lock, put the box into his bag and the key somewhere inside his clothes.

The almost-wind shifted the cypress trees and sent whispers down Main Street. It was a moment found at funerals or at parties where not many people knew each other. A moment encountered before big races and in the back of parents' borrowed automobiles. It was the moment of Waiting For Something To Happen.

The Painmaker looked at his watch and leant against the chair from the diner. "Eight-oh-two. Well, my friends, it's time I was getting off to the station. I see there've been two navy men hanging around town looking for salt water so I'll take them with me and hope I bring them luck. Gloria: your danishes are exquisite. Farewell."

And with a polite abruptness, Professor Joseph Swingler turned his back on the people of Redapple and began walking evenly (that apple box was heavy) towards the railroad station. The crowd followed like a quiet wave looking for a shore.

And as their visitor walked through the station gates, a member of the wave gulped hugely and cry-whispered:

"Stop."

The Painmaker turned just like he knew he was going to turn at that precise point in time and space.

"Yes, Mr Genesis?"

"You're a fine man to be sure, Professor," said Joe Genesis, the juggler. "But what have you given us? Not Pain, surely. We wanted to be introduced to the Pain of the Twentieth Century – but here we are feeling warm and good with ourselves and choking with more pleasure and selflessness than we've had to swallow for ages. You've brought good to this town, Professor Swingler. They'll name a street after you."

"Yes, Mr Genesis. You'd be surprised at the number of Swingler Avenues across this great country..."

"It's true," put in Phil Karrion. "You've packed more positive qualities into twenty-four hours than garlic into a rabbit bake stew. You're a golden fellow, sir, and I salute you."

The folk of Redapple all began to speak, testifying to the Painmaker's enviable attributes and how Pain must be a whole lot better than they'd been told. Gloria rushed up and kissed the Professor a little too fully on the lips and a community blush rushed around the gathering like Christmas lights.

A locomotive whistle echoed down from the Greengage Heights and the Painmaker wiped his face with his handkerchief.

"Well, my fine friends: perhaps here at last, after all these years, I have found a town too good for Pain. Where Pain is constantly mis-spelled and will never find a home. You're all wonderful people and I'm going to do something that I've never done before. Something that I always thought would never get done until World's End..."

The Painmaker balanced his things on top of the stationmaster's gatepost and fished out the cash box. He slipped his hand into his clothes. Slipped them in again, frowning. He might have been saying something but the words were lost as the train pulled in at Redapple Junction. The two sailors could be seen trying to rouse themselves from kit bag pillows on the station platform.

"You'll miss your train," said Ray Genesis.

"Forget the ten dollars, Professor," said Phil Karrion. "Always keep it there in your box and remember us in Redapple, the town that Pain couldn't touch..."

The loco was taking on water, the air moisturising into a warm fog over their heads.

They could hear the Painmaker's words now. "No, I'd like to return your money. I feel it's kind of important..." He continued to worry in his vest pockets for the cash box key. The stationmaster had just succeeded in tossing Mr Poe and his tall hat into the brakeman's van and was peering down at his soon-to-be-late passenger.

Abruptly, the Painmaker popped the cash box into his carpet bag. He pulled something out of his pants pocket and laid its papery weight on top of the stationmaster's mailbox, securing it with a chicken skull that the madman had dropped the previous day.

He looked at Joe Genesis and said: "There. That'll do. Remember me in your road plans."

He winked at Gloria and was gone up the path to the platform and so into a carriage without further comment.

The train hissed, muttered, groaned and began to pull out of Redapple Junction. And as it did so, the warm moisture cooled and everyone realised that it was really raining. That the rain was rather refreshing; that things were going to remain pleasant even after the Painmaker who brought only pleasure had left them. They began to turn back to their own lives then. Coffee shops and garages, rabbit farms and schools and fine apple orchards.

Only the saloon keeper delayed. Jackson Cordobes Stacey still had fifteen minutes to opening time and he wandered over and removed the object that the Painmaker had left under the bird skull.

The sudden rain was petering away now and the single ten dollar bill would dry up nicely.

*

There's still a town where Redapple used to be.

The coffee's as great as it always was, I guess. And if your radiator's been crazy on you for the last hundred miles there's still a place to fix her up.

Folk started off being pretty damn friendly about that ten dollar bill. Folk thought that perhaps Mr Stacey might like to have it, him being the only fellow troubling to pick it up and all. And then perhaps – as this was the selfless town of Redapple – he might like to donate it to some local charity. Redapple had a whole hatful of charities.

But the saloon keeper shut-up shop the very next day. Jackson Cordobes Stacey left the ten dollar bill pinned to the locked bar room door with a note on a beer napkin thanking the good folks but he had to be going and anyone who wanted to take the pick of his teacups and their contents would find everything in the shack out back.

There was some dithering as to who should look after the money. It wasn't as if they could divide it between them. Redapple had no bank. The Genesis Brothers only dealt in hundred dollar bills: they'd sent a special order to Greengage City for the three singles when news of the Painmaker's arrival had been known. It was suggested (politely) that perhaps the ten dollars should be transported to Greengage and there be transformed into nine one dollar bills and two fifty cent pieces. It was then put forward (with warm geniality) that the world out there was well-known to be full of Pain and wickedness and could they really trust their ten dollars to some strange brakeman on the railroad?

No. They would have to delegate one of themselves. But that would be unfair, someone pointed out. The bill belonged to them all. They must all go. What if the fare was a buck seventy-five? It was the only thing to do.

"I can't go," said Phil Karrion, sitting down heavily on an empty barrel outside the locked doors of the saloon. "I can't afford to leave my rabbits. They'd pine even for half an afternoon."

"I'd look after them for you..." said Joe Genesis, who hadn't quite grasped the gist of the money-transported-by-committee argument.

"Meaning that *we* wouldn't?" suggested his two brothers.

Gloria proposed a town meeting. Redapple usually had a town meeting every two months or so – although folk were so brotherly and sisterly with each other that the formality of municipal procedure was rendered redundant. Under spousal goading, Martha's husband slowly thought that making a meeting of it blew the whole episode out of all proportion and couldn't the damn thing be sorted out in the saloon? It was then observed that the saloon was no longer open for business.

Gloria popped over to the diner to get the coffee on. It was going to be a long morning. And there'd be plenty of refills.

*

There's a saying. The saying says: *divide and rule.*

And yet, by bringing those good citizens together as joint owners of one piece of paper, the Painmaker divided and misruled better than any historic nation-seizer. Any Khan or Conquistador. Gloria had reckoned right on refills. *And* she had to heat up the hotplate for more flapjacks. Syrup ran out too. And then Phil Karrion had to run himself, on account of his pining rabbits.

Time spun. It was as if time periscoped backwards into the future. I mean: from that tiny paper object grew the reason for a lot of people to go on living. Their existence began to revolve around a thing, a time, a place...

It's true: no folks died. Unless you count old man Valstoed throwing himself into the river up at Peartree Ridge. And I suppose what Martha's old man got up to with Martha and that razor wasn't so good either.

So it's true: not many folks died. But some rabbits did: in mysterious circumstances, found pinned by their long bloody ears to Phil Karrion's bed when he woke up one sunless morning. Sure, no one got knocked down on the highway: but some of the Genesis trees were found blocking the county road, their new-sawn trunks weeping into the blacktop. Geraldo's tyre dump suffered some arson attacks that summer and I could open an insurance company with what happened to Gloria's plate glass. And those chalk slogans on the Shortlings' blackboard were pretty nasty if you knew what they meant.

Some folk left Redapple. They entered the world of Pain: that dark land beyond the orchards. But by that time it was hokey-doke: Redapple had readied them for it. They were like deep-sea divers coming up slow: the pressure of Pain within and without had been equalised.

*

And what about those Redapples who stayed and survived to maintain a life above ground? Well, they all got worn out with it in time. It all kind of faded. Professor Swingler's ten dollar bill actually got mislaid. Twenty-five years on and folk realised that the item under dispute had disappeared. But no one really cared. They had law firms in Chicago and Kansas City to worry about things now. Like that missing gap between the Red and the Apple in Redapple. They call it Red Apple these days. Two words. Some bunch of lawyers fixed it over a lunch hour when the ten dollar bill litigation was getting slack.

Yeah. You can still get coffee and gas in Red Apple. But folks don't speak to folks so much these days: they let their city attorneys do it for them. The Red Apples are too busy trying to cross the street to avoid each other: silent human bundles of Pain, waltzing in and out of the cypress trees all the way down Swingler Avenue.

In The South

A wedding party moved through the marbled lobby.

It was a strange thing (double-imaged, silent white) and as out of place as a smile in that airport hotel on the outskirts of the city.

The bride, teetering between sleep and hysteria, idled in the coffee shop – the provider of confetti for a prowling vacuum cleaner.

"Such temporary papery weather," she whispered, glancing at her new husband and his friends at another table.

She rose, took up her apron and passed through the service door into the kitchen.

*

The car goes, the bogus Genoa plates discarded.

It rains in miserable November.

Up the creek she comes, paddling her pram dinghy and bearing daddy's hamper (all his favourites – pickles and fruit and a screw-top bottle of wine).

Bustling against the dripping hawthorn, oozing through the slop and dead leaves, she comes to the bridge and ducks under to her father.

He is sleeping in the folds of his moustache all black and rusty red, lost in his heavy jumper and those casual loafers of chains and cement. He is woken and fed. Continually woken as she tries to speak to him. She feels her mouth moving with her fingers, shakes off a single piece of confetti: "*Ciao*, daddy, *ciao*."

As she backpaddles out into the open lagoon, blue birds – tiny kingfishers – dart by her shoulders, eager for the fish in masonry shadows.

Fresh and salty on the new tide.

Backalong in Bollockland
or, The World Made Flush

As recounted by
Mstr. Samuel Trousers *Scallyville* to
Mstr. Timothy Steven *Nickels*, lately of the County
of *Devonshire* ~ Being an Account in Five Books & Several
Asides of *Mstr. Scallyville's* Extraordinary Exploits at the Cusp of
the Wipe & After ~ *Mstr. Scallyville's* Observations on Trousers &
their Contents ~ A Jaffa Cake Crisis ~ Notes concerning the
Congermen of Plymouth ~ *The Customs Officer* who could not
touch the Ground ~ What happened to the *University Bus* ~ *Mstr.*
Scallyville conceives his Theory of THE WORLD MADE FLUSH
with the Assistance of *His Auntie* & explains it to *Mstr. Nickels*
in an Unexpected Aside ~ An Aft'word concerning *Principles* and
their Present Whereabouts, with Special Reference
and Warning to *Welshmen*

*

BOOK THE FIRST:
Backalong.
Backalong it was. Just down arse-side to Auntie's wedding. You
remember. With that Welsh feller. Well, he weren't you know. I

reckon he just bragged about it. Being Welsh. He was a farmer and had breeks full of carrots and live ones most like, but I'm not one for prying. Auntie was a laugh though. She had them Devonport sailor buys in fits before Welshy looked in and knocked her up in a mackerel shed. And not even her own. It was the municipal one behind the Customs & Excise building. Poor old Jones – or whatever his name was. Him and Auntie had a shiner of a time but the poor bugger's dead and buried now so I guess the water's passed over and no mistake.

But blast my airs. Scallyville's my name and I'm down the lane without trousers. I've lost the thread of this tale already. Not that no one would care. But if you're troubling to read this, you're probably buggered with tales of someone else's sparkling early manhood; of thinking our brains and bodies are good for one thing only – and so maybe they were, backalong.

Let me tell you where I'm at. Well, I was but I'm somewhere else now. I moved. I dropped down from Dartmoor out of the Princetown lock-up one night and found me a soft billet with the Marine buys down Stonehouse (down Plymouth for all you out-of-county yahbleedinhoos). Yes, they took me in but who'd they take me *for* – mazed as an 'andcart, all wild and Moorish? They were kind and not in a questioning frame of mind, that's all I know. I'd been screwed up on the Moor for many a month at His Majesty's pleasure and so had to lay on a fib. Said I was a seaman down on his luck who got frisked out of everything in Le Havre. But I was a gaolbird wasn't I, a right Mr James Cagney. I said to the Marine Provost that I had a smallholding as security and suggested that he held it for me. All trousers in them days, I tell you. All the same backalong for Scallyville.

*

AN ASIDE:
GENTLE, George Douglas/ Governor, H.M.P. Dartmoor/Governor's Office/09.25 hrs/04.12.2007

Oh Scallyville. Yes. You want facts. You want to know who I am,

*do you? Very well. Oh, into the mic? George Gentle, Governor, H.M.
Prison Dartmoor. Yes. Prisoner Scallyville. Ran amok in the
paintshop at Devonport Docks. Rushed out into a nuclear sub bay
and sprayed the conning towers pink and yellow. Don't know why.
Quite calm up until then, I understand. No imagination though. Sort
of listless and certainly not Great Escape material. Or so we
thought until he made off last night disguised as my wife with an ID
card cut out of a Jerusalem artichoke.*

*

Yes – in them days, the Channel was sinking fast and rising up
again. They had the sub garages in Devonport opening and shutting
like the business end of a West Hoe pro with a heavy mortgage. All
'cause they were worried about this atmos-pheric stuff. We call it
the wipe now. Sorry. The Wipe. All Big Writing. They had the air
nearly all buggered by then and most of the tars stayed in them
subs so they could breathe right. Yeller, they were. They'd known
that Old Wipe was coming, you see – and they'd known there was a
bit more to it than the atmos-pherics but I'm getting ahead
beforetimes here. Anyhow, them craven sailorbuys had themselves
holed up in Yellerland.

*

ANOTHER ASIDE:
JONES, Phyllis Marie/ Operator, Phyl's Fish & Chips/Plymouth
Aquarium/03.42 hrs/04.12.07

*Eh? What's that, lover? Scallyville? Doing time, ain't he. Wait up.
(50p o' chips? Hang on a mo', sweetheart...) What d'you say? No.
No, I'm too busy now. (No, yer pea fritters are nearly ready, me
'andsome...) Look, you'll have to come back later. It's me busy time.
Yeah. When I close up. All right. Cheers then. (Y'ere, you –
snogging tattoo buy – d'you want this roe or no..?)*

*

91

The English Soil Society

I'd just met up with Auntie Phyl and when It (Big Letters) happened we had to make do with the coffee room at Woolworth's. I'd got turned out of the Stonehouse billet at 6am that morning (fancied them Marine buys was on to me) and I met Auntie quite by chance. She parked her fish & chip van near the Aquarium and was legging it home. She worked all night and I popped out at her like a dream at dawn, I reckon.

"Y'ere, Scallyville, you ghost or no?" (She says this looking up at me from the pavement).

When she got herself together, we strolled along and exchanged news and she told me all about Jones (or whatever) and about their estrangement on account of Jones's departure for the hereafter.

Anyhow, we'd been passing the telly-rental when fifteen Trevor MacDonalds (or whatever) in the window say: "This is it. It's the bleedin' Wipe. Get under cover etc..." Well, he probably didn't say it quite like that; I mean, they really only called it The Wipe (Big Letters) after It had been and gone.

So we found ourselves in Woolie's – open early for staff training – and we get into the coffee room. Light's out so it's like pitch with all them shopgirls shivering, screaming and everything. Hellish it were. And Auntie Phyl talked about the Blitz and Göering and smoke over the Sound. And the Walrus flying boat that spiralled into the Tamar with all the guns in the Fleet of the Western Approaches firing up at it 'cause there was a balls-up big time – but the Walrus made it down all right anyhow. But I'm yammering on again and I'm a bit out of breath too. I can't really keep to a story. I shouldn't have started really. But now that I'm a responsible member and that, it's up to me to chalk it all down for spontaneity. Or whatever.

But we *did* make it out of that coffee room, after The Wipe dragged a third of world water and stuff into the nethers of unGodly space. All sort of sucked away. Me and Auntie really did make it out of there – but only just. Two weeks we were down the coffee room, and them Jaffa Cakes ran out after one. Rum times. Trousers weren't everything. Lucky to have them really. Mazey times – as mazey as a million 'andcarts.

We'd always been split by the seams, our family. There was

brother Steve in the South-West Water with half a million shares in it and cousin Hazel and her fifteen buyfriends: good lads to be sure. I'm not one to pry, as I've made plain. They were mostly fishermen, much taken with hanging about on the breakwater and dangling for conger.

And Auntie Phyl with her chippy van. Or Granny, maybe – no one was too sure, you see. Things were shady and made more so by That Wipe With Big Letters. Before the Aquarium, she ran the van out of Bretonside and then on the new pedestrian precinct where she nicked the cinema crowd off KFC. You could smell her two multi-storeys away. A mothery figure with big milkers and a gappy grin. Tars got on well with her. Tars probably still would if they poked their blue funky snouts out of their bleedin' conning towers down Devonport. Amazing. It was years after That Buggering Big Letter Wipe and they were still down below breathing air from last century. Makes you wonder. Government's still to wankery. Local councillors still cowering in their bunker on the west side of the Tamar, most like. They approved a big air conditioner thing just before It happened backalong. Gets yer wonderin', don't it – but not much 'cause this story's about Auntie Phyl and what she did after the chippy van got sucked into space. But she weren't innit. She was down in the coffee room in Woolie's like I said, with all the weeping shopgirls.

*

ANOTHER ASIDE/TAKE TWO:
JONES, Phyllis Marie/Operator, Phyl's Fish & Chips/Plymouth Aquarium/05.55 hrs/04.12.07

Oh it's you, lover. Caught me clearin' up. Pass us that bunch o' newspapers would you, sweet? Me? Who am I? Huh! Phyllis Jones, formerly of Devonport, latterly of Swansea, lately of West Hoe. Call me missus. Want to talk about Scallyville, my nephew, do yer? Hmm.
Good buy but got unbalanced with this eco-log-i-cal nut stuff.
Sent a few like that, hasn't it. What do I think?
But we've got it coming, ain't we. Been playing with the atmos-

*pherics. Old Jones – my late lamented – reckoned it was all
them English aerosols and car works at Dagenham. And young
Stevie says it's termites farting in Africa and little Hazel
doesn't know if it's Christmas or no unless one of 'er buyfriends
puts on a beard and says "ho ho" and – Eh? You say that
Scallyville's escaped off the Moor with the aid of a Jerusalem
artichoke? No! Yer takin' me on, darlin'... He's such a quiet lad.
And you say I'm about to meet him like he's a ghost behind the
Aquarium and I'm going to 'ave the vapours and faint and then
the atmos-pherics is going to puncture and they're going to call
it The Wipe later on but we'll be in Woolie's and it'll be all right
but the van'll end up on the Moon? Expect me to believe that
do yer? Y'ere, pass us them kippers.*

*

I remember one of them girls. Little tubby cropped redhead with
a nice smile once called Ethel Georgette. Yes. She's here beside
me now helping me to write this, so you can ask her yourself. So
we were eight days into The Wipe and tempers were short on
account of the Jaffa Cake crisis and she says (Ethel, that is):
What about her moggies? And I say (something like): *Yer
moggies are icicles in space now – or lapping up the Milky Way,*
and she says (tearful like): *Don't you think they're in Heaven?*
And I say (convincing – my arse): *Okay, Red, they're in
Heaven.*

You see, I couldn't talk so well then, just off the Moor and
that. They shouldn't've locked me up. They shouldn't have
turned me into a Mr James Cagney. I would have been better
otherwise. If I'd stayed in the paintshop at the Dockyard I
would have done okay. So I painted them subs into a rainbow.
Didn't know what else to do with me, did they? If I weren't
feeling so strange I could have talked more sense with that
poor Ethel about her mangey mog and I wouldn't have felt
trapped in Fumbleland. But look – I'm without trousers again,
blasting off in the wrong direction like an 'eadless chicken.

Okay. Shift on five years after The Bloody Big-Lettered Wipe.

Yeah. Easy on paper, ain't it. Just make a gap:

Well, don't whinge on. Get yer brain goin' and move on up half a decade.

Hazel and her dangling congerbuys lived for a bit in the market opposite Frankfurt Gate. The market used to have a roof once but it don't now, of course. Never mind, lover – life was quite cosy even after every chest freezer in the city had been cleared out. A rum time to be a moggy, Ethel. Yeah, Cat-U-Like. Hazel and her buyfriends and me ran a guided tour business from out of our battered marquee next to the old fish stall. Chief attraction were them battened-down subs: the punters enjoyed knocking a brisk tattoo on the hulls, hoping to lure out the gibbering Hearts of Oak.

*

ASIDE TIME:
CONSTANCE, Hazel Petula/Operator, Hazel's Fabulous Frankfurt Foot Tours/Frankfurt Gate Market, Plymouth/17.37 hrs/03.12.2012

Who's this? Jim, Johnny, Tailend – where are you? I need some help. There's some bloke here. What yer want down Frankfurt? 'Ere, you lot – me congerbuys – where are you? Froggy, Barry, Alan and the two Franks. Look sharp. There's someone here. Stop, you. Yeah – you. Stop. What do you want? Yeah, I'm Hazel. No – just Hazel'll do for you. Auntie Phyl? Well, I heard about Auntie Phyl. Like she's sort of changed. Eh? Well – you know, altered kind of thing. Sort of – you know – well... 'Ere, what you writing then? What's that? Course I got 'air in me 'ead. What? No.
No.
No.
Really.
Maybe.

Oh all right.
But make it a quick one.

*

Anyway, it was early evening one night and Hazel sauntered up and said: "Have yer seen yer Auntie Phyllis?" She rubbed her toe nervously in the dirt. "She's shrinking." Hazel's mouth wrinkled up when she said 'shrinking'. That too bright, post-Wipe moonlight made her look eerie-weirdy.

"Shrinking," she wrinkled again. "She says she's gettin' smaller."

It was a while since I'd seen Auntie and I was tempted to bad where'm to, but I sauntered off up the Western Approach anyway. Auntie had one of the few remaining upright pre-fab things just before the Tavistock turn-off. Lost in The Wipe, of course: thanks, Wipe – did us all a favour there, I reckon. The sky looked all loomy in the moonlight. I thought: *Bleedin' moonlight.*

The outside steps were almost in one piece and I yelled outside her flat door: "Hello, Auntie, are you shrinking?"

"She's out," said a voice.

Turning, I saw the voice belonged to that Ethel from the Woolie's coffee room. Five years on and there she was. Tell yer, stranger than fiction.

"Hello, Red – remember me?"

"Yes," she said, looking as if amnesia wouldn't melt in her mouth.

She told me Auntie Phyllis had gone to the Shrink Therapy Class at the University. Well, what do you say – so I didn't.

"Rude bugger, ain't yer," she muttered.

"Yes I am," I said, all obliging like.

*

BOOK THE SECOND:
There were lots of people at the University, all milling about and looking peaky and worried. The University had had a pig's

arse of a time with That Great Big Pissing Lettered Wipe (you'll excuse me, lover) five years past, and lost half a roof and all its radar dishes that they'd used for whipping Trevor MacDonald (or whatever) off the satellite. A double-decker bus lay like a red house across the canteen and the art students from over the road had done a post-Wipe re-construction mural on it. Lots of rain and sea pictures and choppers dropping helium or whatever they're talking about into the upper atmos-phere. Quite pretty really but I don't know nothing about this art caper. I don't even know what I like. Makes as much sense as a chicken's back legs. We never learnt art from His Majesty's smallholding. That Stonehouse Provost never did give me a straight answer either.

I found Auntie at the shrinking lecture. I gave her a good peer but she was sitting down so I couldn't really tell. I sat beside her and she looked like death. She looked like she did after that wedding night with the Swansea Casanova.

There was a feller called Cleerlap up there on the stage and he was lecturing and waving his arms about like he'd just grown them.

"So you see, ladies and gentlemen, our problem is one of relativity..."

The brain switched off, of course – but I did me best.

" ...Borne of an inverted arrogance, a survival wish feedbacking along the loins of its own creation..."

Oh dear.

The feller with arms paced the stage. "So to conclude, it is not *humankind* that is actually shrinking but our *environment*, the world – our dear *Mother Earth* – that is, in our highly subjective awareness, *expanding*. I assure you, it's in the *mind*. It only *seems* that every non-human cell and crystalline structure is swelling. Evidence is at *every* turning of the *corner*..." He seemed to talk quite a lot in *wriggly writing*.

"My steam iron. I can't hold it no more," wailed a female voice.

"Precisely," agreed Professor Arms.

"Me bicycle – I haven't touched the ground since Christmas." This from a Customs man at the back.

"Exactly."

The English Soil Society

*

THE WILD ASIDE:
CLEERLAP, Gordon Banks/Principle Reader, Biospheric Sciences, Royal College/The Russell Labey Memorial Hall, Plymouth University/19.16 hrs/03.12.12

Christ! What the hell do you want! I've got a situation here. I can tell. It's just like it was over in Barnstaple and Ivybridge. There's a few troublemakers here tonight – look at that woman with the gap teeth – bloody trouble, I tell you. Don't you know who I am? Okay. Gordon Cleerlap, Royal College, Department of Earth Sciences, recently seconded to M.I.T. – now returned to put fire back into the blood of England. Look at them! Idiots! They couldn't understand The Wipe. They couldn't take it all in when it happened so quickly. They were milk-fed on the fifty-year downhill run scenario. You know. Goodbye Bangladesh, hello giant sunflower growers of Manchester. Let's worry about it tomorrow. No. Round and round we went like the Magic bloody Roundabout – round and round and !pop! off it goes. Goodbye atmosphere, hello space. Hello miracle! Only joking. We're still here and we shouldn't be. Oh yes. Mother Earth won out in the end, didn't she. Cor, what a scorcher – but we hung on to just enough air and water. And what more can you win in this week's Big Prize? Well, on offer we've got mass hysteria and a planet on a one hundred-year self-reconstruction project. No, scrub that. Make it five hundred, minimum. So you've got a state of lunacy with people who've lost so much self-esteem that they think they're shrinking. All over the world, you've got people who consider themselves titchy-tiny nobodies... Oh yes, that's right – walk off, run away. Boring you, am I? Too small to talk to, am I? Heard it all from big Trev MacDonald and bloody Paxman have you? Remember them do you? Before they went nuts with everyone else. Yeah. Clear off then. I'll meet you in the bar afterwards. See if we can find a glass small enough to crawl into...

*

The hall was full of these peaky shouts from shrinkers and their complaints of swelling ornaments and underwear. All pretty odd and even the Professor seemed like he was talking to himself. But they looked all right. They looked the same as me. It was rum and dreamlike, sort of like rain used to be when it came all of a sudden at the end of a summer's day. Auntie was on her feet now, milkers wiggling, gap teeth clashing together like clothes pegs.

"Yes! Yes!" she shrieked. "It's too big – the world's too big. The world's blown itself up like a balloon... Shut up, nipper!" She screamed this last bit 'cause I was laughing then.

"Auntie, you're normal!" I said. "You look the same to me. Come home now. Race yer back home and we can hurdle the rubble heaps. Come on, Auntie, race yer."

But Auntie Phyl was all done up. The hall was full of chaos. The Professor was engulfed by his rioting, shrinking audience. The stage gave way. Some grannies had taken over Picasso's canteen bus and drove it straight in the big double doors and out through the locked emergency exit. The lights went out and the hall was bathed in bleeding moonlight.

*

BOOK THE THIRD (This being the THIRD BOOK):

Backalong, it was – but it seems like yesterday.

I had Auntie Phyl out of that hall and up the Approach slippier than a conger caught in a crab pot. Up the steps and past Ethel Georgette, the gaping Cat Queen.

Tea, of course – that's what was needed. We reached Auntie's flat and I scrabbled about under a tarpaulin and found some QuickBrew – though Christ knows where it had come from. All gone in that Buggering Big Old Wipe, most of it.

I called in Ethel. "Make us some tea, would yer?"

Auntie shrieked again when I handed her the chipped Charles & Camilla mug. "Too big," she said. "Like holding a bucket."

Ethel came in from the kitchen to see what it was all about. I was feeling creepy so I said: "How're yer mogs, lover?"

Oh dear.

The English Soil Society

*

ASIDE THE LAST:
GEORGETTE, Ethel Violetta/Journalist/External staircase, Armada
Flats, Plymouth/19.57 hrs/03.12.12

*Yes, I'm Ethel. Ethel Violetta Georgette. And I suppose you'll make
something of it. I was only fifteen when we first met, you know.
Skipped school, lied about me age and found myself in the
Woolworth's Sound & Video Department. I was useless. I thought
Rimsky-Korsakov was one of those indie bands from Finland. And
there I was on staff training when this atmosphere thing happened.
It was just me and Kylie at home. Kylie got spayed the week before
and was a little bit queasy. I was dead worried. I've never been so
frightened. I was stuck in the corner of the coffee room with this
mad convict and his awful aunt who looked like she'd just walked
out of a Carry On. God, he was rotten. His shoes stank and were
trying to walk away without him. Scallyville, he said his name was –
the rudest man I've ever met. And what happened? He eats all the
Jaffa Cakes, strolls out and then strolls into my life again five years
later. I sent him away down to the University after his cacky aunt
and hoped that would be it – but here they come again: up the steps
and past me as if I wasn't there. Probably call me in to make the tea
now.*

*

Anyhow, we settled Auntie Phyl down in her armchair under the
canvas canopy that slung itself where the roof used to be. She filled
out the chair pretty well for a shrinking person.

"What do you think, Ethel?" This was in the kitchen to Ethel, of
course. "Is she smaller? I ain't seen her for a bit."

Ethel was quiet for a time. She took a snort of QuickBrew. Ethel
explained that she'd moved into her own flat two storeys below
about a year ago. She did Eth's Pets' Corner for the old *Evening
Herald* now: the *Herald* went out weekly from a hand-press down

Sutton Harbour. Ethel reckoned there wasn't a cat left on the planet. Nor dogs or homing pigeons or anything else that got caught out in the open. I said the cats probably got sucked out of orbit or they crashed on the Moon like Auntie's chip van. I didn't like to tell her about folk stocking up their freezers with pussies galore.

She said "What's happened at the Uni?" as a distant hum of horror came through the window at us from across the city.

I told her about the Professor with the Arms and how he reckoned it was the world getting bigger but it was in our heads really and how it was all on account of The Don't-Say-It Big Letter Wipe and then I told her about creation and its loins as well. It all sounded mazey sitting there with funny little Ethel Georgette in that dripping kitchen. We went back into the sitting room but Auntie had pushed off.

"Cor, that was quick," I said, searching under the cushions.

"Come on!" yelped Ethel – and she was down the stairs and back down the Western Approach before I had time for a cat gag.

*

BOOK THE FOURTH:

It was quite hectic out. Folk had got word of the University hullabaloo and were throwing up street stores stocked with Action Man's underpants. Everyone was out for what they could get. This shrinking thing had been a bit of a closet caper but now folk were hopping about and moaning as brazen as you like.

Hazel's conger-catching menfriends were well up with it and had taken to flogging them old shrink-to-fit jeans that the Mods used to jump in the bath with. Cider bums wandered around with Tesco trolleys and peered with anticipation into bottles that would soon be getting bigger. There was loose dicker of Argyle re-locating to the manager's uncle's private allotment and herring gulls applying for carriage licences on the Channel Islands route. Shows yer really, don't it. How a sort of fever can get about. I reckon those people were hairier than me that night. People change, don't they.

Ethel collared a brace of mini-floggers, ref: Auntie Phyllis. They'd seen her pass by and told us to try the University again so we went up but it was as empty now as the Welshman's trousers (honest).

Dawn was popping up, all red and arty. Dawn came at different times of day then but mornings were still popular. Ethel and me spent a funny ten minutes in the University canteen, looking over the city in the early light. All the flattened telly aerials and buildings in bits, still untended even five years later. Everything gone to Nowhereland. They say The Wipe might have been brought on by something more than eco-logicals. Professor Arms knew the truth, I reckon. Down the docks, they say it was some sort of Dumbsday weapon thing except that it sort of went off and no one wanted it to. Or they wanted it to, but it was bigger than they thought. Well, that immediately makes yer feel better, don't it. Funny how it all happened really. That's what comes of feedbacking through the loins of one's own creation, I suppose.

We found a couple of bikes in the rack behind the Navigation Department and cycled down to the Aquarium. The streets were quieter now: all the shrinkers had gone off to do it at home.

Auntie's new battery-powered chip van was there with Auntie in it, serving mackerel paté to the Customs man who hadn't touched the ground since Christmas.

"I wanted to have some time to have a think, but it's too late..." She looked up at us after H.M. Customs had buggered off, and she waved a couple of smoked fillets like they were someone else's knickers. "It's all just too late..."

We helped her up to the Hoe and onto a bench overlooking the Sound. The Santander ferry lay beached upside down by Drake's Island: Biscay hadn't broken her but The Bloody Wipe had ripped the guts out of her funnel and blown them halfway to Jupiter. A few ripples passed over the shallow Sound waters: it could have been a so'wester blowing up – but things looked a bit different somehow.

Auntie waggled one of her fingers about, demonstrating how easily her rings fell off – and I suppose she did look sort of shrunken. All sort of curled up. Ethel sat beside her and it made Auntie look even worse: a bit like a hermit crab without a house, all naked and hiding and small.

*

AN UNEXPECTED ASIDE:
SCALLYVILLE, Samuel Trousers/Convict and Tour Guide/Plymouth Hoe/07.38 hrs/04.12.12

Oh, it's you. Well, you know who I am. All right, Scallyville here. No. That's all there is to me name and I wish you'd clear off 'cause I'm doing some brain work. You see it's all making some sort of sense now, as I sit here on the Hoe with Auntie and Ethel the Catwoman. I ain't one for prying into things but I'm realising what The Arms was really getting at with all that universe toshy old stuff. It's all in people's bodies, see – or all in people's heads more like. This Big Pissing Letter Wipe – beg yer pardon – it's been gone five years backalong but it was so Bleeding Big that it's taken all them five years to work its way through. Like that Tigersaurus Rex feller. They say that if you tickled his tum, he'd be corpsing all over you half an hour later. Like – we all think we're so sodding amazing yet The Wipe was too Big for all of us. It's flattened us; it's flattened everything into near-invisibility; like when you mess up a hammer-and-nailing job and you have to curl that nail around and knock him against the wood and hope no one notices. It's the world made flush, lover. Some of us went before it happened, of course. Some of us mazed out beforetimes. Atmos-pherics and modern living, like. That's why I ended up at His Majesty's pleasure on the Moor. Went as mazed as an 'andcart in the Dockyard paintshop. It don't matter now what I did to get into Dartmoor. I was just mazed. I sort of shrunk before anyone else and then I grew again and here I am and ain't it time you sort of buggered off and left me to it?

*

I looked back at Ethel Georgette and Auntie. The new and the old, those big of heart and those small of body. Perhaps some of us would make it for some country matters after all. I checked me trousers.

We were getting up to go nowhere when a klaxon hooted to starboard over from Devonport. The ripples had turned to a muddy rush now and I realised the sea was rising up. Like a great thing it were – like something ghastly, beastly and poetic.

The subs were out of their concrete garages, gay bunting streaming from their blue funky conning towers as if it were a nipper's party. The pink and yellow paint marks I'd made looked beautiful. Those Hearts of Oak were cutting loose of Mother Tamar on the first spring tide in five years. It were a miracle. They trooped proudly out to the open sea like black ducklings, leaving a cheery crowd on the dockside. There was a final bit of klaxon heroics from the leader: and then they disappeared in a big swirl of foam and rainbow engine oil.

And were never seen again.

*

BOOK THE FIFTH (This being the FINAL BOOK):
Seems like yesterday since I started writing this, backalong – but it's taken quite a while. I was determined to do it proper. Chop it up into parts and bits just like them books in the governor's library on Dartmoor. I'm pretty good, you can tell that. I share a birthday with S.T. Coleridge, a good old Devon buy and the best of us.

Well, Ethel and me got involved in country matters and we live in a barn on the north coast now. We don't think much about That Rotten Old Big-As-An-Elephant's-Arse Wipe no more. We have a chat now and again like, and I always look back on them days with a fondness and reckon things were better backalong. But Ethel thinks anyone who says that is talking bloody bollocks and that I talk too much dreamy rubbish anyway. Ethel has a bit of a mouth on her but it's worth it. She's looking at me now and she says: "What're yer going to call this dreamy, bollocky story?" And I tell her – well, I tell her – smirking, like: "*Guess*, Red."

The dawns aren't quite so red and arty these days: sea comes and goes but it usually bads where'm to. Things are evening out now and we all know what happened about that shrinking thing. We haven't seen Auntie Phyl for years but that don't mean we haven't got a microscope: I met Hazel out with her grand-triplets the other day and she said Auntie Phyl had gone north over the Severn Barrage; so I reckon Auntie's into those Welshies like a brock into a hen house by now.

Yes. That Old Wipe. All relative as I said. Well, you've still got yer relatives, like. I've got to tell yer – I had some assistance on this one. That Nickels buy helped me out now and then. He did them **Aside Bits**, bouncin' about through time with his *wiggly writing*. He reckons he's a clever old bugger. But I tell yer, you've got to watch him: he's handsome and all – and I've got me suspicions about him and Hazel – but he'd swear all this is made up...

I still think about That Dreamy Rubbishy Old Wipe. That shrinking thing: was it a dream or no? You'll have to make up yer own mind, I s'pose. I'll just say Ethel's a brick: she really helps me out when I write. I'm not much good on me own – and besides, it takes two of us to hold the pencil.

Just as well I'm saner than I've ever been – even if things used to be better.

Backalong.

~ Finis ~

The Hungry Shine

Amoeba green girl on the road again. She's been so many times.

Can't walk, you see. Like Blanche in the play, like a glamorous cripple, she relies on the kindness of strangers. She finds her friends in the car parks of motorway services or in saloon bars by the sea. She needs a hand up into the cab: or a helping arm to slither her into the passenger seat; a black plastic bag beneath her bum to stop her dripping on his wife's groceries.

At first – in the early days – she whispers to them: "Take me down the coast road, sweetheart – take me to the headland with the single ash tree that free-floats like the seaweed forest of my youth."

But later – her phantom profile hangs in the green glow of the dashboard lights – she merely moans lightly, her mouth open to reveal a hundred white (tiny white) teeth... And she leans closer to the lorry driver or the commuter or the quietly-married man – her mouth touches his ear – and says: "Just take me where you're going..."

And her mind might be full of the anticipation of white toilet tiles as she prays that this man's bathtub is big enough, that his wife won't mind the fish scales around the *Wash & Go* when she returns from her mother's.

And then there are the dark days with the hauliers from the northern hills: a frightening unwashed time of heatwave many miles from the sea. She desperately flushes the lavs behind the transport café, her tail convoluted around the U-bend as she tries to splash her dry peeling body...

One man asks her name once. She doesn't even try to smile as they drive through the grey suburbs of the dull seaside town.

*

And she dreams of deserts... Of unbelievably big skies. Of a *dryness* bigger than the universe. She starts up and finds herself sitting by the payphone in a Little Chef, the receiver dangling from her latest call to some long lost trucker lover... ...one of the few who left his number... ...who may or may not come and pick her up before her tail desiccates and crumbles off the end of her body.

People don't look at her much. She has developed a fine stooping huddle whilst seated, an army greatcoat covering her lower body. It is August now as she sweats a gallon of salt onto the floor by the telephone. Her pale glare tries to pierce the perspex window into the outside where the A303 snakes across Salisbury Plain.

And she prays he won't be late.

She can imagine him with his mates in the coffee room of the dispatch office, the lorries neatly lined up outside. His friends will talk about Michael Owen and bloody mad cows and the pissing French dock workers and the phone will ring for him and they'll say: "Oh, Frank's got that call again. You know. From that crippled sea girl hippy-type. Off you go, Frank. Got a clothes peg for your nose, mate? She could stink the arse off a bloody pig stye, that one."

And all the time, the hippy sea girl – with sad ear barnacles for hippy flowers – will shiver away by the payphone that other customers are now scared to use because this girl's got this look, y'know? And a couple of coppers are having the all-day breakfast in a corner and the waitresses are thinking: *Maybe it's time, maybe it's time...*

Suddenly, Frank is here with the girl in his arms and glaring at the manageress as she rushes a little too quickly to open the door that leads to the outside and the chalky *desert* wideness of Salisbury Plain.

Frank glances at the girl as they get up into the cab. "Where to, sweetness? Can I get you something from the chemist?"

And of course she just looks and looks at him and whispers: "Just take me where you're going..."

*

They drive west.

Hay bales litter the yellow hills. Green valleys with water: she can smell the alien sweetness of the fresh rivers – enticingly familiar, an invitation to pleasurable suicide.

They come to a cathedral town. It has recently been pedestrianised. Frank parks up at the regional office on the outskirts and carries her in over his shoulder. They pause by artificial shrubs and speak with *Big Issue* sellers.

Carefully checking the progress of Hoppa buses, Frank prepares to cross the road but she stops him; tugs gently with her cold moist hand on his hair.

He turns and they catch themselves captured in a plate glass window. He is ruddier than her, a fully-clothed lifeguard. In the reflection, she is reaching out, tries to extend her long luminous arms; tries to claw her way nearer through the air to the silver shoes; the black black – midnight black – boots behind the glass...

He strides confidently into the shoe shop and observes the colour drain from her already monochromatic face. The eyes; the sweet mouth collapses and wriggles into the features of some ecstatic saint forty days out in the wilderness. As he gently sits her on a stool among teenage assistants, he swears that a quiet halo gathers about her seaweed brow...

"What size does the lady take? Is it a wide fitting?" The girls fuss like seabirds as she stares through them at the handsomest, darkest pair of blackest boots in the shop. She sways slightly on her stool. She sways a little more and he gently catches her and whisks her back into the outside in one graceful movement as her eyes slip up into her skull and reveal a shock of white.

The rain starts to fall as Frank begins the long trek back to his lorry. Scooped up from the distant sea, the rain falls now on one of its children: so far from home; so far...

She whispers, she starts to whisper... but then just curves her tail around his body and cries...

*

They are away from the city now. They sit in the middle of the county but can see the ocean: their vantage point is a high one. Sheep crop dully amongst the ancient earthworks that skirt the hill. Bronze Age relics are regularly discovered and exhibited in the city museum next door to the cathedral.

Frank has carried her past the stones to the very top; right below the microwave transmitter that hugs the summit like a rusting flea. Dishes point in every direction. A faint hum slips from the metal heart.

He rests her back against one of the supports so she can see the huge view. Her eyes constantly far-focussed for the murkiness of the sea – shrink back into her head with the vastness, the hyper-image. Fields, hedgerows, flooded ditches and lumps of sheep lick. His lorry – distant windows open – sends up the travel news. And the air. Above everything, the sheer *air*.

Franks sits and leans his head on her shoulder, strangely the weaker one now, the sadder of the two. He sees more than the countryside, the amber glow of the twilight city's street lamps. He looks beyond to a distant headland that dips into the foam of the sea. The shimmer of the sea's surface; it's hungry shine that will one day light up the land and steal it for its own.

"Take me where you're going," he whispers to her lank seaweed hair, his tears sudden and embarrassed. They have been to this hill before. They have agreed: this is where they will meet.

Her tail is drying in the high air. She gasps and tries to speak.

*

The ocean explodes at midnight fifty years later.

Frank is there: his knees buckle as he limps across the saltwater

110

meadows; ancient ankles catch in rabbit holes. A crowd of herons hover over sea-foam as it stretches and gobbles the suburbs of a cathedral city. Frank reaches the hill fort and scrambles up past wailing pissing sheep.

The transmitter still stands, its dishes turned inwards – the dialogue broken with a dozen grounded Comsats. The fine turf has been replaced with marram grass and the blush of sea pinks. The land is ready for the sea: before sprawling on top of him, the ocean has already slipped beneath her dry brother to steal the goodness from his soil.

The moon rises at three o'clock in the morning and halts the tide at the bottom of the hill. A wave-lapped silence, only broken by the distant crash of collapsing cathedral bells. A barn full of drowned chickens floats by.

Frank clutches the metal leg of the transmitter and breathes in deeply. The air is full of mixture-smells: stale seaweed, sweet drowning hay... He closes his eyes. Closes and opens them; throws the pupils far back into his head like he remembers she used to do.

A faint splash. The sheep murmur. A light footstep.

She walks up the new beach. The last bell drops and the cathedral is silent forever.

Mizzlesoft

Sleepy and cliff-clung, he dreams himself into the very centre of the storm system. Or perhaps into a prism within a prism: above him, the Starland Point lighthouse conducts its slow-motion walrus whoops through the thin fog –

*

Mizzlesoft awakes, stands, gapes down into the foam below before beginning his journey villagewards: dry husks of gorse bushes like copper spiders; the seven beams of the lighthouse flicking their fingers behind him.

Dusk in November: red and ruddying the gorse still further as Mizzy gallops down gullies; scarifies the sheep (dyed ochre and blue) with his tattered umbrella.

Mizzlesoft – the weatherman, the corduroyed president of the Morris Minor Traveller Club if only he could pass a driving test – slides by the old town reservoir and into a wood with its mystery of sycamore aeroplanes. He pauses now by the Black Pool, an oily mirror that unoccludes with the passing of clouds: quiet leaves emerge from its pale bottom.

He squats (as he always does) on the same piece of Victorian hydraulic masonry. Several trees have been downed in

113

last night's storm and the woodland floor is greasy with hydrangeas. Mizzlesoft slips again into his own unique mental state: less of a rumination upon matters past, more a vivid foray into the realms of time travel.

The storm only woke him once. Mizzlesoft's place is at the head of a cwym a half-mile inland; a stream running down to the valley mouth. The cottage is guarded by stout larches and his lawn is a wild one of heather and giant thistle. The raspberry canes have long been put away (he murmurs smugly inside his head) and his winter nips couldn't care anyway.

*

There, by the Black Pool, Mizzlesoft time travels fifteen hours into the previous night. The hurricane rushed overhead carrying the branches of lesser trees and possibly a fox cub – for he heard its tiny bark as it passed from one side of the roof to the other. The milky half-moon might have caught it against the gleaming clouds; the hawthorns on the far valley wall reaching up to clutch and hold the fox until the sudden silence of dawn.

In that first long light Mizzlesoft ventured with tattered deerstalker and his father's shooting stick. He forded the swollen stream and rescued the creature, its triangle face an anxious arrowhead in the top branches. He knelt briefly upon the cwym bank, the fox cub cradled against his chest as if Mizzy were a gangling Hazel Woodus. The eyes – weirdly wise – blazed: the cub kicked and escaped up the valley and into the far forest where it remembered the wild pullets dwelt.

*

In the now time – at dusk – he turns and exits the wood by the Forestry Commission gate:

The High Street beckons beyond the village green and war memorial. The branches of two major banks wink at each other as Mizzlesoft edges by. And so past the butchers and the newsagents and those shops pondering the current economic

114

situation by offering a variety of wares.

Midway down the street (in its own little square with disregarded fountain) is the Weather Office. Red brick '60s, a long-ago mosaic mural depicting Wombles in a snowstorm. Mizzlesoft marches briskly in through the bladderwrack curtain.

The Office – although brown – is roomy. Mizzy surveys his domain: the charts, the mercurial instruments; Jane's empty desk, Jane's pencil mug from Athena, Jane's –

*

– Jane collides with Mizzlesoft and they tangle together in bladderwrack. It's 5.53 and she is sports bra'd and gym-intent. Jane wriggles in his corduroyed arms, somehow a vixen herself, redheaded – her bare shoulders indeed foxed with freckles. She tries to speak, thinks better and is gone into the street and onto the waiting bus for West Bray.

"Thank you," Mizzlesoft whispers after her.

*

(Time travel to 11 o'clock that evening: Mizzlesoft lounges achingly in his bathtub. Bookshelves, the familiar volumes, wrinkling and curling in the steam. Kenneth Williams' *Acid Drops*, second-hand Clarkes and Wyndhams from the Brittleport market. Mizzlesoft snuggles into the bubbles with *The Kraken Wakes* – original Penguin orange and cream covers, bookmark eternally stuffed into page 21 [Mizzlesoft's limit before emerging prune-like from freezing bathwater] – but finds himself comparing the flat plains of his easeful life with the mountains and furrows of a life that might exist with Jane. Jane loved showers and used tweezers and cotton buds. Jane knew things that everyone else knew; things that Mizzlesoft had gone out of his way *not* to know. Yet he relished his own bright dusty knowledge, his mind a bird hide living far out on the mudflats).

*

He hangs up his filthy umbrella and sits in the empty Office at 5.54. Framed photographs of notable past cloud formations look greyly down on poor Mizzlesoft who suddenly wishes he *were* a rain cloud: a constant cycle of condensing, rising, falling; of being subsumed into a countless billion bathfuls of seawater. To be lost. To rage at hapless mariners, to soothe in the quiet waterbutts of forgotten monasteries.

*

Mizzlesoft locks the Weather Office and slips over to The Rustless Anchor for a small Guinness and a bowl of onion rings. Hides in a corner with found newspapers. Bland executive positions in the nineteenth pull-out from *The Redundant*. He thinks about looking up the weather (Section 27: Meteorological Update) but discovers that it's been taken.

Should he chance another half? Three women stand at the bar – partial acquaintances as must be the way in this small market town – and he might have to converse. He steals up; teases the beer towel into a map of India as the boy lets the porter sit awhile.

"So Mizzy – anything good in the clouds this weekend? I'm dagging the sheep again and I prefer it dry." Sandy re-rolls her cigarette to the correct tightness/looseness, stuffs it in and Zippos like a demon.

Mizzlesoft is hoarse. "Not so good, Sa-Sandy. Saturday's damp. Big storm Saturday, in fact. Same as last night."

"Yuh, I had trout all over the roses up at the House," says Mrs Rowles in the whine that can wreck a room. Mrs Rowles has been seen walking her estates naked in January. Mizzy observes that she's using the missing Section 27 as a bar mat. "Bloody fish wriggling on the thorns and gasping. All the petals falling down – "

("Roses in November – ?" begins Mizzlesoft, unwisely).

"– Almost like rain," continues Miss Brady, Mrs Rowles' companion.

"The petals almost like pink perfumed rain themselves. Oh

116

dear. It wasn't like this before the war."

And Miss Brady looks from her opaque sherry to the window where the very last of the teatime sunlight peeps through the corporate stained glass, yellowed and greened; the condensation of beer breath softening the autumn outside.

Sociophobia like an egg in his throat, Mizzlesoft turns away from the bar, catches the beer towel in his baggy cuff and takes it with him into the street like a hooligan fop. A moped almost runs him over. A small dog has a go at his brolly.

Mizzlesoft promenades the High Street and passes the crossroads at the town hall. Since before the Age of Dissent this has been a thoroughfare of oafs and unlicensed smallholders. The sort of folk who allow their geese to stray onto the property of another.

Mizzlesoft is in the lane by the graveyard: he pauses, peers over the wall at the stones of past Mizzlesofts, Muzzlesocks and just plain Mizers. His weather-reading ancestors are buried thick in this yard, an underground ghostly ganglia of phantom nerve endings. Mizzlesoft enjoys being in the family business: he hears them occasionally; listens to them a little less often than that.

He passes through two fields and finds himself at the head of the little valley; the rhododendron jungle, his own little piece of the Himalayas. He gazes up to the forest further out; imagines he sees a smudge of fox.

Mizzlesoft feels peace. The weather hangs quietly over the country.

He thinks in a dream:

Kettle's already on in the kitchen and Janey's putting the finishing touches to a lemon drizzle cake.

Mizzy enters his cottage, looks into the yellow-grey interior at the cold kettle and cakeless kitchen; uses the old Hacker to warm his hands as the valves glow and breathe life into Radio 4.

Rain frets the windows.

Things will be fine on his quiet plain. Boiler's on, bath soon. Tea now. Some toast. Marmite or Rose's lime marmalade.

Janey – Jane – has some boyfriend who works at the school. Tall and attemptedly moustached, neck adorned with a white towel. A PE teacher. Mizzlesoft has seen him; he drives something blue called a Toyota Corolla that Jane sometimes alights from in Weather Office square. Mizzy squints and wonders over his steaming tea: how could he tell that the PE man was tall if he was sitting behind the wheel? Eyebrows stuffed through the sunroof? Nose nestled on knees?

*

Mizzlesoft writhes gently – an electricless eel – in his bathtub. The radio mumbles up from the low-wattage dimness below. It is 11 o'clock: bookshelves, the familiar volumes, wrinkle and curl in the steam. He closes his eyes and Jane comes out of the fangled shadows. She is aglow in apricot moonlight. Freckled; fine hairs shimmering up her belly. Gym legs taut and ropey. She slips into his bath. A tidal wave swarms down the side, floods the lino. Mizzy feels floppy, full, idiotic: the overwhelmingness, the sting, an ectoplasm through his torpid Radox.

*

Jane lopes up to the attic, crawls out of the skylight and raises her head into the new wind. She attacks the hurricane with her hands and flies like a fox through the dream of Mizzlesoft's weather.

Her bathwater trail dries quickly on the stairs.

*

"Lemon drizzle, Mizzy?" Jane stands with a paper plate. "I made it special."

Mizzlesoft (immersed in his precipitation logs) peers confusedly up at her on the following morning – but takes the plate anyway.

"You told me it was your favourite. Ta ever so for taping that Radio 4 play."

Mizzy smiles.

Jane hovers, smiles too and departs for her desk with its lovely

collection of old almanacs.
   Mizzy recovers:
   "I love you. I mean, I thank you."

*

"Drizzle, Mizzy?" Jane slouches with a paper cup, texting. "Or nothing special?"

It's the morning after and Mizzlesoft (adrift in his rain charts) peers up at her confused – but listens anyway.

"You told me drizzle was your favourite sort of weather. You saw a documentary on Channel 4."

Mizzy tries to smile.

Jane sighs and turns away to her desk piled with *heat* magazines.

Mizzy remembers just in time:

"Thank you."

She turns back. "What for, Mizzy? You're always saying 'thank you'. Like *so* what for?"

Mizzlesoft gulps, closes his eyes and thinks of whirlwinds off the coast –

*

Dale – Jane's track-suited suitor – is suddenly there and stands in the doorway of the Weather Office. "Hey J, are you ready?"

Mizzlesoft's eyes are open. He imagines the tornado slumping back into the sea and almost smiles.

Dale is sweaty and uncertain and looks smaller standing up.

"Janey, are you ready?"

"Ready for what?"

"The lecture. The weather lecture at the school. Remember?"

"Well, whatever."

Mizzlesoft is standing. "School? Weather?"

Dale unzips his top a trifle. "Janey – Jane's giving a weather talk at the school this morning. Um. As you know?"

Jane has her pink thing on and a baseball cap. "Yeah. He knows, Dale. He's such a sweetheart. Ain't ya."

And Jane's hand slips like a frozen breeze over Mizzy's cheek. "I'll be back this afternoon. Or maybe you can get started on those spreadsheets yourself. Ha."

They're gone, the Toyota a shiny blue whale as it slips past The Rustless Anchor.

Mizzlesoft ponders his frostbitten face in the black screen reflection of the computer. He rubs the warmth back and thinks he might need to nip home for something.

*

His storm is re-forming off the Starland Point lighthouse.

Severe Weather Warnings are signalling their way up and down the coast. Bulk carriers cower and the rescue helicopters are ready.

The Mizzlesofts sleep silently in their graveyard beds. They are untroubled by this spat; this love; this slight emotion.

*

Mizzy is at the cottage and hauling out his ancient Raleigh.

He applies cycle-clips and is away on his three gears. He descends a narrow lane bearing leg-lashing nettles. No matter. The air around him becomes fuller by the second. The molecules are packed in. Carbon dioxide has nowhere to go except back into the human body and Mizzy's lungs are full of condensation.

A single fork of lightning slices down the charcoal sky and splits a hawthorn in the near-distance. It is Mizzlesoft's particular and favourite tree and he swears; surprises himself as if he's snorted lemon drizzle up his nose.

*

He has cycled hard and can see the car as it dips in and out of sight. It scurries now, no longer a whale but a buzzy blue kingfisher. Jane probably yaps and smokes and complains of this unexpected date with difficult and disgusting schoolchildren that may indeed have been noted in the organiser that she left in those bloody loos at God-knows-what-club-or-other-or-whatever.

Mizzlesoft imagines Dale's reluctant foot on the accelerator; thinks he really *can* catch the Toyota if he pedals fast enough.

But the wind is coming at him in mad eddies across the stubble-ugly fields. Hedges are disintegrating skywards. A family of herring gulls whizz by upside down.

*

The bicycle trickles to a standstill. It's too much. Mizzlesoft tries to take deep breaths, tries to slow his respiration – happy now to even halt his heart.

Anything to stop the weather. *His* weather: that nose-thumbing sprite, that spat on legs...

Objects are leaving the ground on a regular basis: Mizzy's stricken hawthorn sails across the road; farm gates flap into the air as if they were grey misshapen crows.

Jane and Dale spin up out of a valley: the car, a sycamore seed itself, twisting and yawing right into the depths of the sky. A blue kingfisher penetrating and succumbing to the axis of the runaway storm system...

*

Mizzlesoft bestrides his old bike in the sudden silence of non-weather. He glances aloft and breathes. The sky is dim. The Starland Point lighthouse begins to moan happily, its seven creamy beams fanning out in that grey lunchtime to France and a flat stormless sea.

*

And back in the blue sky of his bathtub that evening Mizzlesoft munches Marmite toast. His nettled ankles smart and he doesn't feel like Kenneth Williams.

(In the hour-ago past, in the aftermath of a fresh downpour, Mizzy has tripped over a tail-light cover in the remains of his raspberry patch: something remarkably like an exhaust system is

121

glinting from the bottom of his stream; a car's CD auto-changer is caught by the moonlight in the very middle of a field.

(And away and up in the forest, a fox cub freely barks).

He glances over at the sad umbrella hanging on the toilet handle; with this new heavy weather, he might be needing a replacement.

*

The following morning: Saturday and the local paper.

Mizzlesoft risks a third ginger beer shandy and a noisy perusal of Mrs Rowles' *Cuttings from a Kitchen Garden* on page 17. Although its author leans at the beer pumps facing away from him (intent it seems on the fish tank, its tiny occupants like wavering brush marks from China), Mrs Rowles has eyes in the back of her head.

No, she really has.

The newspaper is quiet this week: it is that under-time between bonfires and Christmas. A mammoth multi-agency cliff rescue for a single sheep; bald tyres, no MoT. Ah, but here beneath Mrs Rowles lurks a small and curious meteorological item that hastens Mizzlesoft's heart as he begins to read –

"Still a big storm on for tonight, Mizzy?" Sandy is crowing through his concentration. Cigarette papers are scattered over the bar like albino sycamore seeds.

"Mmm." Mizzlesoft squints: the ginger beer is a little peppery.

"Raining cats and dogs, then?"

Mizzlesoft turns the page:

"Maybe."

Boo

Once, in the quiet year that followed the world's very first breath, there lived a creature called Boo.

It was of silent habits (having no fellows to gossip with or to inform against) and scampered happily about the forest floor on its four legs, slurping on dewy leaves and foraging for berries that sprung in the Springtime back then. The creature was an ingénue; an angel of innocence. It existed in a continuing mist of surprise at the unfolding wonders that the world had to offer. And it realised that it had a part in this world so it gave itself a name. It called itself *Boo* in honour of its constant state of startlement.

Folk living today – the distant relations of that faraway creature – cannot imagine the depth of its innocence. The first Ice Age was still many thousands of years ahead of Boo, yet the driven snow would have been like coal dust against its unsullied soul.

One day, Boo was sniffing through some low shrubbery and considering the next evolutionary leap (perhaps a neck extension to facilitate grazing on elevated succulents) when it came across a lake that stretched right across the valley. The creature turned from its meal and approached the lake with some trepidation. Boo sniffed the air: this was certainly a strange plant with its huge single shiny black leaf and gently shimmering ways.

Boo trotted forward and peered into the lake. The peaty soil clouded the water and made the bottom invisible. This might have been a pivotal moment for the species: water as energy source; water as mode of transport... But Boo just peered and peered. And the creature on the surface of the lake peered and peered too. Boo flicked an ear and the lake-creature flicked back. Boo attempted a sort of juggle with invisible balls and the creature juggled almost as well.

After a while, Boo tired of the game and returned to its snug nest in the woods. Having a non-retentive brain, Boo promptly forgot about the lake and its curiously peering juggling occupant. It proceeded on its business: inventing this and that and trying out some recipes on an awkward bonfire. Birds were beginning to appear and Boo began to imitate bird song, limbering up its larynx for the more serious conversational stuff that would be needed later on.

The first of the world's leaves was falling when Boo returned to the lake by chance. It had been chasing a humming bird through the wood: Boo was fascinated by the tiny creature with its wings of smoke and illusion. Boo had rushed out from the branch-roofed dimness and the lake was suddenly there. It appeared as a new wonder. In our own cleverness, in our mastery of written words and our ability to read them as we are doing now, we can afford to smile at Boo's lack of memory. Yes, it was purely subjective: for this small-brained creature the lake was a New Found Thing. In these early years, the brain had yet to acquire the jaded irksomeness of misused memory.

Boo wandered up to the still waters. But Springtime was over and Autumn filled the air: little genetic time bombs were beginning to run down deep within Boo's unthinking body. This time, Boo had visions of filling some of the big seed pods that lay around the lake with water... And perhaps (Boo's brain was all a-quiver) transporting the wet stuff to a place of utmost convenience. It dreamed about having a bath. Its brain cells traded microscopic lightning flashes at the thought of sailing away across the lake in seed pods to see what was on the Other Side.

A pod was heaved over to the water. The pod was heavy and Boo was wheezing at the water's edge. As Boo bent down to massage aching rear ankles, it caught a glimpse of something in the lake. Something that was bending down and fumbling around with its back leg too. Boo thumbed its nose and the lake-creature thumbed back. It scratched its ear and the watery double vigorously reciprocated.

Boo became somewhat disquietened by this odd vision. The disquiet had a name but the name had not yet been invented. Sometime after that first Ice Age this mere disquiet would be called Jealousy. Boo couldn't bear the thought of sharing the beautiful world with anyone but itself.

It tossed a petulant pebble into the lake. The interloper broke into a million exploding stars before shimmering back into its original form.

Boo strode out into the lake with alarming results. The Stranger had attached itself to Boo's legs and was scowling up meaningfully. Boo brought its face down to the very surface of the water. And the Stranger elevated its hideous excuse for the same right up to meet it. The Stranger was indeed exceedingly ugly. It wasn't at all like the wonderful flowers and shining insects that Boo was familiar with. Boo waded out of the lake in a huff and ran about the trees in a sort of murmuring craziness. This horrid creature from below must be stopped. Its ugliness precluded it from any involvement in paradise.

So Boo worked through the rest of the Autumn to dislodge the odd and frightening rival. Stone bombardments became de rigueur if Boo had any business (which it frequently seemed to have) around the lake. A smothering of the Stranger with fallen leaves was attempted: but it just kept re-emerging as the November winds scurried the leaves across the surface.

Winter came. Paradise hardened. It wasn't a proper Ice Age but Boo was scared. The succulents stiffened and became unfriendly. Boo took to burrowing in the hard ground for roots. It had its first Big Cry – and great sympathetic tears of whiteness blew down from the sky on freezing winds. In its hardship, Boo forgot all about the lake and its enigmatic inhabitant. In the night blizzards, Boo screamed out in pain and fright and was innocent no more.

And just as the white weather became so completely

overwhelming – just when it seemed there had never been any other sort of weather – the white weather stopped. It was a morning of silence. The stillness was stunning. The world remained white: drifts of the sky-fallen white stuff lay in scarifying heaps all over the place; icicles dripped from trees like glass fangs.

Boo ventured out from the safety of ground hollows. It capered in the still whiteness. It thought it had known what beauty was: but now it knew the true nature of beauty. Now that the world had changed so drastically it felt it could elucidate each one of those changes. Boo felt the true, hideous, gorgeous power of *Change.*

Boo ceased its forest dancing. It was in a place it had now learnt how to recognise. It was by the lake. Swaying with the euphoria of change, Boo rushed on in – intent on exciting every nerve ending in the icy waters. But – Boo cried out loud! – the lake was not giving way. Boo was running on top of the surface, sceetering around in a long spiral fall that ended with a bump. It was flat on its face, nursing a nose bruised by the impact of the frozen surface.

Boo had to share this. It had to tell someone. Everything was too extraordinary. Boo peered down into the lake – and straight into the wondering eyes of its old adversary. The Stranger had changed too. It was shivering now, spittled coat snapping under a layer of hoar frost.

"Come out," whispered Boo, rather unexpectedly. It cleared its throat and spoke louder. "Come out. It's all right. I must show you this."

Boo tapped on the ice. The Stranger inside the lake tapped back. They both hammered like crazy things. The air cracked. The glass water blossomed into a clouded fracture; it snapped and parted. Boo helped the Stranger pull itself out of the hole; helped it stumble across the winter beach and so on into the frozen forest.

*

And a time came when the world was wise.

The world thought the Age of Surprise had passed. The

knowing of knowingness filled the air as thickly as that first piece of white weather all those years ago.

Churches became science museums and science museums became nurseries for Einstein toddlers choking on rusks and logarithms. And schools ceased to be because ignorance had been outlawed. The carpet industry still thrived: enough problems remained to be brushed out of sight. But problems had become a tomorrow thing. And – curiously – when tomorrow came, next week beckoned. And when next week arrived – well, what was a further fortnight to Those In The Know?

And at some time-point in the new wise world (perhaps halfway through the week after next) an anomaly was detected. It wasn't detected on or under or quite nearly over the planet: the wise worlders had that all sewn up. No. There was something rather odd going on *Out There*.

Out There had been abandoned for lack of finance. *Out There* had been a logistical headache. Evidence of the wise worlders' foolish forbears still existed *Out There*: floppy flags and footprints on the Moon and Mars; plus a whole big buzzy bag of malfunctioning satellites on the way to Who Knows Where.

Out There was a bit of an embarrassment.

However, and by way of a gesture to sentimentality, the wise worlders did maintain an old orbital telescope. The telescope – named after an astronomer who pre-dated even the foolish forbears – had had a particularly chaotic and financially disastrous operational baptism. Hence the wise worlders' mirthful inclusion of it on their preservation list.

The telescope was still in partial operation and it beamed a signal down to a dusty basement in Texas where an earth station of sorts ticked-over. The janitor peered with interest at the binary figures spooling across the screen. A semi-retired official was summoned. After some hours boning-up in a disintegrating manual, the official managed to relay the figures to the computer terminal of an octogenarian living in Florida. The octogenarian was called Augusta Santi and she was the only person left alive to have worked with the satellite telescope when it had been fully operational.

In truth, Augusta hadn't worked on the telescope very seriously: she had only been a student invited in by a benign and media-savvy scientific agency. But as the figures slipped down the optic from Texas to hopscotch across her screen under the yukka by the window that looked out at the swimming pool that she'd never swum in, Augusta Santi sensed an irritation at the back of her mind.

She shook her grey hairs – sparkling under their coat of anti-UV hairspray – and went to the old work cupboard where she kept her ancient notebooks and prized electronic calculator and ticket stubs from the Pearl Jam farewell tour. It didn't take long. Her fingers played across the calculator with the remembered nimbleness of girlhood. Augusta gave a little smile for the benefit of herself.

She peeped out at the sun just sinking into the Gulf of Mexico and gave another smile.

Augusta was old enough to remember when the world wasn't at all wise: when it had been foolish and had known it. Augusta gave a larger grin.

She went down to the pool and smiled so widely that her friends looked up from their loungers with some interest. People in the wise world smiled quite a lot – but usually only little quivering snakes of knowingness.

*

They came and interviewed her just before The End.

The media were the wisest of the wise. She couldn't tell them a thing they didn't know already. As the day of the sun's detonation approached, they scuttled to her like insects with half-formed, barely-ready-to-listen ears.

When Augusta completed her calculations and news of the solar cataclysm was revealed, the barest of shrugs passed through the population. The wise scientists couldn't be wrong, of course. But maybe it would be next week or next month – or even in a decade or two. People purchased parasols and promenaded up and down the world's boardwalks in a droll manner. Sales of sunglasses showed a downward blip in a gesture of wry contempt for a nature surely only half as wise as mankind.

But news was scarce. An apocalypse was a significant event unattended by trivia. In this follow-up story desert, Augusta Santi was an old and foolish oasis. The messenger not the message: a fossil from the age of pre-wisdom.

So they all sat around the swimming pool with their palmtops and disc recorders and boom mics like fugitive furry limbs. The swimming pool had dropped two metres in as many days. Little curly lizard carcasses had fallen out of dead or dying trees to be crunched underfoot.

And the colour of the near-the-end sky was very colourful indeed.

The reporters goaded Augusta harmlessly. She smiled. And smiled again. They made snide references to her existence in the formerly foolish era. Wasn't she pleased to be alive in this new wise world? Yes, she was very pleased. Wasn't it an honour for her to be the harbinger of something that might happen *Out There* next week – or even next century maybe? Yes, quite an honour. What were her hobbies? Oh well, these days she just sat around reading the insert notes of her old grunge CDs and just kind of bathing in the radiated wisdom all around her. Yes, she was lucky to have survived into this modern age.

They left her then and filed up the drive under the pale, pale shadows of the ghost palms. Augusta rose from the deck chair and made to go back to her room when something caught her eye in the shrunken swimming pool. She leaned on the rail of the ladder and peeped into the forgotten water.

She reached her hand in.

*

Larry came by with ice cream ten minutes later. Larry was the community's head gardener and Augusta's special friend and was almost as old and foolish as Augusta was.

"Augusta?" Larry called, looking around. "Augusta? You're okay, honey. They've all gone now. Oh Jeez..." He noticed Augusta's pink flip-flops neatly waiting by the diving board. "Oh Lord..."

He crept closer to the water's edge.

"Hey, Larry."

Larry must have sensed rather than heard the words as he watched Augusta and her reflection swimming together at the bottom of the pool. The two women turned on their backs and formed a kiss with their lips. Larry squinted closer. It looked like a single word.

What *were* they trying to mouth up at him?

The English Soil Society

It was a good day for air-brollies. Marion and Betsy owned a model with dodo-wing stabilisers.

Bidding farewell to their Father, they caught Hurricane Kettley's downdraft to the foot of Mount Bonington. The lungfish hansom still wheezed and waited without comment. Army sappers were presently engaged on a canal building programme for the huge gasping creatures: the lungfish needed water, air and cabbages to remain mobile and a sizable portion of the Wessex downs had been given over to mud lakes for their Winter hibernations.

The stench of foetid cabbages lay heavy now as the girls' mount wriggled its way through a railway tunnel containing Blitz survivors and so up the suitably serpentine drive of Florey House.

*

Miss Clementina Casewell　　　　　　　　*The English Soil Society*
Florey House　　　　　　　　　　　　　　　　*Nitrogen House*
Bridchurch Canonicorum　　　　　　　　　　　*Dorchester*
Dorset　　　　　　　　　　　　　　　　　　　*Dorset*

3rd March 1863

Dear Madam,
　　I hereby beg to inform you that one of the Society's Inspectors will

be visiting your area within the next month. Should you wish to make use of the Inspector's services please communicate with our Office at the above address. A nominal fee may be forfeit.

Assuring you of our utmost diligence at all times.

Yours faithfully

R. E. Ezekstein, Founder

*

The House itself seemed deserted: Nurse Evelyn was taking in the Gaieties at Weymouth; Mother was on a walking tour of the freshly revealed Pacific plate systems and was not expected back at Florey before the end of the decade.

However, the scratch of topiary shears from behind a hedge heralded the presence of Julius the gardener. *Gardener* was an honorary title: Julius had been known to potter along (and indeed through) the crocus borders and patches of red-hot pokers. Cricket pitch rotovation between lunch and tea was a speciality.

Julius revealed himself with a flourish and gave a half-hearted salute to the departing lungfish. The gardener had a great affinity with animals.

"Julius Caesar!" trilled Marion with genuine delight. She deposited her hatboxes on the gravel path. "Shall we play?" And she was off, skirts held daringly above the knees.

"Seize-her, Seize-her..." imitated Julius, managing to caper upright in his chasing efforts with Betsy close behind. All three raced about the conifers and across the ornamental pond before collapsing inside the old greenhouse next to the Soil Pile. The sunlight through the few remaining panes made the interior glow magically. A rack of test tubes lingered in a corner and the designs for Uncle Arthur's long-abandoned satellite programme were pinned to a rafter. The girls lay about drowsily – Betsy, plumply proper, retained her bonnet. They chuckled as Julius juggled plant pots with his feet whilst his hairy hands were engaged with something inside his unmentionables.

*

Miss Clementina Casewell
Florey House
Bridchurch Canonicorum
Dorset

The English Soil Society
Nitrogen House
Dorchester
Dorset

20th March 1863

Dear Miss Casewell,
    Further to our Inspector's call at Florey House – and to your subsequent telegraphic communication – the Society has deemed your soil worth preserving. Our Surveyor's full findings are to be found elsewhere in this letter but in summation the affected loam is as follows:

    3 yards NNW from the corner of the abandoned greenhouse
    8 yards surrounding your ornamental fish pool

    Each trench to be one yard in width and one yard in depth.
    Our Inspector reiterates his desire to excavate beneath the pool – and acknowledges your wishes for due recompense, in respect to the fossils found by your late uncle there.
    The Soil will be collected by myself at the soonest instance.
    My warm regards to you once again.
    Your Servant –

Ralph E. Ezekstein

*

A figure passed across the sun, passed back and remained, casting the gathering into shadow.

Nurse Evelyn: returned disastrously early from the Gaieties in the company of her middle-aged young man, Herbert Softness. Nurse Evelyn stood atop the Pile of English Soil like a starched colossus; Herbert lingered behind her, an unhappy greyness.

"Marion and Betsy Ezekstein. Go – to – bed..." Nursie grimaced. "Go... now..."

The English Soil Society

She glared at them through the shattered greenhouse roof;
her face flushed beneath the snowy-white beard that faded into
gills and back again even as they watched. The girls were transfixed,
too terrified to move – but Julius was gone, a rakish figure swinging
away on his long arms through the oaks and beeches.

*

Tuesday morning –

Dear Miss Casewell,
My thanks for your very kind note – and your medical advice is
sincerely appreciated. It is a while since I last wielded a shovel in
anger – but I am sure the strain is not a bad one.
I am afraid that my knowledge of literature is modest to the point
of paucity – but your included lines of poetry do seem very apposite
on this occasion.
I remain Yr. Most Affectionate Servant –

Ralph Ezekstein

*

They didn't go to bed, of course. They had to help Nurse Evelyn and
Auntie Bridie with the carpet moss in the dining room. Nurse kept
giving the Pile of English Soil well-laundered glances through the
French windows. Mr Softness had been sent out for an earthing
spade.
"That Soil's throwing a whoopsy, children," brooded Nurse
Evelyn. "Try and take no notice. Once young Softness has done
a little mulching with the earthing spade things should be back
to normal. Work a little faster with that hoe, Miss Bridie – there's
some moss growing under the polyphon."
Auntie Bridie – a small and curious person – gasped and paused
to wipe her spectacles. "Goodness, goodness me. What a to do.
All hot and bothered. No rest for the wicked. All's well that
ends well – but only for some. In for a penny – and what's *that*

got to do with the price of – "

Auntie Bridie abruptly devolved into a deep-sea fish with gaping mouth and blind eyes. Her spectacles glowed eerily. The low pressure of the dining room was too much for the depths-dwelling creature and Auntie left a nasty mess on the oak-panelling. Nurse Evelyn fingered her atrophied gills and sighed.

Mr Softness did nothing to lighten the mood by returning empty-handed from his earthing spade expedition.

"We're in England," he buzzed unhappily, trying to scrape the chrysalis shreddings from his wings. "They were closed."

*

Doctor Ralph Ezekstein   *The Head Cashier*
Florey House   *Hulot's Private and Commercial Bank*
Bridchurch Canonicorum   *31 McDonald Court*
Dorset   *London W*

12th June 1865

Dear Doctor Ezekstein,

I write to you in connexion with the five safety deposit boxes that you acquired in the name of The English Soil Society this January last.

You will realise that we commissioned especially from Geo. Watkin & Nephew five new boxes to accommodate your bespoke requirements. You must recall that these boxes were several times larger than our customary model and the lead lining you requested incurred some small expense on our part.

Whilst appreciating your financial strains (of marriage, an infant daughter – and, indeed, as you write 'the prospect of a new expectancy') the Bank cannot help but take a dim view of your abrupt termination of our services. In addition, the spillage of earth upon our vault floor prescribes the Pro Forma invoice contained herein.

Further, one of our junior clerks – Mr Saltover – is instructing a private lawsuit against you in respect to damages incurred upon his 'very soul' whilst undertaking night duty in the vault. Saltover is

135

young and excitable and I would hesitate to comment upon his accusations here: he reported some 'disturbances' from your deposit boxes and that is all. It is only in respect to your long association with the McDonald Court branch that I mention anything to you now.

On behalf of the Bank, I thank you in anticipation of a remuneration upon your soonest convenience.

Your Servant

J.S. Swanby, Hd. Cashier

Addendum: One of your boxes seemed in a parlous state and – under the terms of our contract – I took the opportunity of disposing of it for you – J.S.S.

*

The moss had now thickened and grown into a primitive maidenhair fern. The girls closed their eyes, aware of a sudden tickling in their bloomers. The fern's growth slowed, stopped and the feathery fronds began to curl and brown into bracken. The girls became women. Middle-age flew up at them from the floor like dead leaves.

The dresser collapsed as it curled into an acorn. The silk wallpaper sucked itself back into a million long-dead caterpillars and sent a framed copy of *Pegwell Bay, Kent – a Recollection of October 5th 1858* by William Dyce flying to the new forest floor. *Pegwell Bay* stared up at the verdant ceiling, the picture's faded hue, fine line and odd positioning of haunted, unsympathetic characters a cold reminder of *un*-change. Within the picture frame, the broad stripes of shawls and skirts rustled motionlessly over rock pools; a pallid comet streaked lazily across the angeline sky.

*

URGENT *** EZEKSTEIN TO SWANBY *** WILL
BE TRAVELLING LONDON UPON 18TH INST *** ON NO

ACCOUNT REPEAT ON NO ACCOUNT DISPOSE
OF FIFTH BOX *** ENDS

*

Florey House was shaking.

Originally late Georgian on Jacobean foundations, the building regressed to Romanesque before proceeding apace to a system of henges and barrows. Mr Softness selected his favourite mammoth harpoon and departed with Nurse Evelyn. Marion shrugged on bearskins, tottered to Uncle Arthur's greenhouse and invented fire. Betsy clung to the vast oak where the dresser used to be and flung herself into the future: hands softened, stature grew to the human female optimum of five foot, seven and one half inches. Her hair fell out. There was a brief thunderstorm as she stepped out onto the frozen sea of a briefly far future Florey. Icebergs calved and her snowshoes flubbered into walrus flippers.

Hurricane Kettley smirked far above; Cyclone Fish murmured on the other side of the world.

The Twentieth Century pulled up in a six-horse landau, stayed for a light supper and departed on a solar-powered microlight. Alexander Fleming and the Lords Attenborough began a tea dance that would rage for millennia. William Morrismen waltzed up the walls of England and laid their paper there. Michael Powell and Paul Weller walked arm in arm from the burning daylight set of *The Kentish Christ:* the two Marys – Kathleen Byron and Toyah Wilcox – strolled once more in the garden. The Stones remained unrolled. The Muslim Breakout began two centuries earlier and the world was decimated by man-made plague in 1803. Cricket was never invented. Kate Bush was a welder's mate at Tilbury Docks and the weather stopped.

In 1861, The English Soil Society isolated sentient schist in Dorchester. Two years later, the Pile by the Florey greenhouse wilted and grew and settled and re-excavated itself. Normality reigned with the sway of a light June breeze at teatime.

Weather crept back into the conversational agenda and frogs fell briefly. It was Boxing Day and the sisters went to visit their Father.

*

Dr R.E. Ezekstein
Florey House
Bridchurch Canonicorum

Eastern & Northern Railway Company
Rocket House
Leicester

6th January 1883

My Dear Sir,
    On behalf of the Company and myself, I would humbly wish to take this opportunity of extending our most sincere condolences on your recent and profound loss. Our Inspectorate is still carrying out enquiries and the possible presence of livestock on the track has not been dismissed. You can be assured that any further evidences will be relayed at the soonest instance to yourself and to the families of all the other passengers involved.

    With the Deepest Respect –

    Thos. Yates, Controller, Eastern Section

*

They tried not to tread on the Auntie Bodies when visiting their Father. The Aunties were distant relations whose evolutionary path had forked from their own several generations ago. They lay now sullen and unwashed at the top of Mount Bonington; tiny-fanged and insolent, their beds of self-knitted cardigans crinkled on a sub-strata of Delia Smith recipe supplements.

    Marion crimped and zipped-up her drysuit. The Auntie Bodies fumed, their blue rinses garish in the light of late afternoon. "There there, dears," boomed Marion inside her diving helmet. She produced a small packet of dark chocolate digestives and the Aunties fell upon them hungrily.

    The entrance socket's scum parted to Betsy's hand, scudding and steaming in the warmth of the air hanging over the mountain top. She withdrew, a fascinating patina of ice crystals coating her fingers. Betsy jangled the crystals like jewellery, crouch-spun in a corkscrew and disappeared head first into the socket leaving barely a ripple.

The water closed around her and Betsy dropped like a stone through a world of darkness and distant lights. She plummeted for half a mile before slamming her head into Father's drawing room carpet and rolling under the aviary table. Small bubbles evacuated themselves from the joints of her drysuit and her eye followed them up to where Marion was beginning her own descent: more cautiously, more *elder-sisterly*. Betsy grunted and pulled herself out and peered at the glass domes on the tabletop, surveying the finches and flamingos inside with fear and distaste.

"Do you eat these, Marion?" she asked, as her sister threw out hand anchors and pulled herself nearer. They touched helmets. "Do you eat these, Marion?" she repeated.

They stared at the stuffed blind-eyed flamingo together. "Certainly, dear sister. All of God's creatures were put upon this earth for our enjoyment. Our gratification is their point of existence. If we weren't here, nor should God's creatures. You know what Father says."

The drawing room was a homely place. Persian rugs flopped around the clawed feet of desks and divans. Mighty portraits of noble beasts hung midway between floor and imagined ceiling; douglas firs swayed under cargoes of Christmas baubles and sweetmeats. All made magical in the shimmering light of the *underwater*.

The sisters anchored their way about the drawing room seeking out their Father. Living so far from the Pile, Father's form remained especially inconstant. He never appeared the same way twice. A Huxley essay lay upon the desk, weighed down by a group of ammonite fossils. Betsy juggled with them as Marion searched through the desk drawers: feathers and fairy lights floated up from curling lining paper; well-thumbed copies of *The Dandy* and *The Eagle*.

Betsy threw down the fossils in disgust. "Do you think Father's out visiting? It *is* Boxing Day." She looked past the stag portraits and out into the gloom where the glimmerings of other drawing rooms glowed. There was little movement save for a houseboy who darted from light to light with memos and fresh seltzer syphons.

"It's the usual game," spat Marion. "Hunt the Father." She swung in the swing chair, glancing into every nook and cranny. "Hah!"

She rose up and partly swam, partly staggered to the Christmas tree. "Darling Pater," she warbled. "I believe I espy you on yonder branch!"

The spermatozoan detached itself from the tree and curled through the water in a playful manner. It glided between their thrashing arms and wriggly-waltzed to a tallboy. Carefully, with the girls' help, a pen and vellum were taken from a cubbyhole. Father's tail took hold of the ink pen and the two girls steered the entire assemblage to the desktop. A hydrophone floated into view.

Writing backward and blind he managed to scribble out a greeting:

No ti eMALB

Wryly, the pen scratched a maze before:

NOituLove

The hydrophone cut in with gurgling abruptness. "Ah! Brrfff... (gargle...) ffrrdiddlediddle. Branson told me he'd fixed this. Evolution, dears. Schhh..." The sperm coughed and continued. "Tell me what has brought you back here so soon. Mount Bonington is a private club, strictly gentlemen only – except on alternate Thursdays when we let the landgirls in to drain and clean the water. The other fellows are curious. You know that in the perfect (gurgle) social system the male has one function only. The other coves think we might be m-m-m..." Father had some trouble getting the hydrophone to behave. It was tuned to a Victorian frequency. "...Conjugating," he concluded stiffly.

140

The girls recounted all that had happened. Father seemed distressed to hear about the insect-regression of Mr Softness. "Mmmm. Drone mentality," the hydrophone murmured. "Well, I always suspected that the Soil was unstable; that isolating the potential memories from the loam was fraught with frustration if not out and out danger. I never mentioned this in my initial correspondence with your mother. It only came out later. The Pile is susceptible to any dis-location. And the fact that we find ourselves here seems to be an anomalous aside in the Ezekstein way of thinking, I have to admit. And the fact that we are aware of our existence is something that has kept the other club members on port and cigars for years. That's certainly something I'd never considered when digging up the Florey garden.

"These memories – or memories of memories or memories of memories yet to be (gurgle)... all things from all ages, even those before man had conducted his glorious pilgrimage from the cradle of Africa. Those memories – those ghosts – are obviously getting loose on the Estate. Nurse's young man has never undergone a pupative state before – am I correct?"

The girls mumbled inconclusively.

Father proceeded: "It's a shame about Aunt Bridie. She was a good sort and her truisms were rather priceless – but now she's joined the mulch of eternity..."

"The march, Papa?" Betsy asked nervously. She had become aware of activity in the surrounding drawing rooms...

"No – the mulch, my dear. I believe that potentially all tissue can break down and join the English Soil, thereby enriching it with every passing generation. As in the actual world, so within the memory world of the Soil. But I think Frank Reeves might help you. My old student conscience. I think he has some grasp on all of this. Go my children – go to him. Begone and find the ghost of England: for I believe it must be the very fibre of Albion that has loosed itself upon you. Might I suggest a short but pithy hymn prior to your departure to the upper world?"

The hydrophoned voices of the other fathers carried movingly through the dim waters. The girls looked back as they swam up to the daylight: drawing rooms stretched away as far as the eye

The English Soil Society

could see, infinite oil lamps like dank musty stars...

*

Doctor Francis Reeves   The English Soil Society
The Croft Museum of Wetland Antiquities   Florey House
Taunton   Bridchurch Canonicorum
Somerset   Dorset

3rd July 1883

My Dear Reeves –

Please forgive me. You must have stared at my letter last Tuesday with an understandable askance.

You will think me foolish and perhaps a little sad as you look upon this strange delivery to your museum door on Angel Street. And how sweet that street's name seems to me! Since the loss of my three girls my thoughts have been turning increasingly upward. Do you think me too pat, too music hall? One just does not know where to go or how to be. The death of a wife – even taken before her time – possesses some sort of gauge in the human mind; a motif, an expected reaction, ungerminated but waiting. But the deaths of children. The deaths of children to this cursed age of rail and steam! I wander here and there, doing some minor chore, some tiny task –

You must know that my health is failing daily – and of course you will recall my student reveries from so long ago; those curious dreams we shared in the '40s must seem like wrinkled misshapen fruit to you now. But now the fruit lies in your hallway awaiting a home in your venerable cellars.

Tragically, we have lost one of our samples – but nevertheless   I dream of this English Soil sleeping next to the Saxon spear, the Beaker stone pillow, the ancient and modern texts of science and literature – and, indeed, your wonderful sprigs of appleblossom!

I salute you, old friend.

Yours –

Ezekstein

142

*

Doctor Frank Reeves lived atop Windcheater Hill, a short blow from Florey beyond the new canal project.

His gardens were awash with permanent appleblossom, his mansion corridors a nasal paradise of beeswax. Doctor Reeves was considered a kindly man for an exorcist and wore a shell suit and trilby. He yodelled to his kippers at breakfast. Kippers were his weakness. The house was festooned with them. Doctor Reeves enjoyed the challenge of cleansing their long dead, always dead, smoky souls.

The housekeeper – a slight man with negligible moustache – glided down the stairs and ushered them into the sitting room with the haunted air of a gazelle at a waterhole. A George Formby record could be heard from an upstairs room.

Doctor Reeves was wrestling with dental floss. He glanced up from the girls' calling card on his desk. "Old man Ezekstein again is it? It happens occasionally. A rogue Pile. A breakdown of the silicon or micha schist or whatnot. Never know why though. I kept them as best I could at the Angel Street museum – but you couldn't really tell if anything was amiss or not. Here – hold this could you, um – Betsy, is it?" He proffered a dripping hank of floss to Betsy. "Hold tight, my dear..."

Frank Reeves took a deep breath and flung his head around 720 degrees. Betsy – a temporary satellite – spun with him and relieved the mantelpiece of several family portraits and a fish knife.

The Doctor shivered briefly and, dabbing his raw gum with a piece of ectoplasm, led the way through to the kitchen garden. His housekeeper had been Digging for Victory at the weekend but a baled-out pilot had parachuted into the tomato canes and he'd lost heart.

"I just want to show you that the most stable Pile is not immune to these curious fluctuations. Mr Colpepper – " The Doctor indicated his nervously hovering housekeeper "– was starting up the manure with some kipper renderings and down popped the parachutist. I thought we might have got away with a bit of mulching but the Soil is terribly sensitive. Heaven knows what would happen if it received a more severe jolt. The Soil is a living thing. Here, let's go inside and see if Mr Colpepper has our tea ready."

Mr Colpepper disappeared like smoke into the kitchen.

Over Assam and kipper mousse, Doctor Reeves told them more. Going to his study, he returned and unrolled a large map of the district, pointing out the many spots where Piles had become unbalanced – including the tidal road to Holy Island and several Foreign Fields. Doctor Reeves fancied that the example at Florey House might represent a complete digging: most of the other Soils had become dispersed. He told of the increasing appearance of bio-phenomenal anachronisms like the lungfish and he even had one of the original pamphlets from the English Soil Society in a glass case: at the bottom of *A Foreword – Thoughts on This England and the Sentiency of its Soil* the brown signature of Ralph Ezekstein curled like the eccentric tail of a spermatozoan.

"I'll certainly pop over to Florey for you, dears. Often all that's needed is an earthing shovel, but I'll bring a copy of the Society's Instrument of Disclaimer just in case. It runs to three hundred and twenty-seven pages and that usually settles things down if I have enough throat lozenges. Mr Colpepper will see you out, dear girls. Your Father was a broken man when you died, you know."

The distantly heard George Formby scratched to an abrupt silence as the housekeeper slid past them to open the front door.

*

Scutt & Son, Auctioneers
Cliff Place, Minehead, Somerset

This 12th day of October 1923: Notice of sale – the goods of the late Frank Reeves of Taunton... ...Four Fine Hessian Bags in Fine Egyptian Weave. Bags contain quantities of Earth totalling approximately 600lbs in weight. Earth may be removed with small injury to bags...

*

The girls returned to Florey in sanguine mood, their steps made light by Doctor Reeves' words and a band of English longbowmen who gave the maids an impromptu lecture in woodcraft along the way.

The sunset was glowing to sepia as they skipped up the drive. In the twilight, harvest mice were growing leathery wings and slipping into the sky. The girls felt a new tingling trickle through their bodies. The grass seemed to slip over itself and shrink away...

But the land wasn't falling.

It was being rolled up.

They tumbled back into the high road, hapless carpet tacks on a disappearing Axminster. Mr Softness hovered unhappily above the gateposts of Florey as they shot through. His wings were only just missing his bowler hat.

"Girls, girls... Try and – "

But they were gone, tumbling down the valley where the land was vanishing into a tiny khaki blob; bowling through a mobile copse, the crack of infinity only a hundred yards away.

*

Mrs Amanda Cartwright   *Divisional Commander*
Shadewell Cottage   *North Somersetshire Home Guard*
Coombe William   *G.H.Q.*
Dunster

Our Ref: SHD/AC/53PL19456VB/Std.Apgy.
Clearance: Restricted/Duration

5th June 1942

Dear Madam,
    Further to your letter of the 1st inst., I can but apologise for

the conduct of my men. The dissembling of your Anderson Shelter under blackout regulations is inexcusable. Our Area Commander has authorised an immediate apology, both through the agency of this communication and a complete re-build of your shelter by sapper regulars.

Incidentally, it was discovered that four of your bags contained earth – as opposed to the suggested builder's sand – and we return these to you intact on the understanding that you will carry out the Ministry's recommendations.

In answer to your pertinent question, I am not authorised to furnish an explanation until the secession of the current Emergency. Unofficially, I would say that the theft of your sandbags and the staging of the Combined Forces Novelty Sack & Egg Race on the day after are two wholly disconnected occurrences. Your kind enquiry is noted: the Porlock Platoon romped home with a ten point lead.

My apologies once again.
Yours sincerely

Major S.H. Dickenson, Officer Commanding

*

"Marion!" Betsy crossed the copse from tree to tree, clinging like a crinolined limpet to each quaking trunk. She could see her sister knotted into a root system perilously close to the chasm. "The edge! The edge is just here..."

The sisters stretched out hands and Betsy hauled Marion painfully up. The chasm gurgled and thundered mere feet away, throwing out autographed David Jason scripts and part of the moving staircase from Goodge Street Underground Station.

"Time to be leaving, I think. But to where I'm not altogether sure. After you, dear Marion."

"No, no. I insist, sweet sibling."

"You are the oldest and prettiest, beloved sister..."

"Nay, nay, me darling girl, you – "

The countryside – the old countryside – disappeared into a pin prick of forever. The girls were thrown into the air – and kept on going...

"Can't... can't hold on much longer, miss... miss missus missuses – ses – ses – "

Mr Softness gasped as his wings purred and blurred above him. The effort of holding them aloft and fumbling for the unmarried plural was almost too much.

*

Lady Florey   Department of Geology
Florey House   British Museum
Bridchurch Canonicorum   Bloomsbury
Dorset   London
DT7 3AB

15th March 2008

Dear Lady Florey,

It is with the deepest pleasure that I return these sacks to you. Your letters of provenance were quite unnecessary: the attached notes of your great great grandfather were more than sufficient. The circumstances of the sacks' arrival at the Museum remain hazy – although it should be remembered that we lost many of our records during the War.

The story of The English Soil Society is indeed a remarkable and eccentric footnote to the history of Victorian gentlemen scientists. I just hope that Dr Ezekstein would appreciate our efforts at preserving the samples – whilst respecting our less than one hundred per cent belief in his theories! The concept of soil sentiency is an attractive one, I'll freely admit, but one doomed to a shady existence in the murky realms of psuedo-science.

Nevertheless, it is good to know – from an entirely human point of view – that these items are finally coming home to rest.

With Kind Regards

Herbert Softness, Department Curator

*

They rose up over the swiftly inflating countryside. Like a lively tissue paper, the woods and football pitches uncrumpled into moist, rain-fretted greenness. The English Channel flooded across the Florey Estate before retreating back to its customary level. Far below, on the new old beaches, life was crawling ashore: the sea caverns beneath Mount Bonington had been flushed out, the drawing rooms and their contents helpless flotsam washed-up now in the coastal estuaries.

Mr Softness deposited the girls on the esplanade at Weymouth and flew off in search of Nurse Evelyn. Eric and Ernie were headlining the summer show with David Bowie; the promenading crowds were candy floss-thick and excited.

"My children..." said a pale voice.

A dripping figure focused itself into a small man with rumpled suit and absurdly mis-tied cravat.

"My children," the stranger squeaked unimpressively, leaning on his shovel. "Welcome home. My name is Ralph Ezekstein and I am your father." He pointed behind them. "And look who I have brought with me..."

They turned. The clouds cleared. The sun came out. Blue birds twittered over the white cliffs and the whistle of a steam train echoed through England's infinite hills.

Tooley's Root

Buccolia stirred on her one hundred and twenty-eighth birthday.

Dreams had come with difficulty and they had smelt of salt.

The rock behind her head teasingly murmured Buccolia back into wakefulness, the nester mites scuttling from her hair and ears. Podlett crabs remained, scraping away the dried lacrimal wax from her eyelids. She lay still and listened to the rasp of their tiny working claws.

The ante-oestrus stiffness was still on most of her body although the exo-skeleton that sheathed her abdomen was unaffected. Buccolia knew that only a few days remained until her fluids ceased to flow. The pain that she had been able to soften by sleep would be replaced by the ache of cursed instinct. Then there would be no rest. The glands in her neck and thighs would swell and throw a chemical mist through her body – stimulating the stem of her brains, the root of her loins. Already, she felt the itch of her tri-clitoris as it sensed the onset of appalling oestrus.

She slipped back her eyelids, sending the podletts floating away across the gallery. The cave was pitch black. Buccolia leant against her rock and phosphorescence brought a magic dimness.

Tooley had been while she slept. He had tidied her toys, rearranged her books and put the picture-page of Stannerwitz's Christyman on the wall next to racks of drying seaweed. Tooley was unable to differentiate: he called books toys. They played with them together, making strange book patterns on the cave floor. A lake, perhaps, or the shape of the sea. Neither of them could read.

Buccolia knew she must pull herself upright. It had been such a long time. Her legs resembled pencils, the coarse black hairs like nails. Buccolia had pencils and nails. She knew what they were. She raised a meta-carpal up to the rock meaning to gain support but received a sudden vision from her old friend. Her rock was murmuring with others all the way along the fault line that ended at the scree slide on the cliffs. Buccolia could smell the sea, could refract the image of it. Night lay across the ocean. Shooting stars trailed towards the pink horizon.

*

She felt a shock go through her abdomen, almost making her fall. It would not be long now. Under the new Moon, the Prickermen would come. They would slip out from the surface of the sea and scamper across the black sand to find her. Following the reek of her musk, they would scrabble into the crannies and fissures of the cliff, slide through impossible cracks and finally come to her spawn-gallery.

And she would no longer be alone.

A sigh echoed and she started. It had come from her own mouth, the jaws opening to let out the trapped air within. She staggered from rock to rock, knocking off cuttleshell ikons and the picture of Christyman; she circled the gallery searching for her mirror. Tooley must have taken it. He was a fool in many ways and yet softness sat easily on him: he had taken the mirror so she would not see.

*

The Ochre Way was a steep passage and Tooley had to make the descent six-handed, the seventh clinging firmly to Buccolia's scrap of mirror. He had only just made it. He had murmured to her and knew that her body was slipping off its sleep; a body that was bloated and changed.

150

Tooley was worried. He was terribly scared. He had a pickled expression on his small face, a wrinkled fright. It would never be the same now. Not after the Prickermen. Tooley gasped, felt his guts loosen out. He raced to the passage-gutter and pelleted uncontrollably. *Things are getting out of hand*, he thought.

Biaritz and Torlado – females of young Stannerwitz's acquaintance – passed by, giggling at Tooley as he squatted in the gutter. Babies, he thought, just babies. Just like Buccolia had been. He could recall her now – rolling in the short turf that covered the cliff top, laughing in the sunlight among the sea pinks. Buccolia had loved sunlight. She had loved wind; she had loved the ocean.

He stood upright, checking the mirror. He inserted a carpal-nail into a skin-flap on his chest and slipped it in for safety. He knew this would never do. His life was a quiet one but he had to get on – at least until his next hibernation. Tooley touched his chest again and slowed the pumping organs within. He leant against the wall at the Ochre's junction with Shedding Way and stopped breathing for a while.

*

Sceela was feeding when he got back to his home-gallery. She squatted in the corner below an especially bright piece of phosphorescence. Sceela was careful with rocks: she only murmured when she really needed to. She had fooled them. Rocks were her workers, not her friends.

Tooley slipped back the dried sugar-wrack curtain and entered, taking his own food from where she had left it. It was small and gritty: the scraps. He moved to an opposite corner and fed in silence.

He still wondered why he had dry-spawned with Sceela in the first place. Others did too. It was not as if any offspring would come of it. He'd been silly, really. Socially, she was above him in The Levels and he knew that the other Gardeners laughed at him: Tooley the bumbler, the sterile fool. Few Gardeners shed semen anyway and what there was went into the Gardens at Springing-time as a gesture to Good Luck. Sceela held a position of some importance. She had been born bi-clitoral and had been visited by

Prickermen twice. She was so pleased about this that she had removed her scutellum plates permanently so everyone could see. Tooley glanced sullenly over at the object of her self-adoration and pelleted. She was so unlike Buccolia. She had no toys for him to tidy. Sceela played host to hibernation crèches and he had to clear up after those instead.

He swallowed the last of the food, spat shell fragments onto the cold floor and then thought better of it. He shovelled them back into his mouth as Sceela looked up darkly.

I don't want you here for a few nights, Tooley, she murmured, wiping saliva from her closed lips. *I'm entertaining.*

He thought of answering her vocally – to amuse her – but couldn't as the shell fragments scraped painfully down his crop. But she would have continued anyway.

It will soon be your sister's time, yes? Her very special time. I'm sure we'll all be happier then. Poor Tooley... She crawled over, laid a stinking carpal on his nose. She brought her mouth nearer to his. "Poor baby. You're so worried... so worried..."

She moved her mouth away, sank her grey teeth into his ear. *Be sure I'm the first to know when Buccolia's time comes, Tooley. Tell me first when it happens... There's only one reason why I dry-spawned and murmured with you, Tooley, and that reason is about to happen...* Sceela was thinking about her position in the High Garden: bringing first news of the Prickermen would be a social *cachet*.

"Poor baby. Don't forget – never forget who I am..." She grasped his wrinkly face and thrust it down her body. Tooley hated this. He really hated it. *Remember who I am...*

Tarsal scrapes came from the tunnel outside but their owner passed on by. Sceela dropped him, turned and pelleted. He smiled dismally and began to tidy up while she went into the shedding-gallery to peel her old skin. She was especially irritable at this time, he thought.

Perhaps she wasn't to blame.

*

He picked up a large shell fragment from where she had been

feeding. It was violet and yellow and shaped like a porpo's fin. Buccolia would like this for a toy.

He murmured to it. Squatting there in the cave he could see the fragment as a whole, as an armour for precious life. The armour-shell was a fantastically designed valve and pressure mechanism. It was honeycombed with air-cells that protected the owner from seasickness.

Tooley murmured again. The creature was an androgene, smooth and waiting for its partner in the hugeness of the sea. This particular creature had never fulfilled its destiny, had never met another of its own species. Using the ocean currents and the jet-thrust of its own valve mechanism, it had travelled the World's oceans: from friendly warm waters to the frozen surface tensions of the far north. What a wonderful World, thought Tooley, as he brushed the fragment. How strange, how beautiful –

He dropped the shell with a gasp. There was a stirring from the shedding-gallery but luckily Sceela hadn't heard. He closed his eyes once more. The shell creature had been in the deep darkness of a maritime trench. A freak down current had pummelled it towards the very roots of the Earth. The pressure was tremendous.

But there – his brains shrunk at the recollection – there swam the Prickermen. It was so dark that he stretched himself to the limit, murmuring to photo-nerves and memory endings. But he was sure. They hung in clouds like podlett crabs floating across a cave. They seemed to feed from the plankton-rich water. They cavorted amongst the curling strings of their own oxygen bubbles. They were coming closer to the little shell creature. Closer and closer... Tooley hastily un-murmured – an extraordinary act. He looked down at the shell; looked down at Buccolia's toy.

A groan came from the gallery. Sceela appeared in the doorway. She was drenched and blotchy and she held him with her dark eyes. He could tell that she was unable to focus her brains in their skull of new skin. Her mouth worked with difficulty, the ugly lips curling. Her throat rattled as air passed through it in an unfamiliar way.

"Go now," she said.

*

He went into the Garden.

The route was circuitous. Tooley descended even further through the Earth along the Kelp-Shedding Mainway, doubling back along a narrow underpass blackened by the Great Fire Experiment. This was a place of blind lichens with their attendant parasites. Thin white roots thrust their way in the semi-darkness, swaying with delight as Tooley touched them.

He came upon a party of young larvals – the issue of the Prickermen's last visit – in the Pool Room. They were playing charades – but immediately busied themselves with transparent shrimps and sludge samples in a rather too earnest manner. Tooley smilingly left the students to their studies and carried on up the underpass.

The Garden was set in a vast gallery among towering piles of sedimentary rock. Vari-coloured layers almost disappeared into the roof far over Tooley's head. The roof was peppered with holes, blue from the sky outside. It must be a sunny day, he thought. Light-shafts rained down into the Garden, made solid by the podlett crabs that hung in an eery suspension. He remembered that the Sun was very beautiful and he thought of sea pinks.

A purring came from the Garden. Along the rows of domesticated grasses and seaweeds, the Gardeners lullabyed lovingly. Every root and stem was touched; every pod and fibrous cell murmured by an adoring carpal.

There was something in Tooley's plot. It was an odd figure, swathed in dried kelp, encrusted with tiny shells. A curious deformity sprouted from one side of the intruder's head-shell; gullbeaks hung from ponderous earlobes and rattled unpleasantly. The figure looked up and broke into an odd choking, chuckling cackle.

Tooley came forward and they murmured.

Uncle Greenblade. I didn't recognise you. You've skinned again.

Greenblade was an enigmatic figure in Tooley's life. He was

some sort of relation to Sceela – but in the complicated genealogy of the Garden, Tooley wasn't sure if this actually made him an uncle. Greenblade came and went. He was often found in the depth-galleries beyond the Sour Reaches, murmuring with the blind things that made their home there. A keen teacher and symbiotic, he often played host to myriad onboard eco-systems that went beyond the standard crabs and anal mites.

And he sometimes went outside.

Come closer, my boy. Look. He rubbed a carpal over the odd protuberance on his head. The bubble shivered and sighed. Tooley bent down so that a light shaft passed behind it and saw the life held within.

A porpo in his porpo-sac, Tooley. A little interest of mine. I've been showing it to my pupils. They're doing marine field-studies.

In the Pool Room? I passed them by.

A tribe of small crustacea scattered over the porpo-sac and disappeared into Greenblade's ear. *Oh yes, vibrant youth. We come, we go and we remember.* He gestured to the sac. *Not unique, of course. It's been done before, but I see it as something of a personal triumph.* The Uncle pelleted with quiet satisfaction.

Tooley located his bone-tiller and began to loosen some soil. He noticed that the occupants of neighbouring plots were looking over at Uncle Greenblade with some curiosity. Tooley felt a small wave of embarrassment: his life seemed to be made up of forced lust and eccentricity. He busied himself to his work, turning over the soil and sifting out pebbles.

It's almost time isn't it, my boy. Greenblade put down his customary clutch of books and took up station on a chunk of basalt that chose to ignore his murmured overtures.

Tooley carried on tilling.

It's been a long time since the last over-spawn. Not since I was a boy.

Tooley – envisioning the larval Greenblade – glanced up with some interest.

We had that under-spawn just a few seasons ago, of course. I tried to question some Prickermen before they left but it was no good. Unresponsive lot. Only one brain apiece, y'see.

The English Soil Society

Tooley had heard things, but like most Gardeners contrived to time his vernal hibernation to coincide with the under-spawn. The Prickermen remained a mystery to him: creatures of deep ocean and nightmare. He thought of the shell fragment and shivered.

Greenblade was being over-murmurative, as usual: Buccolia is an exceptional person. I've spent quite some time with her. I understand her very well. She's having trouble focussing her brains on this over-spawn business. She doesn't need those stupid toys, those idiotic books...

GREENBLADE!

The shriek of Tooley's murmur echoed silently across the Garden. Faces appeared from behind grass borders. He felt a gut-surge and pelleted; controlled his brains, quietened himself inside. *Greenblade...*

I fear you're too close to Buccolia, Tooley. Her path is different now. Different to you, me and Sceela and her gossiping bi-clitorals. I look at her and see the past. I can sense the eons.

Tooley's tiller scratched on. *You've deep-murmured?*

Well, no... The Uncle was uncomfortable on his cold rock. *But sometimes an outside eye is useful. The larger view as you might call it. You must remind me to tell you about my Theory of Mankind...*

*

A savage jolt snapped through one of Tooley's arms, rushing on up into his brains-stem. He could see the bone-tiller shrinking and inflating and realised that he was in the under-reality that preceded instinctive coil-up...

Regaining consciousness, Tooley found himself sprawled out on the earth in a plot two away from his own: flattened weed stalks gave testimony to his violent passage. He sat up and looked around. Dodd – the plot's Gardener – lay dry-spawning nearby. He peered at Tooley with mild interest before resuming his position: Dodd's six partners were young thirty-five year olds, their scutellums tinged with the yellow of maiden-oestrus.

Greenblade had left his rock and was examining the bone-tiller when Tooley crawled back. The tiller – chiselled from the thighbone of a sea-dog – was still in one piece. The Uncle was mumbling to himself and raking the earth, setting out pebbles and shells in portentous patterns. Tooley snouted him with a carpal and tickled the porpo-sac but Greenblade was obviously in some sort of small-hibernation.

Other Gardeners were gathering now. Tooley – who was somewhat inept socially – felt awkward. Wishing to busy himself, he bent down and gently scooped his phalanges across the sandy soil. He made some patterns that brought great satisfaction and realised that Greenblade's trance was contagious. He pulled his carpal back quickly – and as he did so something flashed in the light earth. It was extraordinary. It was blue. One would have called it the brightest, darkest, deepest blue: in its profundity it was nonsensical. A mad blue.

Tooley bent closer, not daring to touch. It was transparent, he was sure. It was like a piece of still blue water. He sensed the anticipation of those around him. Someone handed him a piece of weed-cloth and he gingerly slipped the find into it.

A new toy for Buccolia.

His arm still ached but he knew he must search some more: he had to keep scratching the earth. He had to find what was buried there. Greenblade dazedly scratched with him. Onboard parasites scuttled from the Uncle's joints and abdominal recesses: the embryonic porpo stirred in its head-shell womb. Others bent to help: Dodd and his lovers; some Middle-Agers from the levels beyond the Great Fire Experiment.

The light-fingers from the World above dimmed as the Gardeners scrabbled and cursed. Evening was slipping down onto the Earth. Tooley touched the blue toy, safe now in a skin-flap. The others were finding more fragments: red and green and colours he couldn't quite place. But the blue belonged to him. He would keep it safe.

A small mountain was growing beside Tooley's plot. Sand, weeds and the bones of small fish. The Gardeners had murmured to the rocks and a green dimness dusted the scene: even the excavation mound glowed.

They kept on working and several of the party induced skin-shedding to facilitate easier digging. As the night wore on, the plot was littered with wasted exo-skeletons and the tiny writhing pools of dying symbiotics.

At the very centre of the night they found The Root.

They all knew that it wasn't a root, of course. But even the esteemed Greenblade was unable to furnish a more accurate description. The Root was a vertical *something* made of a flawless white stone. It stuck out of the pit bottom and was surrounded by more of the coloured fragments. It seemed to the Gardeners like a magic island set in a rainbow sea. Tooley lay flat out on the pit edge and reached a carpal down to scratch away surrounding soil, being careful to touch neither Root nor fragments.

There's something else here, he thought. The phosphorescence was especially dim and he stretched his nerve-endings out before him. He worked a carpal-nail carefully into the darkness and a small rubble-slip revealed a little more of the find. Tooley ran his senses to their limits.

It's some sort of under-root, he murmured up to them. *Although –* he scrabbled some more *– Although, it only seems to be on one side. It's like a bundle of thorn-grasses all knotted and curled up together into a ball. But it's only on one side... Oh, it's like –*

They helped him up. Tooley gasped for breath, inhaling with his rarely used patella-valves. *It's almost like –*

"We need someone smaller," said Dodd unexpectedly.

One of Dodd's ousturi leapt unprompted into the hole and disappeared from view. The pit sighed and partially collapsed. Dodd hurtled in – head first – after her, flailing loose his normally recessed pudendum. The hapless lovers were finally dragged out to lie gasping and embarrassed on the edge of the excavation.

Tooley looked down at the tangly under-root in the hole: *It's like a head. It's like a head in a book...* But his murmur was turned inward and no one heard it but himself.

Greenblade staggered to his unresponsive rock.

"We need Stannerwitz," he whispered.

158

*

The blind eel slithered past his body, sprinkling the new skin with electric shocks. It was a nightmare journey: the water was freezing and the air trapped beneath his carapace made sub-aquatic swimming difficult. Tooley found himself bumping into the submerged rock ceiling, leaving his dorsal ridges scraped and bleeding.

It wasn't that Stannerwitz lived far away from the Gardeners, but the seawater-filled passage that led to his cave *did* make regular contact difficult. Stan was young and essentially gregarious: his choice of home-gallery remained an enigma.

Tooley located an air pocket and stuck his snout into the narrow space between water and ceiling, breathing desperately. Stan had scratched encouraging directions on the rock: it wasn't long now.

The passage narrowed before it widened and he had to squeeze painfully between submerged boulders. His bowel stretched and he watched wretchedly as the pellets floated up like small brown bubbles.

Stan was napping on his beach when Tooley broke surface. Biaritz – the giggling youngster from the Ochre Way – was lying on her front, leafing through a book. *She* couldn't read either, thought Tooley. But he must have inadvertently murmured for she looked up and gave him a ghastly grin. Gum-crabs danced across her incisors.

Tooley waded ashore, water pouring from his recesses. The eel burns stood out brightly on his arms. Stan opened his eyes and brushed away the mites.

So. The toy collector, he murmured, not unkindly. *A pleasurable visitation – is it not, Bia?*

Biaritz peered at Tooley darkly. A distant cousin of Sceela's, perhaps?

Stan rose up and traced idle patterns in the sand with a dirty tarsal. The cave had changed little since Tooley's last visit. The vast book collection had been shifted to one side and the new pride appeared to be a muddle of transparent containers. Their construction material was shiny and – although of a greener hue – not unlike that of his new toy. The containers were narrow at one end as if the owner didn't want anything inside to escape. Stan noticed the direction of his guest's gaze.

Fascinating, hmm? I discovered them just below the Middle-Age levels. They were full of black water and a book-page was slapped on the side of each one. No use for that, of course – so I dumped all the inconsequential stuff and hung on to the interesting bit. Rather pretty, we think – don't we?

Biaritz gave her snarl-grin. With a start, Tooley noticed that she was bi-clitoral. He must have a quiet word with young Stannerwitz – but now more important matters were pressing.

My boy, we have a problem. A digging problem in the Garden. My bit of Garden... he murmured, with a slight blush. *Uncle Greenblade recalled your excavation prowess and wondered, if you weren't – er – well...*

Stan licked an ear absently. *Have a go, old friend? Well – I would like to carry on with that dig under the Middle-Ages, but...* He worked a nail into a troublesome flap. *Hmm. Important, you say?*

Biaritz tossed aside her book with a yawn and Tooley's eye caught its cover. It was a familiar one: Buccolia had a page-picture from the book propped up in her spawn-gallery. The out-page featured a very odd and beautiful person who was murmuring with some others. Mystery-writing decorated the top of it and a jolly red beetle-mite sat on the bottom. He remembered the title of the book: Stannerwitz had spent many seasons poring over it and the translation went on.

THE MIRAKLEES, he thought. *THE MIRAKLEES OF CHRISTYMAN.*

You reckon it's a biggy, Tool?

Tooley shook himself. *Um, yes... A very powerful murmur. Quite intense.*

Well, that seems to settle it. Stan adjusted his rakish neckerchief. *Count me in, you old pellet-in-the-night.*

*

Mercifully, Stan kept several caches of equipment throughout The Levels. A sub-aquatic journey hefting tools from his home-gallery would not be necessary.

A day and a night passed before Stannerwitz had completed his tortuous inventory. *Be prepared*, he had murmured mysteriously. But Tooley and the others almost went mad with impatience. Gardeners had by this time brought in relations and friends and the plot was gaining a distinct air of being lived in. Pellet latrines had been dug and emergency hibernation-lines were beginning to cobweb their way across the Garden Levels.

Tooley took to stalking unfamiliar passageways during this enforced hiatus. But his wanderings soon found him at the entrance to Buccolia's spawn-gallery. He moped outside, straining to hear any movement within. There was an occasional grate of chitin on rock but nothing more. He grasped the blue toy in his chest: the flesh had begun to grow into it and removal would soon be difficult. But he daren't disturb Buccolia.

Tooley realised that he had lost all sense of time. He was beginning to cut his memory into small portions, unable to grasp them as a significant whole. The coming of the Prickermen could not be far away now. He remembered again his ammonite-vision: he imagined clouds of them rising up from the ocean depths, hungry for their spawning landfall.

He returned sadly to the Garden.

Stan's preparations had come to a crisis. A complicated system of supports and derricks criss-crossed the excavation. It was difficult to see The Root at all now. Stan had attached himself to a hemp-rope and was swinging down the short distance to the pit's bottom. There was much scrabbling and grunts and calls for odd tools.

Crowds had swelled for the event: Greenblade's larval pupils milled about the diggings and made further field notes. Tooley even thought he could make out Sceela among the hordes as she absent-mindedly copulated with a Middle-Ager of his slight acquaintance.

There was an especially loud grunt from the pit. The throng

strained to catch a murmur of discovery.

"There's only one way to go with this pelleting thing," said Stan's distended voice. "Under it."

*

Sceela still had plenty of home entertaining to do and the Middle-Ager was only part of it. She received the news quietly – but with a look that cursed Tooley to a lifetime's skinning in half a minute.

Through a complex tradition of genealogical debt and favour, plots and home-galleries were often acquired at the same time. The ideal arrangement would be for a plot to lie directly above a home: the lucky Gardener could then cultivate the gastronomically-prized mazey roots through the roof of his kitchen-gallery. Tooley was just such a lucky Gardener – and Sceela huffed off to the Sour Reaches.

In the meantime, Stan weighted a line with a pebble and dropped it down a hastily-drilled bore hole. The happily glowing pebble swung now from the ceiling of Tooley's feeding-gallery. The audience was delighted and moved down a level. Stan shed two skins and followed them. He erected bone-scaffolding and scrambled up.

At first, digging was difficult. Stan had to import extra lash-mites from willing donors to protect his eyes from the descending dirt and mazey roots. Then the soil took on a more gooey texture and didn't separate so easily.

Increased moisture content, murmured Greenblade to the enthusiastic gathering.

That enthusiasm dwindled, however, as it became clear that a swift denouement to The Root Mystery would be unforthcoming. The gathering shrank and some of the larvals resumed their game of charades. Indeed, Tooley was on the verge of brewing some communal mazey broth when an audible scream came from overhead.

The scaffolding groaned and the bones twisted and snapped. A great sound ripped across the home-gallery, filling the air with dust and the yelps of Gardeners as they tried to make a swift exit.

Some made it out into the Shedding Way and disappeared down obscure under-passes. Others obeyed a deeper instinct, curling into armoured coils and stopping their hearts: it would be many days before they could revive themselves. Comatose Gardeners lay about the gallery like sandy lugworm spirals.

Tooley felt his gut distend but nothing came out.

He stared upwards through the settling debris. Stannerwitz floated above him as if by magic. The young archaeologist had been thrown from his perch and had grasped the first thing that he'd come across: the glowing plumb-line. It had been a risky thing: he didn't possess as many hands as Tooley. The line was fastened to a sturdy derrick up in the plot and Stan swung now, unsure whether to laugh, pellet or curl into an armour-coil like the others...

The line snapped.

Stan squeaked, fell and landed on a concussed and rambling Greenblade. The Uncle groaned: he stared past Stan and up to the gallery ceiling.

"Look," he managed to rasp out loud.

The collapse had created a deeper recess. The Root jutted down at them – thin, angular and dirty white. The straightness of it was unbelievable. There was nothing like this in Nature: in comparison, the smoothest mirror rock pool was awash with ripples. The three stood or lay in wonder. Greenblade tried to murmur but was swiftly put down by his companions.

Something was attached to The Root: perhaps an adhering remnant of clay, thought Tooley. He murmured to his optical-canal, murmured to his brains to shrink the distance. No, not earth. Something else. Taking his bearings from the plumb-line, he realised that this odd appendage must be on the same side of The Root as the tangly head. He focused in closer. What was it? It didn't seem to be quite the same as what lay in the plot above...

The others helped Tooley up onto their shoulders and he looked closely. There were two of them, folded across each other. Smooth, of course – yet somehow organic, each of them fanning out into five stubby tarsals. Could he believe what he was seeing? Should he tell the others? But it was too late: they had detected a murmur through his body, a spasmic hint.

They lowered him down and an eager – if one-sided – debate ensued. Greenblade fancied it was a hoax – a fraud laid down by frivolous ancestors. He gave them full credit for imagination but the feet were simply too smooth and unrealistic. True, they corresponded in size to their own but the design as a whole was obviously the work of a deranged maniac. Then again, The Root could represent a longing for an ideal: the perfect creature. A construction, of course – but the skin carried not a hint of shedding and the flesh looked hard and unyielding. Nothing like this could have existed in real life. It was a hibernation-dream.

Tooley just kept looking up at The Root and its Feet. Perhaps the attached stone-creature had been planted so it might grow; perhaps he should go and find his bone-tiller. But then, even then, he knew and he leaned against the rock and murmured. His thoughts passed through the Earth and into The Root. He closed his eyelids. He could almost feel his brains squeezing together. The Root. The Feet. The Head in the plot above. No one would ever know what Tooley saw there in his gallery. He gasped, almost passing out.

"Buccolia," he whispered. "Buccolia must come here... She must come here before they get her – before it's too late..."

He leapt over the armour-coils and out into the Shedding Way.

*

The Levels were deserted. The whole population was either in shock-catharsis or had made its way to personal hibernation-lines when the ceiling caved in.

He shed some joint-skin and ran. The rocks around him flickered with phosphorescence as they reacted to his fevered murmur. It was as if a green sun raced before him. He could hear a scrabble from behind and realised that Stan and Greenblade must be following – whether to help or to hinder he could not tell. He just had to bring Buccolia to this place. The blue toy throbbed in his breast but it didn't matter anymore. He clawed his way into the skin-flap, ripping away the blood-soaked fragment of stained glass.

The sudden pain made him slow and stop. Tooley's breathing was rapid: his patella-valves were wheezing too. He leaned against the passage wall and noticed a recent rockfall. Oddly, the earth seemed to have been forced out under pressure rather than to have collapsed under its own weight.

Tooley listened intently. One of his brains could detect the running steps of the two companions: another could hear nothing. But Tooley sensed it was a very important nothing. The silence was as solid as a rock.

Stan reached him first. His joints were sore under the new skin and he'd discarded his neckerchief. He lay on the floor, gasping. *Tooley... you one-brain pelleting fool. Leave your sister. You can't move her. You'll kill us all...*

Something slithered through Tooley's solid-as-a-rock nothingness. He looked down at Stan. He spoke aloud. "Come with me, boy."

They moved slowly forward together. Rock-murmuring brought no response. The air tasted different – but without the twin-senses of smell and murmuration the Gardeners were confused.

There were further rock falls ahead of them. They leapt over the rubble and galloped on faster, both aware of some unknown crisis. The Gardeners were almost foiled by a mammoth collapse blocking the entrance to the spawn-gallery. They worked at the mound like creatures possessed, blood freely flowing from their carpals.

Buccolia had gone.

Her cave was strewn with the beginnings of book patterns and uneaten food. The picture-page of Christyman lay in three pieces. Again, that strange taste filled the air. Tooley crawled around the gallery braying uncontrollably while Stan returned to the entrance and peered out into the passage. The odour was strong and salty. He went back and pulled Tooley up by his dorsal bumps.

"Come on, you old pillock," he grunted.

They carried on up the tunnel. An odd chirruping suddenly echoed ahead of them. They came to a halt and there was a slight pressure-drop.

A wall of crustacea was rushing down Shedding Way. It came

like a wave. Crabs, mites, sea spiders: tiny, small, huge. The noise of their rush was breathtaking: the chitinous clack of claws, the wet thump of ten thousand dead men's fingers. The two friends leapt wildly at a ledge, searching for a carpal-hold. The deluge rushed by and Tooley and Stan could feel their own symbiotics scuttling down their bodies to join it. The mass of legs surged up the large rockfall by the spawning-gallery and were gone.

Gone in the direction of the sea.

A small figure stepped out into the tunnel ahead of them: it seemed to raise a thin arm in farewell. The arm froze in mid-elevation and the Prickerman crouched. It turned its head from side to side and bounced back into a sub-gallery.

*

The fissure was a small one. How Buccolia had managed to work her way into it was a mystery.

Tooley lingered with Stan in the Shedding Way. They couldn't stop staring in. Her appearance was shocking: ecdysistic skin had grown over her eyes and she was blind. The legs were crippled under the fantastic weight of her bloated abdomen: fluids dripped where she had forced it into the tiny crack.

The noise was intense. In the usually near-silent world of The Levels it was a sound from hell. Buccolia herself was screaming incredibly. Her jaws had telescoped into fearsome mandibles with which she crushed and snapped any Prickerman foolish enough to get too close.

And the Prickermen: a hiss rose up like the ocean passing over shingle. They almost spoke. They almost had brains. There were swarms of them – as many as the retreating crabs. They clambered over the rock outside Buccolia's fissure, trying desperately to get in at her. Frenzied, they tore at their fellows with toothless mouths and mounted each other in the madness of their instinct.

Fascinating, quite fascinating –

The murmur came from the passage behind them. Greenblade had made it at last. He was pale under his head-shell and the porpo-sac had abandoned him. *I have a theory, you know –*

166

The mass of Prickermen turned for the first time. Their hissing quietened to the surf of very distant seas. One of them came forward with that odd bouncing movement they had noticed before. It was perhaps half the height of the Gardeners and smoothly skinned, with an iron-lipped skin-flap running vertically down its chest. The head was glob-blossomed in a curious wavering shell of air. Inside, a snout wriggled slightly and then with more vigour. The air-bubble wobbled and the Prickerman gave a light snort. The sight was almost amusing.

Greenblade took a step forward. *The creature has smelt me, my friends. This never occurred during under-spawning. They're more sensitive now. I am beyond Middle-Age, you see. Bits and pieces of me have dried up. I have ceased to function in many areas. The poor brute sees me as female. For every ten under-spawnings there is only one like this: there's only one like this every hundred years...*

He was a larval last time, you know, Stan. Tooley was curious at his own conversational manner.

The Uncle proceeded, as ever: *The over-spawn must be a trying time for the Prickermen. Their seed carries not the germ of Gardeners but of their own rarer kind. Buccolia will give issue to a clutch of larval Prickermen. All rather sad. We come, we go. You must remind me to –*

Tooley and Stan barely had time to duck before the Prickermen were in the air, bouncing off the ceiling, leaping from the walls. The sea-hiss grew and filled the gallery, threatening to rub the very air molecules out of existence with its hideous rasping:

.........SSSSSHHHHHHHHHH.........

*

The sub-gallery was empty.

Buccolia screamed in her fissure: Stan and Tooley crouched on the ground; a few maimed Prickermen shivered and shrank into the gloom. A distant hiss echoed around The Levels:

......sssshhhhhhhh......

Buccolia was soothed into silence. Oestrus had brought on nervous collapse in at least one brain. Most of her body was paralysed. It was fantastic she had made it this far.

The two Gardeners struggled to ease her ballooned carapace from its refuge. It was a terrible weight. Tooley, already on the verge of hibernation shut-down, had only the thought of The Root to power his aching limbs. They managed to get her to the entrance of the sub-gallery before stumbling and falling together. Buccolia groaned and put up an odd high-pitched singing.

Stan's brains were obviously faded. He spoke with difficulty. "Stuff it, Tooley. I say leave her to the Prickers. It's crap, I know – but she's *got* to go with them. She's *got* to birth out more bubble-heads. And then if we're lucky, they'll swim back and shag Bia and her bi-buddies and we'll have us some new Gardener larvals..." Stannerwitz was pacing the borders of madness but his words were true. "It's the way of the World, Tooley. It's how it all works. If they don't get to her you're wiping out the whole pelleting race. Don't you know it could all end here?"

Tooley worked his jaws: "Yes, maybe it *will* end here. Maybe it will. But didn't you see what they looked like? Didn't you see their bodies? Don't you look at your own picture-books?"

They struggled up once more and carried on. The burden of Buccolia was on their shoulders, the weight cutting down one side. They had to stop often to change ends. Tooley was delirious now, Stan just scowling and silent.

The salt-smell slid through the air again as they approached Tooley's home-gallery. A small red heap lay in their path. It was crumpled and flat, its armour crushed into a thousand pieces. Tooley stared at the remains of Greenblade and felt an admiration for the Uncle's proven Theory – whatever it might be...

And in the dimness beyond lurked the Prickermen.

Some were already convulsed in the death-spasm that followed over-spawning. Greenblade's sham mating-odour had caused confusion: lost figures shuffled around uncertainly, engorged prickers absurd against their midget bodies. Buccolia was eyed with trepidation. Their limited cranial capacity had not prepared the Prickermen for two possible spawn-mates.

The Gardeners leant against the passage-wall. Their shoulders were now senseless and they hung on to Buccolia with a dull determination. Her breathing came in short gasps.

"Give her to them," hissed Stan. "Give her to them..."

A Prickerman approached. It was their friend with the long skin-flap. A leader, perhaps? Had Greenblade's Theory included a social structure among the creatures? The glob-blossom slurped and glistened. It adjusted its neck and the air-bubble slid away revealing the small face beneath.

"Yes. Give the Mother to us. Give her to us and we'll go." The Pricker spoke quietly and carefully. The nostrils flared, drawing in the unfamiliar Levels air with distaste. "You people – what more do you want from us?"

And without warning, Tooley found himself murmuring with the Pricker-leader, found himself tumbling into that small, smooth head: *I want to show you something.*

The Prickerman gasped.

Don't be frightened, ocean-swimmer. Tooley swung into deep-murmur. He raced back through Pricker-life, using the Prickerman itself as his alley, to inform and translate, to devolve each magic element of strangeness.

Tooley sensed an ache within the Prickerman:

Flashes and twinkles: Glimpses of Prickerbabies on smooth-floors strewn with picture-books, toys and wrapping paper: Flashes and twinkles: Forgotten songs that sang again: A flash: And the Word became Flesh and dwelt among us: A twinkle: And a smooth Prickerwoman came closer, trying to smile, trying not to think of the dried-up nut womb that dwelt inside its stomach and the stomachs of all its kind: But in a twinkle of his own, Tooley was already racing back with the Pricker-leader across the sea and through the drowned entrance of the great cathedral: Slipping through the cracks, using fire-jelly from skin-flaps to detonate those too narrow to carry them...

It was the work of a second. Tooley gasped and fell back against the rock, almost dropping his sister. The Prickerman seemed puzzled. It wheezed, almost smiled and turned away before twisting back slowly, the nearly-smile fading, the mouth moving:

"You shit, you insect..."

Buccolia sighed.

The Prickerman hunched and sprang. Stan went down under its lightning attack. Tooley also fell as he tried to cover his face, his body crushed by their burden. The Pricker had grown a sort of shining iron-tarsal and was throwing itself at Buccolia's swollen abdomen. It had gone mad; flashing, twinkling mad. Through the hideous lubrication of blood and embryonic juices, Tooley managed to slip out from under his sister's body. The dismal throng of Prickermen backed away and he realised that he must make a fearsome sight. Tooley raised all his arms into the air and screamed. The pathetic creatures scuttled away into the darkness.

There was a terrible sound from behind and he turned just in time to see the Pricker-leader's head go flying across the passage. Its body shivered briefly and then fell away from Buccolia's mandibles. Tooley looked down at the Pricker's feet. They were smooth and the flesh was firm, quite unlike those of the Gardeners.

They looked like The Feet of The Root.

He dragged Buccolia over the senseless Stannerwitz. A crash came from his home-gallery. Dust fell out at them from the doorway as they staggered through it together. Tooley stared upwards: The Root had sunk further into the cave. It almost reached the floor now.

"Look, Buccolia! Look at The Root. See how it's grown..."

The Feet had now lengthened into smooth Legs: Legs bereft of nail-hairs and patella-valves. In the green rock-light, they seemed to be almost transparent.

"See. See The Legs..."

Buccolia crawled forward, her carpals ground to stumps. *I cannot see, my brother. I am blind. I cannot see –*

He helped her forward, pulling her across rubble and the armour coil-humps of sleeping Gardeners. There was little point in their waking up, he thought. The World had ended now.

They lay together on the rough floor, mere skin-widths from the base of The Root. It was as smooth as a pool at the Centre of the Earth: Greenblade's dream work of a maniac artisan.

Tooley held his tarsal in front of his eyes. The twin-pincers clenched, the stiff hairs rasped against each other. *Things can be better than this*, he thought. And the flashing-twinkling memory-murmur came back to him.

"Things can be better than this, Christyman," he said.

He glanced at Buccolia then stared up at the beautiful Body.

And wondering what would happen, they touched The Cross together.

Lusheart

You might not think much of me now but I loved a girl once. Andrea. Andie. Oh, she was lush. Real lush. I liked watching her smile. I invited her over to the hostel and she brought some change for the meter in my pacemaker. She'd go shy and watch telly. Her stomach was like a balloon but it didn't matter to me. I never asked. I'd plump up the sofa and Andie would let me suck her blood umbilical as she searched the shopping channels.

If we saw each other down town or caught eyes in the hospital during a donation session – well, that was different. We'd be strangers. I might look at Andie a little longer than she tried not to look at me. Defiant. Men are the ones. We're stronger. And I *am* a man whatever might be said.

*

The social worker – Gary – meets me a few years after Andie's death. "You're a man, Charlie," he says, and the little laugh he gives isn't so little now. It has grown as he has grown. He opens his mouth so wide I can see his sperm teats. "Have you got a new girl, Charlie?" he says and I look right back and say: "Maybe!" and everything's cool between us. He has an in-car CD and offers to drive me home.

*

Gary had heard about Andrea back then. At least I thought he'd heard. Gary seemed to know she was pretty lush. He was a real chill. A laugh. Hardly any teeth, of course. Lost them in some girl. She pulled away too quickly and left Gary to shampoo the carpet. But Gary still had a donor who worked down Somerfield's. A supervisor was Gail. Looked like Drew Barrymore. Paler. Drew on drugs maybe. I think she gave too much to Gary. She wore a hat like a gangster except that it was white. Got to guard the streaky bacon and all. She could get shitty. Gail was on the till once when I was there. She waved The British Heart Foundation tin in my face. "Have a heart," she said. Yeah, shitty, like I said. I poked my tongue out at her, mouthed: *Shitty shitface.*

I almost got a job at the store but my lips were a bit cracked up from sucking Andrea and the management was nervous about the pacemaker. It was one of those noisy ones that come cheap out of Romania. And I couldn't reach the top shelf, of course. Gail was okay about it. She was caught in the middle. That dark place where almost-good people have to go sometimes.

There were three of us at the hostel: Darren, Stevie and Charlie. That's me: I'm Charlie. Both Darren and Stevie were up for a heart once the pigs had done growing them. Darren still went to school, of course. Government paid for him to have an oxygen cubicle next door to the boiler room. Teacher found him messing with his sperm teats one time. Tricky.

Steve and me, we missed out on school. We dodged education. We were just happy waking up alive. About the time I tried for Somerfield's, Stevie went to his mum's for the day knowing full well that was as long as he'd be allowed to stay there. She wouldn't even get out her umbilical to oxygenate her own son. Stevie went into hospital full-time soon after: lasted loads longer than anyone thought he would. I took Darren and some Cadbury's to see him in his titchy little bed in a long ward packed with titchy little beds, each one with it's own wee whirring pump and blood bladder.

Darren was pretty brainy and wanted some GCSEs. Gary – the social worker, remember? – gave him some special exercises though he wasn't really qualified. Gary was great then. He drove an old Beetle with Gul and Quicksilver stickers on it. Not one of those poncey new Beetles. Really. He was just so cool. I would have died to be Gary. I would have died to be older. Gary used to reckon that if *he* got any older his teeth might even grow back. Right. He said he'd seen it on *Horizon*.

*

Gary took me and Darren up to the north coast. He drove us in the Beetle with Gail. Gail didn't speak, just played with Gary's girly-yellow mobile, just stroked the text-faded keys. We walked along the promenade trying to look more invisible than we already were. Darren went to sit in a shelter by an odd little seaside railway track with his inhaler. The shelter had a WOMEN ONLY sign and the bench was a bit too high but it was winter and there was no one about.

The rest of us danced on the red shingle and watched the surfer girls. Gail looked a bit odd away from the supermarket. She had a few goes at small talk and skimming stones – but it was difficult with Gary still attached to her, his ankles knotted around Gail's bra strap, blood rushing to his upside-down head, the remaining teeth embedded in her umbilical.

It struggled to rain – 'sea fret' reckoned Gail when Gary had finished with her – so we joined Darren in his shed by the shutdown miniature railway with some melting ice-creams. It was all getting funny in a mucky kind of way when Gail suddenly knelt on the ground in front of Darren and me and put a hand on each of our chests like they were one of her bloody avocados or something. Girls were always doing it, weren't they? Did you find that? I mean, what the bloody hell were they looking for? Christ, it was hard enough remaining conscious. It's not as if we were big enough to fend them off or anything. It was just so sodding annoying. Liberal girls? Conscience girls? Stare-a-cripple-in-the-face girls? Was that it? Yeah well, you could have just left us all alone if you had a conscience. Given us what we needed, then left us all alone.

Anyhow, I swear Gail was about to swing into her 'have a heart' routine when Darren got into a right barny and reckoned aloud that he should grab her umbilical and tie it into a bigger knot than last year's Christmas tree lights. Gail just laughed – but I could see that the poor little bugger had hit home as he wheezed through the inhaler and his pacemaker screamed like a modem from hell.

We all watched the bloody rain fall into the sea for a bit and then Gail said she had a daughter somewhere else. She said it quietly. The daughter stayed with her dad and he lived off her. Perverse, if you ask me. Could never do that. Anyhow, Gail used to go around pretty often until the ex turned rough. He wouldn't stop feeding off the girl. His own daughter. Gail tried the police but the dad went to the European Court and the judge was Italian and they're always doing it over there aren't they so *that was that*. And now she just sent little gifts for the kid. Books mainly. She was twelve, her daughter. And loved reading and writing. Gail was sort of seeing her through their book choices. She had sent a battered old Puffin paperback called *The Lion, the Witch and the Wardrobe*. It was all about a lion and its heart, Gail told us. And I realised that maybe Gail wasn't bitchy and shitty and shallow after all. The daughter often sent some oxygenated blood in a Jiffy bag that she'd managed to hide from her dad. Dead weird. But magic really. Yeah? Y'know?

Anyway, Gail told us this last bit about the Jiffy bag on the way back to the hostel and Darren wasn't mad after that. Gary said nothing as Gail spoke of her daughter, leaning over to us from the front passenger seat. I could see Gary's face in the mirror and I supposed there might be something there like in a film. Significant. You know. His tongue might have been jacking-off his sperm teats but I couldn't be sure. Gary kept on driving and *that was that*. Life's full of *That Was That*. You start off – don't you – with the *Big Thoughts*: oh, I want to be a shelf stacker or a helicopter pilot. Steve wanted to be a helicopter pilot with the navy but then he found they'd only let him crawl inside the engines to fix them. He'd bi-valved a girl who could strip a Lynx helicopter twice and put it together again all in one morning. Now that's lush. Yeah.

*

"Who needs girls, eh?"

Gary said this one day as we lay out under the biggest oak tree

176

in Arrington Wood. Arrington Wood actually only had three trees. There were quite a few empty cider bottles though.

Gary was smaller than me. His head was the size of my kneecap and he kept gobbing on my stomach, trying to get a gummy tooth-hold. That was okay. Gary meant nothing by it. It was just an instinctive thing like schmoozling babes at parties about their red blood cell counts or blinking. Gary gave me a corner look out of his eye, his cheek resting on my stomach; as if the Men Thing was his personal *Big Thought* that had maybe never left him.

"Do we need girls, Charlie?"

And I said "No WAY!" which was a bit stupid, of course. So I said: "Or maybe just a part of them."

Gary didn't speak. He looked and looked. Maybe I should have said something else but I could see his teeth-stumps were beginning to hurt, a trail of sperm and sputum on his chin. Gary couldn't stop looking at me. Gary and Gail: maybe they'd had sex. But it seemed unlikely.

I thought about Andie then and smiled. And Gary watched me as I smiled.

*

Gary wanted to lie out in Arrington Wood the next weekend, but I'd fixed up with Andie and Andie's buddy Chloe to go to a gig at Bristol Uni's Anson Rooms. We staggered up the A38 in Chloe's sky blue Fiat 500. Chloe'd put her dad on a stool and he'd sprayed it sky blue for her. She'd turned the car over twice on the roundabout. Only one bloody roundabout in our town – but Chloe had spinned once and then done it again in that Fiat. She'd gone to court to contest the twenty-two quid ambulance bill. As if she actually asked for the sodding ambulance to turn up.

Anyhow, the show was pretty lush: a girl band – all bellies and soft brown arms – with a couple of boys sort of hanging on. The three of us managed to get right up against the barrier and all needed to pee like anything. I'd forgotten my iron tablets and the girls took turns with me, making sure I didn't faint away. Andrea was so cool. She let me suck her slowly: I felt the salty red osmose

from her body as the teeny-bop moshers glided over us. It was
really great to be with her again. She seemed pleased too, but tried
not to show it. Gave me a corner-wise kind of Gary-type look. I
knew. She sort of fell against me during the encore and got her
finger stuck in my ear. Lush. Mmm. Dreamy.

"Two hearts are better than one, Charlie," Andrea said to me
later in the back of the rattling Fiat, letting me touch her rugger
ball belly. And I might have said "Three are better, Andie," if it had
meant anything. Already pregnant, she needn't have let me lamprey
onto her umbilical: the commerce was as one way as the Bristol
traffic system. The sperm nipples in the roof of my mouth were
meaningless to her. But Andrea let me drink her body anyway, use
her heart, trusted me not to take too much, acknowledged that
romance slept in a shallower sea than we both might have wished.

*

One of the rear wheels was in the air at the last roundabout before
leaving the city.

We slipped from the sharp amber night into a gentler, more
floating world that showered our rear seat with Werther's Originals
and insurance documents; tumbled us back and sideways down an
incline into the entrance of a pedestrian underpass. Weirdest thing
in my life, but it seemed all right. I just lay in the crook of Andie's
arm with Andie flat up against the back and all I could see were
Chloe's lime Converse wriggling about in the smashed windscreen
like a pair of fat eels. Chloe was actually dead, though I didn't know
it at the time. I mean, there wasn't much blood or anything, but her
neck looked funny, almost as if she were leaning back to say
something. Very hairy nostrils. Those Werther's wrappers slowly
became twinkling leaves of rust in the faraway lights, hypnotic,
warm and sleepy.

And then I was being pulled out of the rear window. Andie's
big hand was around my denim collar, nearly throttling the life out
of me in her efforts to drag my midget man's body from the
wreckage. We made it back up onto the road and slumped down
on a bench under a sign for the M5. Andie's umbilical was poking

178

out over her hipsters. I felt my mouth moisten but her belly was moving now. She was close. She might have been pale beneath the tangerine halogen.

I stroked her forehead, touched the prickling slickness of sweat, fumbled for a mobile that might be in her jacket, cursed the lack of phone credits as I realised I was okay thumbing in 999, as I remembered I'd seen the phone's shade of girly-yellow before. And Andie just looked at me, her pupils tinier than a pinprick from the world's tiniest pin. Her breath was fast, her lungs breathing for two. Yeah, she was lush. If I had a heart I would have given it to her. Even then.

I rode in the ambulance. I suppose the paramedics clocked me for some sort of pound-an-hour bloodsucker. Some blokes wouldn't have it any other way. The thrill, y'know?

We shot through casualty's buzz of striplights; a quiet lift; a murmuring maternity suite. Nurses never ask questions. They're brilliant. You get toast afterwards and maybe an ambulance bill for twenty-two quid. I don't remember now as I think of Andie lying there like a glowing saint, her baby girl nuzzled on her dead chest.

*

Gary asked me up to Arrington Wood today. It's been a few years since we've really got it together – though I guess we've eyeballed on the street now and then, Gary slowing his new Beetle to a crawl so I can keep up with him. He's still a chill in his own peculiar way. A *dude* of sorts, I suppose. But he finished with Gail. She became area manager and got me a stacking job at the depot: I get to call her 'shitty shitface' quite a lot now but I never ask about her daughter. I suppose Gail and Gary finished long ago. Even before we'd played on the red shingle beach. He had still been one of us then – but now he drinks in singles bars with the girls, just to let them know that he doesn't need them anymore.

I was already in the Wood when he turned up. Gary might have grown a little. His teeth certainly had. He flashed them. They were white, the red of the gums a natural red. He leaned on a dead fridge without a door and unbuttoned his shirt; revealed the long acid-white scar on his chest to the winter air.

Lusheart.

Andreaheart.

Andie's heart.

As I'd stood there in the dimness of the maternity suite, Andie's heart had already been blue-lighting its way down the motorway on a journey without her: through the cold night air into the chest of another.

Gary did himself up and smiled and looked at me. Ah, the smile. And that look. Remember? He said: "I know who got the best end of the deal, Charlie."

I'd brought a bottle of Strongbow and we both sat down under the oak tree. We chatted about the old times for a while.

We certainly had no new times to discuss.

*

Gary gives me a lift home. He lets me play with the CD for a bit then lifts me out onto the pavement. He thinks I'll invite him in but he's wrong. I'm out of the hostel now and in council accommodation. I make my way up the cold community stairs to the third floor. They've promised me a stairlift soon. I've already got a new-to-me pacemaker from the People's Republic of China. I fumble for my keys; but she's already at the door and has it open and she looks just like her mother in the winter sunshine.

We go inside and she says she'll fix me something.

http://www.straight-talk.net/evolution/anglefish.htm

Another Summer

I won't forget it.

On the big screen, the brown and white river flows strongly as the soldiers swim in its chocolate waters. Horses move on the path behind them. The horses are in pairs, a postilion rider for each, as they canter on back to the shelter of their canvas mews.

The soldiers look up as we steam past. Many are naked. Their bodies are tight and thin; the ribcages topographical. Penises dangle and drip as their owners pee and wash undergarments; forty-year olds with big moustaches that leave chins in shadow; boys with too-open faces. Absinthe merchants chant soundlessly among the troops; I remember foul French curses and entreatments. Christ, how the soldiers hate the French. One seller carries a field telephone, perhaps claiming to have cornered the contents of a brewery in the north. Another is dressed as a woman, lips smeared into the rosebud kiss of America's Sweetheart.

I remember Marjorie saying how art imitates life. She was our war artist and it wasn't such a tired expression then. I begged to differ with her as we smoked on the after deck, peering back at those pale, scrubbing bodies. I said that life limitates art. After all we'd seen in the past months I could still say that. I could still feel that the only check on man's potential was man himself; as he screamed and tore himself into pieces under the still unchanging eye of the universe.

The English Soil Society

I could still think that then.

And I won't forget it, watching that sepia river flowing by once more on the big, silent movie screen: sitting in the picture palace stalls with George Silken beside me. Captain George Silken: astronomer and coward, madman and lifesaver.

And the life he saved was mine.

*

The barge docked at teatime and medical officers were first ashore with the casualties from the coastal fighting. There were quite a few bodies wrapped carefully in muddy linen, the heads like mummies. Some of the corpses were rather small – or warranted two or three linen bundles per stretcher.

We – the non-combatants – sauntered into the town and inspected the shattered buildings. The cathedral was rather picturesque in its destruction, the masonry fingers clutching heavenwards. Harrington observed that a spirit of the early church might herein be engendered. The cathedral was occupied by cats and children who howled at each other.

Our hotel stood by the railway station. The station had a façade like a music hall, with hoardings that featured fifteen identical posters of a young Ellen Terry admiring handfuls of Lux Flakes. Trains hadn't arrived or departed here for six months. Marjorie was intrigued by this monument to inertia and sketched the deserted platforms and the railway lines. The rails stretched away across the ruins and out into the frightened countryside. Marjorie always called it 'the frightened countryside' – as if the countryside was a stupid child that should know better.

The hotel was full of drunken screaming nurses. Three of them were getting married the next morning and carried poppies in their hair. One of the brides knew our Sergeant-Major, who seemed displeased at this recognition. He was familiar with the district, but – perhaps a little like Marjorie – tried to keep the district at a distance.

I decided to leave them all to it and strode out into the town.

The cracked pavements clutched the atmosphere and made it muggy. An observation dirigible hung in the air like a moon.

I passed across the deserted square and so on to the path of a quiet tributary of the river. The path was treacherous with horse dung. A lock keeper's cottage was almost lost among huge piles of munitions. From a hole in the wall, drink was being dispensed to soldiers and civilians alike.

The soldiers were silent, hunched on armchairs strewn about in the undergrowth. They seemed to be held together by nothing more than their webbing. The townsfolk were more animated, not sure whether to be happy or sad or anything at all: wondering if the mothering presence of troops simply brought the war closer.

I thought of the coast and the fishing village and the people we had seen there a couple of days ago. They had been quieter. Some had dirty shoes; others had clean – but most feet were bare as they stuck out from under the tarpaulins on the marsh road.

*

We had first encountered the Sergeant-Major then. "Meet the locals," he had said, raising the tarpaulin with some small ceremony. Marjorie didn't faint for half an hour. Young Zeb Watling wasn't quite so lucky and I had to carry his moving picture camera for him. The village – two jetties, one row of houses and a flag pole occasionally used by the coastguard – had sustained a five hour howitzer bombardment.

Officially, the war had ceased to exist in that sector three months previously.

*

The dispense on the riverside closed at eleven-thirty. The town drinkers ambled off but the military remained. I walked back along the path, only turning when I reached the square: the soldiers were like distant ghosts already, collapsed in silver armchairs amidst the tiny sparks of flowering ground elder;

dreamless or dreaming under the full moon and its dirigible shadow.

*

Harrington was breakfasting in a room full of mirrors when I came down. He was alone save for the two nurses sleeping under a far table. He'd been trying to wire New York by way of Newfoundland. Harrington was a Hearst man and had worked with Ambrose Bierce. He was a good enough reporter but his newspaper was notorious: we all secretly wondered if William Randolph Hearst had started the war as he'd done in Cuba, dispatching his journalists like pencil-wielding mercenaries.

We ate bread and drank tea, watched by our twelve-year old waitress. The morning sunlight shafted through glazeless French windows and the cathedral was awash with a fabulous chiaroscuro: early risers scuttled through the speckled morning sun like minnows in a pool.

One minnow resolved itself out of the bustle and smartly marched across the square. Even upon so brief an acquaintance, I was struck by the enigmatic nature of the Sergeant-Major. In many ways he had dropped straight out of a trapdoor at the varieties: a ruddy nightmare, the comic bellower. But several times over the last couple of days I'd caught him looking blankly into hedgerows and ruined farmyards. And perhaps only I had seen his eyes as he replaced the tarpaulin on the marsh road: eyes that waited for his brain to catch up; two severed halves of a slow worm that might one day come together under some damp dark stone of victory or defeat.

"Good morning, Sergeant-Major," said Harrington, brightly.

"Mr Harrington, Mr Brock – a good day to you."

He left the French windows open. The waitress slipped through it with a school satchel and some bread stolen from our breakfast table. The Sergeant-Major helped himself to tea, firing it with a flask swiftly secreted back amongst the folds of his tunic.

He raised his cup. "The King and Mr Asquith."

184

We raised our own and said nothing: a secret silent response, perhaps – but only because we could think of no reply.

One of the nurses started snoring.

*

Harrington went off to try the telegraph office again and Zeb Watling joined us. He'd been out at the supply dump since before dawn with his camera and was very excited. It was being run by Senegalese troops with French officers. He had striking tales of warehouses fleshy with hams; of silos with so much flour that it was as if he were looking down onto a tropical beach, the Senegalese working far below like exotic mirages. There were also four cartloads of apple saplings, two of female and two of male. "They're going to re-plant the whole damned country," enthused Zeb through mouthfuls of tea. "It'll be like Johnny Appleseed! It'll be like the Garden of Eden!"

I smiled shortly.

The Sergeant-Major looked into his cup. "Perhaps you'd care to help with getting the stores on board, Mr Watling. When you've finished your tea. Of course."

The American journalists were a subject of continued debate among the General Staff. Many considered their presence scandalous; others felt that history would be thankful for these subjective recorders of unfolding catastrophe. In any case, it seemed prudent for Watling to obey the Sergeant-Major's suggestion, no matter how casual its delivery. I decided the young photographer needed a little moral assistance so we arose as one and stepped out into the sunshine.

*

In the square, I put down my valise and adjusted the locking strap. The strap was a tough old thing, and – wearying of it – I stretched my arms and peered back through the paneless window into the dining room.

Marjorie was starting to sit at a table. The big looking glass behind her – ugly-framed and eccentric – caught Marjorie's reflection and threw it around the room, tossing and re-tossing it from mirror to mirror. The gilt frames bloomed with a million Marjories captured in the act of sitting down, of bending to retrieve one of last night's poppies. The mirrors wriggled with ten million fingers tapping on white tablecloths; tapping and waiting for the schoolgirl service that would never come.

*

One of the horses got loose mid-morning. It skidded and limped on the foredeck, screaming its head off. Harrington was trying to get a good shot from the top of the wheelhouse with a buffalo rifle.

Several crates had gone into the river, along with Corporal Selby: I managed to hook him with my umbrella and Harrington nearly fell off his perch, helpless with laughter. The Sergeant-Major approached the horse from behind with an army blanket and a revolver. Harrington blasted off again, loosening a chunk of decking. The creature shied right into the waiting blanket and the Sergeant-Major fired twice. They fell down together, the horse sliding off the deck into the water almost taking the man with it.

"The dentist's," murmured Marjorie.

"I'm sorry?"

We were aft, towelling down Corporal Selby and drinking cocoa from billies. Selby still gripped the umbrella as if it were a holy relic.

"The horse. It belonged to the regimental dentist. He raced her for the Force's Cup at Chepstow in 19–. The white blaze on the rump is quite the giveaway."

"Did it win?" Zeb's flippancy was instinctive; he was shivering with shock.

"No," said Marjorie, looking just past my ear. "No, she didn't win."

*

Our journey had begun in the salt of coastal waters.

For the first time, a successful path had been cut through the mines at the river's mouth: and how fortuitous that the press had been at hand. Disembarking from an ironclad five miles out, an oyster ketch sailed our party into estuarine creek systems before transferring us to our present supply barge, under the command of the Sergeant-Major.

We numbered less now: another war artist had left us shortly after the incident on the marsh road and had cut across country in search of his family. He was a Fundamentalist and his eyes glowed in the dark. Three journalists – they were on different publications but had seen the war through together – had belatedly elected to join him, tumbling like maniacs over the side. We were at an isolated bunkering point between high dunes and two men lost their brain cases to sniper fire as they tried to scramble up onto firmer ground. The third turned back to help but took one in the leg, leaving the prophet-artist to carry on alone. He made it cleanly to the top of the dunes, waved once and disappeared.

We left the wounded man where he lay.

*

Our ultimate destination was uncertain. We worked in the perverted idiom of the military. All proper nouns were in code: we dreamed encryption. For instance, the bombarded fishing settlement was Utopia; a blameless village with its satellite two-house hamlet where we'd camped on the first night became Sodom-and-Gomorrah. And the great metropolis that might herald the end of our journey had been christened Jerusalem.

While the river – the river...

The river was just The River. That lifeless snake: that fevered navigation...

*

I presumed that the journey would end for my companions in Jerusalem. But for myself, I was not so sure.

During a final chart briefing aboard the ironclad, a tacticians

187

officer had pointed out an astronomical observatory just downstream from Jerusalem. The observatory had been a signalling station at one stage but was now devoted exclusively to scientific research. The officer had been dismissive, comparing the astronomers moving amongst their instruments to monks wandering their bee hives, oblivious to the ravages of war. Half-men, shut-eyed men. But the idea held a certain poetry for me, and I had longed to seek out these hermits in their sanctuary of brass and prisms.

*

The memory of the horse lay heavy.

The air flowed past the barge like warm glue and we all complained of headaches. I thought I could smell bracken fires: the Sergeant-Major said it was probably the dregs of the latest nerve agent drifting down the shallow valleys.

Zeb Watling cranked some footage of us cavorting on the afterdeck in swimming-suits. Marjorie had her hand on mine but I could not see her face at the time: the eyes perhaps watered out as they surveyed her frightened countryside; the dark hair drifting in that warm atmosphere. Her mouth moving – maybe even speaking –

Zeb had worked with Griffith in New York and still had dramatic aspirations. He had persuaded us to attempt the can-can (Corporal Selby was rather good, I remember) when a howitzer battery suddenly opened up to starboard. The resin-air seemed to dilate for the shells as they screamed over our heads and into the low hills on the other side of the river. We were on our hands and knees, laughing and crying and realising all at once. Only the Sergeant-Major remained upright, peering at the seven-mile trajectory of the ordnance and sniffing the cordite like a lurcher.

The howitzers were heavy and hungry. The railheads that we had been bunkering were essential for their continued mobility. Those gunners were fast, by God. We were perhaps a hundred yards away and could see them yanking, cleaning and avoiding ejected casings. I became aware of a rhythm to their work; of a man bellowing and keeping time: "Hilda – get – yer – fookin – skirts – dan – na – Hilda – get – yer – fookin – skirts – dan – na..." And on each 'na' the fusee wire would be tugged and the shell would be away. 'Hilda' would see the spent casing go flying and 'dan' would be the split second it took to check the wadding in the breech before plunging in another lumpen shell from the munition shops of Birmingham or Lancaster.

Not all of the soldiers were involved in the bombardment. Quite a few lounged by the river with improvised fishing poles. Marjorie pulled her colourful beach gown a touch tighter. One man was nearer to us, ankle-deep in water. His hair was cropped short: the face and head seeming to share the same hue of mottled brown; foxed like an old book. He looked directly at Marjorie and we could read the words he said to her silently beneath the roar of the howitzers.

"Hello Hilda," he mouthed.

The bombardment ceased. Our hearing came and went, the sound of the very air circulating and revolving around our heads. I remained on the afterdeck with the Sergeant-Major. He had grazed his cheek badly on the sacking after his encounter with the dentist's horse. Presently, we both became aware of a movement on the bank. It was the foxy crop-haired gunner, dodging behind trees and discarded shell casings in a bizarre attempt to remain sniper-invisible whilst trying to gain our attention.

"Way-o! Bunkerin' bucket, way-o there!" He had a West Country accent and was still barefoot. The Sergeant-Major ordered a complete stop: Corporal Selby dropped a drag anchor and our barge swung into shore as the two privates took up station on the Vickers gun.

The Sergeant-Major winced as his cheeks moved, the caking wound cracking and weeping. "What is it, sunshine? Crabs get yer?"

"No, Sarn't-Major. Buggers know better'n that. Lieutenant Lofthouse says you're to take three gasees and a section case up to Hill 80."

"Blast him. Oh, all right. Tell the officer we'll wait but I want to be sure we'll get no ruction out of this section boy. What's yer name, sonny?"

189

"Gunner Cooke, Sarn't-Major. No, he's all right – well, depends what you mean by all right. He's a soft 'un. I don't know what they got him for. Mazey bugger."

They all appeared a few minutes later: the three mustard victims shuffling in the familiar crocodile. They hummed the Hilda tune and laughed shortly every time they hit an obstacle. Their throats were hoarse from laughing. Behind came Gunner Cooke armed with a fishing pole: he escorted a tall man with dark hair who wore an enemy greatcoat.

"The boys gave it to him," Cooke explained about the coat, apparently not feeling the need to say anything further.

The crocodile was helped up onto the barge while the prisoner took the gap between bank and gunwale in an easy lope. He presented himself:

"Captain George Silken, King's Salopian Volunteers. That graze needs attention, Sergeant-Major."

Silken's long features lengthened even further in an effort to avoid smiling. He pulled a beautiful yellow silk scarf from his pocket and placed it carefully and deliberately into the Sergeant-Major's hand. The Sergeant-Major looked at Silken and then back at his hand as if it were about to explode.

"Let me have it when you've finished, there's a good fellow. It belongs to my great aunt and she'd kill me if she knew." Silken's slow words seemed to catch in imaginary amber; one could almost see his words hanging.

A kingfisher buzzed by like a blue bee. A pair of moorhens clattered into some trees and I felt – rather than saw – a tiny flash over to the left. "On the deck with you, Mr Brock," murmured the Sergeant-Major, still clutching the yellow scarf.

Gunner Cooke raised an arm in farewell – then pulled it back quickly, the hand spinning away like a whirling red starfish. He gazed at the stump, just looked and looked. A vast rattling filled the world: the deck sounded as if it were awash with dried peas.

The Sergeant-Major held scarf to cheek. "Shrapnel ordnance. Corporal, move the civilians under cover. Leakey, Barkworth – get the for'ard machine-gun lined on that copse, portside, three hundred yards."

Selby ushered the rest of the journalists down into the coal bilge. Marjorie's eyes looked as wild as the dentist's mare as she descended; Harrington was curiously calm, almost as if he suspected the attack as another ploy of the yellow press. I was trapped on the far side of the deck behind a pile of hemp and two of the strangely still horses. It was difficult to know what to do.

Another shrapnel bomb exploded to the aft of us. I could see the Sergeant-Major standing upright, supremely confident in the enemy's inability to get our range before we steamed beyond the trench mortar's arc of fire. It was a more than mild gamble on his part: the factory mortars were a known threat but these latest home-made stove pipe weapons were dangerous and unpredictable. The mortar units were trained to harry 'targets of opportunity' – a new term that held overtones of brutality and bravado.

Leakey and Barkworth were struggling with the Vickers gun: some of the loose hemp had jammed the chamber and Barkworth was shoving his hand into the breach, losing skin and fingernails. The Sergeant-Major peered through field-glasses, his mouth constantly moving.

A hand touched my shoulder. Captain Silken. He smiled gently. I would learn later that I was screaming my head off. Silken leaned forward until his lips brushed my ear. "Plays hell with the trout, this. They haven't landed a decent fish on this stretch for two seasons, apparently."

The Vickers finally opened up with short uncertain bursts. A last junk bomb came over and sank a clump of bulrushes fifty yards behind us. The Sergeant-Major thundered in the sudden silence. I turned to Silken. His chin rested on the gunwales; and his eyes were slitted to keep out the sun as he peered deeper into the sparkling waters.

*

We passed the night at anchor by the riverbank and posted a sentry. It was Leakey's twentieth birthday next day so he undertook double duty to enable him to enjoy celebrations to the full.

We sat in the long grass away from the horses and dined on tea and bully beef, with tinned peaches for the journalists and Captain Silken. Silken managed to identify thirteen grass varieties without rising from his elbow. The gas cases sat apart and took very little food: they laughed less now. Their brass buttons were caked in a green residue. One man had no buttons at all and his tunic was held together with parcel string. The Sergeant-Major ate by himself on the barge, perhaps having only enough rum for one.

The stars were very bright. I lay on my back amongst ferns and water voles. Marjorie came through the trees at midnight and sat laughingly on the edge of my blankets, trying to de-lace her corset. I could just make out the charcoal stains on her artist's fingers in the moonlight, her arms very thin as they twisted up her back. She finally fell across me, her elbows still at strange angles. I could see a tobacco glow on the river so I drew myself out and left her there; curled-up and snoring in the beach gown I'd bought her on Blackpool pier.

*

George Silken was on deck, sharing one of Private Leakey's cigarettes. He leaned over the rail to me.

"You're Gerald Brock, aren't you. Come on up."

I nodded and carefully crossed the plank onto the boat.

"I was sorry to read about poor Sallinger, silly bastard. I knew him you know." The cigarette glowed. "Briefly."

His accent seemed slightly forced, naturally public school with studied Cockney overtones. He gazed heavenwards. "Tell me how you met. Tell me about *you*."

I was not sure how to respond to this suddenly intense man on his way to a court martial. I began to froth about my one year at university championing Chatterton and his pursuit of the perfect representation; about the crippled lung – Silken snorted – ruling me out for service; and of somehow finding myself on *Allbright's Magazine*, the well-known periodical dealing with scientific developments in a popular and droll manner. *Allbright's* mixed serious fiction with frivolous fact: you may recall the adventures in picture form of Professor Albertus

192

Understeam by Sallinger & Brock. I am that same Gerald Brock. Arthur Sallinger – a genius of the rude and smelly type – died of gastric influenza at Gallipoli, his brushes tossed away for a rifle and his native New Zealanders.

Silken snorted again, still peering at the bright sky. "Sallinger's up there now, you know. Up there with bloody creation. That's what you're looking at, Brock. One day it'll all stop. Like Very lights, those stars will blast out to a certain distance – and then they'll have to fall back.

"Some scientists – mad ones, naturally – say that those falling-back stars might even meet their upwardly-moving selves, still bursting with brightness; that the incomers move quicker than the outgoers; that time moves differently for those coming or going." He tossed his cigarette into the river, a shooting starlet winking out. "Do you think those old stars would recognise their former selves, Mr Brock? Not quite a mirror image. Things might turn out differently on the way back."

I thought about the broken mirrors in the breakfast room, ripe and fractured with their infinite possibilities; wondered if I might even survive to the end of the war to write about it.

"Brock..?"

I must have appeared to be dozing.

"...You can only see the beginning of things when you've lived life a little, Mr Brock. When you can stand back a bit. Sodding obvious really. The long perspective. The long road. You're a London boy like me, ain't you. It's called living and learning."

"It's a bit late for Arthur Sallinger."

"You miss him?"

"No. No, not really." I felt an urge to tell this man nothing, to answer only with opposites and lies. I said: "He's on a longer road now. The longer perspective."

It was a useless empty remark – and even as it left my mouth I realised that Silken had been on the verge of some sort of confession or deeper intimacy.

"Sodding right, mate," was all he said as he walked away to steal another fag off Leakey; and I suppose I deserved it.

I went back down the gangplank and into my woodland hideaway but she had gone. In the distance beyond the hills, Very lights rose up and danced.

*

I awoke suddenly.

A memory-dream. Like Zeb Watling's film looping back on itself.

There was movement beside me. I reached out and touched wriggling coldness. Under the moon's gaze, I could make out dozens of drowning fish in the undergrowth; moving together like living shining black roots, their spent fellows tumbling back into the poisoned river.

Not a good year for trout.

Silken had been right.

*

We made Hill 80 soon after dawn.

Swallows swooped before our bow, skipping the water like curled stones. George Silken sang to them as I sat on the hemp and cleaned my teeth with a corn cob. In spite of our progress, the river appeared so still and unmoving that Harrington managed to lean over to shave in its unbroken reflection.

Hill 80 wasn't a proper hill and it was difficult to decide where it began and ended. Silken explained how Hill 80 had been taken and re-taken, the local population fleeing and returning and fleeing again. They were experts on Hell: every time they returned they felt more qualified to define it. A plague of graves dug ever more shallow until the dead outnumbered the living.

"And we can all go home when that happens," said Silken, watching with interest as Harrington dabbed his bleeding chin.

Facing the river at the foot of Hill 80 was a laundry works. Being only ten miles from Jerusalem, the laundry represented forward headquarters for the sector and received occasional visits from junior General Staff members. A curious miasma lay to the right of it; a brown cloud that glinted. As we steamed nearer,

I realised it was a vast dump of barbed wire that clawed high into the air like an ancient forgotten wood. Marjorie came on deck tying her beach gown. Zeb Watling followed closely and began an odd, redundant sort of inspection in the aft coal bunker.

The morning was full of bright angled light that caught every remaining blade of grass, every web of every remaining mutated meadow spider. A hand touched my shoulder and Silken leaned against me, trying to follow my line of vision. The ball of the sun rose abruptly from behind the laundry, sending the shadow of its chimney scuttling across the broken landscape.

"Hill 80," announced the Sergeant-Major as the world turned. He stashed the hip flask in its tunic recess; I caught a flash of yellow scarf. "Changes hands more than a bad penny. Shitty dump. Lousy billet. I was here six months ago. They've taken it twice since then."

We docked at a wooden quay littered with waterproofed baccy tins and spilled cigarettes. The gas crocodile disembarked first, laughing and falling over in the slippery bloody mud beyond the quayside. There were several soldiers on the bank, picking through packing cases of sodden millet.

"Booby traps all over the place," explained the Sergeant-Major. "Spring-shrapnel in dirty playing cards, incendiaries in sacks of sugar..." He unexpectedly held out a hand to help Marjorie down the gangplank.

"I expect we do the same, Sergeant-Major," she said, not taking it. "But then again, I'm not so sure. I mean, we'd read about it in the newspapers. Wouldn't we." She pinned her correspondent's pin to her beach gown. "Thanks for the hand."

A lieutenant came along from the laundry to be our guide through the mines. He approached us like a rabbit: short fast runs followed by slow strolls with his head down. He saluted briefly and introduced himself as Lieutenant Bainbridge. He wore skiing boots and his pistol holster was empty. He didn't really look at us. His eyes were constantly watching the mud and sky: the middle ground of human contact seemed to be unnecessary.

We left the horses on the barge and crossed the quarter mile or so to the laundry, trying to be rabbits like Bainbridge. The gas cases sang *Clementine*: their knees were bloody wrecks. Silken and Private Leakey came last: the prisoner had manufactured a birthday card out of an egg carton for the boy. Silken fell into an easy stroll compared to the rest of us. He took in the hectic architecture of machine and body parts with a mild expression.

We gathered in the main drying room with its snaking clothes lines and beam-dwelling finches. It was unbearably hot and the rain of droppings and feathers was constant. The gas cases were led away to make-shift wards, while Captain Silken – accompanied by Leakey and the Sergeant-Major – disappeared without fuss to see the Section Board. The rest of us – upon the Rabbit's recommendation – wandered up the spiral staircase onto the roof.

The roof was rather pleasant. It was flat and the previous occupiers – or possibly those previous to them – had organised it into a duck-board spa with deckchairs and metal ironing tables taken from the laundry below. A postcard depicting *variété* diva Zena Dare as a woodland fawn had been set in sapper's resin and served as a paper weight. Zeb Watling even found a gramophone and wound up Miss Dare's wistful lullaby, *Another Summer.*

We could see for miles down the long heat-hazed river valley. Back to Hilda's howitzers and the ruined cathedral; imagined we could make out the sea and the rest of the planet. Zeb gave me his precious canister of exposed films to hold while he shot some more footage.

His fingers were trembling: Marjorie's mouth smiled.

I joined Harrington among the nest of deckchairs. A sniper cracked away in the woods below us. Harrington offered me a cigar. "Of course you know who George Silken is, don't you?"

"Something of a mystery man?" The cigar was cheap and difficult to draw.

"No. Not such a mystery. One of Hearst's Sacramento papers did a piece on Mount Palomar two years back. Silken had gotten himself up there in the mountains too."

"Silken's an astronomer?"

"Seems so. Or thinks he is. Had a real set-to with the college

196

men up there. Some crack-pot theory or other. He's something of a chickenhead from what I heard."

I recalled the previous evening. "He thinks the universe is moving away from itself..."

"...And it might even come back one day, Mr Brock."

It was Silken who had spoken; suddenly standing at the doorway onto the roof, smoking one of Leakey's cigarettes with gusto. Leakey hovered behind, nervously.

"It's the lad's birthday," Silken continued brightly, walking towards the edge of the roof. "I'm helping him celebrate. And, oh, I'm to be executed by firing squad in forty-five minutes."

Silken took a long draw on his cigarette, winked at me and stepped off the roof backwards.

He didn't make a sound as he sailed over the edge. The mountain of barbed wire rose up to meet him: to suck him silently in; to turn George Silken – finally – into a clutching, shrieking, bloody, slowly-dying insect.

And then, oddly, Silken's cigarette – dropped in mid-air – rose up towards us. It was a freak gust of wind in the summer morning. But it appeared to me as if Silken's universe had suddenly reached a climax and was reversing itself. I imagined the stars falling into each other; I could actually see – for an instant – time running backwards. Could see it running in a different way; could conceive of time not even running at all. The cathedral re-building itself; the eyes of the mustard men unglazing; the guns swallowing their own shells like circus seals gobbling pilchard.

The cigarette slid back down the air and lay smouldering in the shaking wire.

And the silent seconds stretched and dropped like bombs.

*

The roof door slammed open. The Sergeant-Major was breathing hard. "Bloody enemy's got a big push coming this way. Daylight too, the buggers. Bloody Selby and Barkworth have taken the barge back downriver. Shoot them myself if I had the range. We'll have to hoof it along the bank. What's happened here?"

197

Zeb Watling started to answer.

"Forget it, Mr Watling. If the Captain's making a nuisance, I'll be thanking you to take care of it yourselves and to be looking after the lady here as well. Now downstairs quick."

We followed him down through the drying room and out into the courtyard. Apart from scattered small arms fire, there was a peculiar almost hypnotic silence. The enemy had gambled their hand – and won – by not laying down the calling card of preliminary artillery bombardment.

Soldiers were running towards the river, guided by the scampering Lieutenant Bainbridge. Our gas cases were not among them. Downriver, I could make out the bunkering barge in a halo of steam. Selby had succeeded in turning the boat around and was re-covering the water we'd navigated that morning. Trench mortars opened up from over the river: our friends from yesterday, those seizers of opportunity.

The Sergeant-Major began his bellow of instructions. We struggled across the old battlefield, tripping over telephone wires, heedless now of hidden ordnance. We were filthy, mud-coloured shadows by the time we reached the riverbank. Enemy sappers with poles were swarming down the hill on the opposite side: far away we could hear the roar of engines.

An overpowering heat-surge sucked at our limbs then spat us over: when I finally looked up, the bunkering barge was falling back into the river in steaming pieces; stray strands of hemp lingered on over the water's surface like mayflies.

The Sergeant-Major was flat on his back, de-lacing the strap of his rifle and laying out ammunition clips on his stomach. I realise now that I was on my knees biting at the ground with my teeth. Through screaming numbness, I could see Marjorie bending low as she dragged Zeb Watling into a shell hole: his chest had disappeared.

I stared at Marjorie through the dust, thinking of her in the mirrors at breakfast time – catching herself on the way back. She would never scream, I knew that. She would just stare back at me over the lip of the crater with her smile of huge disdainful knowingness.

Fear came then. Just fear. The thickening of the throat, the lead weight that drops into the root of the intestines. The realisation. Absurdly, I recognised it as the sensation one feels when someone loses their temper in public and you know they really mean it. I clutched the film canister closer and glanced over at Marjorie, remembering. But she had gone now.

The Sergeant-Major slid down the bank and used a holed dinghy for cover. The water was steaming as tracer flared into it. He was roaring. None of us could hear but we followed him down anyway and scrabbled through the reeds and old swan's nests. Everyone tried to will themselves into invisibility. Or into being somewhere else altogether.

I peered over to the other side of the river:

The enemy had captured one of the new Lincoln caterpillars and it crashed down the incline, rising and falling like a sounding whale through the trenchworks. It gave off a grinding snarl – an overheated gearbox perhaps – and beached itself some fifty yards from the riverbank. The laterally-mounted machine-gun swung blindly sending great plumes of mud into the air. Harrington was bleeding heavily next to me: bloody balloons were inflating and exploding from his throat. I couldn't close my eyes: they had dried open.

And then – with dragonfly lightness – that familiar hand was on my shoulder: caressing it, grabbing it, dragging it. I was hobbling up-river on the shingle with Captain George Silken striding before me; expounding on wetlands flora and his twilight boyhood rambles through these ancient beds of reed and bulrush.

We'd gone perhaps one hundred yards before I turned back. Several enemy mortar companies were spreading across the old trench workings in front of the caterpillar. The Sergeant-Major had stripped to the waist and held his rifle high, bayonet fixed. He began to ford the river towards them, heedless of the bloody hunks of horseflesh. Silken looked at me with his pale long face and maybe he smiled.

We staggered on through the mud like madmen and perhaps we were then. I was screaming and screaming while Silken yelled out the chorus of *Clementine*. We were lunatics trying to dance on the water as we raced the swallows all the way up the brown river to Jerusalem.

By dawn of the next day we had reached the observatory but it was deserted: those dreaming half-men were dreaming elsewhere and the lenses of their precious instruments had become frosty and imprecise.

And so we were ancient stars falling home, returning to the place where we had started. In the sunshine, the London boys walked again through the old warm streets of their city by the river.

The Last of The Dandini Sisters

Henry Dandini was born on a sewing table in the laundry room at the old Palace Theatre, Plymouth. He had a make-up box for a cradle and a midwife called Norman. Henry's head was haloed in caked Vaseline: it was 1.15 on the morning of Saturday 25th December 1959. A doctor had been called – but had left ten minutes before the birth to attend a concussed Argentine midshipman in the salt-rusted toilets of the Swan Hotel. Henry – despite obvious and obverse evidence – was registered with Equity as the third and last of the Dandini Sisters.

Henry's birth and early life was greased in the very stuff of legend. His first fifteen years of existence was spent with his two elder siblings, Sheila and Wilhelma. Shee and Willy were identical twins and had made their own entrance in the back of an ENSA five-tonner during a Cinderella tour of the Western Desert in 1943. The sisters were immediately stage-named in honour of the Prince's friend and confidante.

Their mother was Bluey Craven, the Siren of Cirencester. Her real name was Krakia Brackewitz but she changed it when she discovered in a forgotten bed near Suez that bluey was Desert Rat slang for the dune desert: Craven came from the cigarette that was her favourite because the machine always gave you an extra one 'for a friend'.

Bluey was dead in 1961, yet her unseen presence continued to hang like an acrid smoke over the Dandini Sisters. They carried bits of her wherever they went: framed programme covers, ticket stubs from Malayan camp theatres and tiny signed photographs of plump girls in sailor suits.

There was also the magic coathanger.

"In the land of laundry the coathanger is king," had been a famous Craven saying, carried over from Eastern Europe by Brackewitz ancestors. The magic coathanger was singular in its pedestrian anonymity: Henry would often leave it swinging in a swiftly-left dressing room, only to have it re-appear at their next venue.

"It's magic," Shee would solemnly intone. "It's the magic coathanger."

Henry wasn't a very good sister. Shee and Willy attempted to administer motherly affection (an exercise which ended in a significant but still obscure crisis in Henry's early adolescence). At first, the elder Dandinis tried to incorporate their curious younger sister into their skip & tap routine, with Henry looking on as a sort of proxy audience member. He would wander the aisles, clapping wildly and distributing boiled sweets.

Henry – thrust into a gingham dress, his head crowned with a pair of wiry pigtails – was certainly a sad and misplaced figure on the pier shows. But that's not to say that he didn't collect a certain cult following. In 1967, a beach donkey at Minehead was christened Henry in his honour: the naming party (courtesy of Mr Frank Gargle, 'Donkey Master of Clacton, Bournemouth and all points west, love') collapsed into a Vimto-fuelled brawl over *Thunderbirds* swap cards. By his early teens, Henry was quite the toast of the south coast with his energetic displays of exploding pigtails and precocious ventriloquism and was often to be seen nursing a sweet sherry in the company of well-groomed men of middle years.

The Dandinis occupied a curiously capsuled world during the '60s and '70s. As the turbulence of those times increased, so the little boat of the Dandini Sisters whirled in a perfect circle of club, panto and Summer show: always revolving, never proceeding. A three-minute slot on *The Black & White Minstrel Show* in 1973

might have led to an easier life but Willy's pre-breakfast bloody
marys were taking their toll: and in any case, the Dandinis'
routine and delivery – and of course the Minstrels themselves –
were perceived by the public as a faintly tragic embarrassment
from a former age.

A reasonable Puss in Boots run encouraged the three of them
to club their meagre resources and lease a flat in Torquay. The flat
belonged to an old boyfriend of Shee's. It was their first permanent
home but it wasn't to last. Willy was found with her wrists
slashed in a Babbacombe bus shelter in 1975. She was a thirty-
two year old virgin: the autopsy drained enough Smirnoff to down
a beachload of Frank's donkeys and her dancer's knees were
those of a septuagenarian.

Henry played *Funeral for a Friend* very loud all night and when
they got back from the service a few days later, they discovered
the magic coathanger was missing. It had been supporting a set
of tails used in the Broadway Lullaby routine: the tails lay in a
sable heap at the bottom of the wardrobe.

Louie Kaufmann dropped down from Denmark Street a fortnight
or two later. He brought sympathy and sweet peas for Willy's
wretched little memorial on the dank east wall of the crematorium.
Louie had been a rather distant figure for an agent. Their relations
had been largely telephonic. But he was a kind person: like them
an outsider, the faded representative for a fading era. He was
sideman to Texas Sid Draper before the war and had the
tomahawk scars to prove it.

"Still got the magic coathanger, Miss Henry?" The Channel
wind blew up the Tor Valley past the crematorium, animating the
old agent's beard. "That gorgeous mother of yours always talked
about it. Cor, she was a turn. It was me that christened her the
Siren of Cirencester. Course it was 'si-reen' in them early days.
We never knew how to say the word till Hitler taught us. Yeah,
that bloody old coathanger. Came over from Europe after some
uprising or other."

Henry was inspecting neighbouring epitaphs. "In the land
of laundry..." he murmured unhappily. His new wedge soles
were already scuffed.

"Yes, Miss Henry. 'In the land of laundry the coathanger is king'. You're lonely, aren't you? You're a bit of an outsider, boy. You should have some friends. A boy should have some friends..." Louie Kaufmann gleamed for a split second – the time it takes for a single raindrop to follow its fellow to the ground. He looked different. He floated, his brogues seeming to *brush* – rather than crush – the gravel.

The rain was beginning to soak their coats: Louie's smart camel hair, Henry's blue anorak with the zip that worked sometimes.

"We'd better get back to Shee, Mr Louie..." Henry realised that he couldn't talk properly. "Look, we'd better get back..."

They found her sitting behind the wheel of the Mini. Shee Dandini had Henry's fuse wire out of the glovebox and was making tiny perfect silver coathangers. All glinting – like little sparks of magic – on a dank afternoon in February.

*

Henry went on bumtime.

He was even considering going to school when the barman ad popped up three seasons later. It was rather a quaint and tedious dive just up from the harbour on Union Street, with a matt crimson paint job in the loo and James Dean posters. It was called *Dorothy's* and a pair of ruby slippers hung over the pumps. Friday was Mother's Night so Henry started on Saturday morning with a bin for the broken glass. A bloke called Dudley ran the club with some shady figure who had a postal address in Luton. Dudley insisted on calling Henry 'Hen' and referred to him as 'my new little bird'. But this was a familiar environment for the newly-hatched Hen: the glamour of disintegration, an ease of acquaintance and a plummy horror of the Health Inspector.

Hen managed to visit Shee in the hospital a couple of times a week during that late Springtime. It was back in the countryside and Dudley drove the Mini for him. Hen watched the tiny coathangers take shape under his sister's ugly hands and form into a vast slithering pile on the hospital bedspread. They were like the ribcages of baby chickens.

"They call me Hen now," he said.

July dropped in and the sands exploded with flesh and ice creams. Night time Union Street throbbed like a great black heart, a scuffle or couple in every doorway. The coppers raided *Dorothy's* toilets late in the month and shoved everyone into Transit vans. A bunch of skinheads chuckled and lazily tossed a lager can at Dudley's head. He managed a faint, bloody smile at Hen before being hauled up into the van.

It was a poorly organised hold-overnight job and the police were later criticised for their handling of the raid. A semen sample held in evidence turned out to be the emulsion medium that Dudley used on his lunchtime art course over at the Tech. There would be talk of lawsuits but Hen rather enjoyed it – and the single cell was a novelty.

He picked up his things from the desk sergeant at dawn. The police hadn't bothered putting effects into individual envelopes: the sergeant produced a battered biscuit tin – *contents may differ from photograph* – and invited Hen to peer inside. Hen only had a couple of quid in silver, plus the valued Equity card – but something else glinted in the sickening buzzing tube light.

"Turn that bugger off, Tom," said the sergeant. Tom, a rather intense young WPC, rose to comply and in the natural light of dawn the glinting resolved itself into a tiny perfect coathanger.

"Action Man'll be all right then, son," smirked the sergeant with good humour, but Hen left the words behind him as he slipped the coathanger into his blue anorak pocket and stepped out into the Summer morning alive with the sound of birds and mopeds.

He turned the corner into Fredrick Lane just in time to see a small figure reaching into the back of a milk float and making off up the road in his direction. The figure presented a curious aspect to the world: it was dressed like Anne of Green Gables and its head sported two waving antennas.

Hen stopped and tried to undo his anorak but the zip was stuck. He'd been waiting for this to happen and now that it was, it inevitably felt like it was happening to somebody else. Which he supposed was only natural.

The milk thief ran up and stopped, puffing hard.

"Hello, Henry," said Hen.

"Hello," said Henry, as he dropped a milk bottle trying to straighten his pigtails.

*

Hen had the flat to himself now so Henry wouldn't be a problem. They travelled home on the bus and the conductress gave them a grin.

She was from Wolverhampton and Hen knew her slightly. "Enjoy yer day, chuck," she said to Henry who was looking thoroughly miserable. His gingham was morose with spilt milk.

The pair made it up the communal staircase without further incident and Hen set out two bowls of Frosties. They used to be his favourite. Henry removed his pigtails and sat on the sofa. He peered at the photographs on the nest of tables by the window. He struggled up to choose a picture: Shee, Willy and Henry in full Broadway Lullaby get-up wearing best studio grins courtesy of Mr Louie. It had been taken days before the suicide.

Hen was starting on his cereal. "Christ, so bloody sweet I was then." He paused. "Weren't we."

Henry tucked the picture into the bib pocket of his dress, went to the table, ate two spoonfuls of Frosties without sitting down and left the flat. Hen finished eating and waited. There was a light knock on the door and Henry re-entered, his face askew with emotion. The forgotten pigtails were gathered up and the happy wearer skipped away once more.

Hen rose and looked out of the window. The first beach tourists were coming down the street; in the overcast, their rolled-up windbreaks shone ever so slightly.

He smiled as he finished Henry's cereal.

Magic could be found in the oddest places.

*

Christmas limped in with a special Mother's Night early in December. Dudley had booked a stripper called Vince deRiva who worked the ferries out of Weymouth part-time. Vince was holed up in Cherbourg courtesy of a French dockers' strike and things were getting ugly: James Dean was stolen by weekend bikers toting duty-free boxes of Marlboro and Dudley hid in the kitchen making cross-Channel calls and chain-eating peanuts.

In the bar, Hen kept things moving but earnestly felt like giving the ruby slippers three taps and going home. The skins came in at 9.30, the Bill at 9.45. It was the annual policeman's ball and the coppers looked like they'd stepped out of Busby Berkeley. It was the end for Dudley and Luton, of course. Most of the skinheads were let off with a warning but Dudley had to do twenty-eight days in low-security for keeping a disorderly house.

Hen made it out all right. The desk sergeant recognised him and said it might be as well if Hen left town for a while. WPC Thomas was being seconded to the Met for special duties – so why didn't Hen travel up on the train with her, hmm?

He had to pay Shee's bloody boyfriend three months rent which was a drag but there it was. Pictures were piled into suitcases, notes were written and the railway station reported to.

WPC Tom waited in the ticket office, intent and beady. "Mr Brackewitz?"

"Er..?"

She softened. "Henry Dandini? I'm your personal goon squad. Fancy a sandwich?"

Tom was quite jolly underneath it all. She had a thing about oak trees and her mum used to do a variety run somewhere in the north. Over Maxipak coffee and a shared cheese and cress sandwich, life began to change for them both.

*

So they were innocents in the city.

Tom got transferred to Greenham but then came back. Hen circled naturally into the MacLaren/Westwood galactic core like a comet, designing for X-Ray Spex and working on the first Stiff tour.

A garden flat in East Putney became theirs and they lived like pirates, whooping into the early eighties and glorying in the great Fox's theatrical sale, so everyone – at last – could glitz it like the Antboy or Steve Strange. And it was a time of names and places: before that great fade to grey even the smallest of them would make their mark. And Hen Dandini, a gatherer and giver of favours, sailed through with his policewoman at his side.

Tom was doing late duty one freezing night in January and Hen went partying at a squat just off Wandsworth Road. Bananarama were holding court in the kitchen but the bog didn't have a door and the jungle garden concealed a half-buried safe that the Krays might call back for one day.

He cycled out of Brayburne Avenue at 5am and headed west on a graceful cruise home. He loved this ride down and up the Hills: Lavender, St John's, East and West. The wide streets, almost deserted; the lights changing with no one there to take any notice. Past the betting and kebab shops; the building sites armoured with corrugated iron. And the high flesh-glow arc lamps stretching away, clouded by his winter breathing, steady, mesmeric...

A distant half-heard hum leapt into a roar as a souped Capri ripped past him at seventy and jumped the red lights at Plough Road.

"Wait up, Hen."

The voice slipped out of the abrupt silence.

"Over here, Hen. Wait up."

A shadow broke from a tobacconist's doorway and swayed under the high lights. The man was dressed smartly and warmly in expensive clothes – yet they didn't seem to fit too well or perhaps the wearer had worn them too long. Hen stopped but didn't dismount. The face, the familiar face... It was lived in, ancient and comfortable with itself. Familiar... So familiar...

"She loved us. We were the best thing in her life. It began with a sandwich and turned to the deepest trust; she wanted to give us the whole of everything. Remember that, Hen. We were always the kindest of men, weren't we? Always ready to give a mixed-up kid a room or a bowl of Frosties."

"Wait – who..."

But even as the figure faded into the darkness, Hen knew.

*

They'd cordoned the street but the officer recognised Hen and led him through, arm over shoulder, past the terraced bedsits and hydrangea bushes.

The driver had been lucky. He'd caught Tom out in the street. The front door keys lay by her side. There had been a witness and the police had checked the description with Tom's log book confirming that she'd clocked a '73 Capri with a re-bored engine beating the lights at Hammersmith two days ago. They dragged a rug over Tom's poor body: Hen recognised it as Shee's old one from the panto days.

The officer was talking. "She really loved you, you know. You were the best thing in her life, son..."

The hydrangeas whispered; their petals like thin dry Frostie flakes.

*

It started in earnest then. The *hauntings*.

Hen was almost embarrassed at the word – yet it conveyed much beyond the traditional knee-jerk baggage. It carried intimations of a shared fear between factor and vendor; between the haunter and the haunted. A lingering, possessive quality. A coldness, an under-fear, a crook in the neck from too much turning and twisting for the over-the-shoulder unknown.

After Tom's death, Hen lived in a changed city.

Barely a week – and then barely a day – passed without a casual or not so casual encounter with himself. An infant Henry might be spied at the end of a school crocodile; a familiar teenager in greased-down pigtails was occasionally nabbed for shoplifting sweet sherry from Sainsbury's. And the older Hens, middle-aged and beyond, stalked the night time streets of south London in council donkey jackets or elegant evening wear. A nude Henry

Dandini was even encountered by a policeman on the Albert Bridge. According to the short end-of-the-news item, the officer estimated his age at something over ninety years. The pensioner had handed him a coathanger, danced a tap routine and proceeded northwards.

Hen's work suffered. He'd previously managed to keep several jobs on the glitz periphery: barman, designer, cabaret person and known by those who should know. He'd been halfway through a Jarman project down in Dorset but had to let it go. He rarely left the flat now, preferring to pore over an *A to Z* with an ashtray full of map pins, tracing the patterns of his various past multi-aged manifestations.

He dwelt in a city of haunted mirrors.

In the summer of 1987, the doorbell rang for the first time in a year. Hen was living out of the freezer and the bank and waiting for both of them to expire. Three Hens lived in the garden now: two youngsters and a man of fifty who introduced himself as Henri, hinting darkly at a wedding in Nice in 2023. Henri sailed through the French windows to open the front door while Hen shivered behind the sofa.

Henri ushered in the visitor and disappeared back into the garden.

"Hello, Miss Henry." Louie Kaufmann slowly paced the room before settling into the sofa. "How are you keeping?"

Hen scrabbled from his hiding place and lay flat and breathless on the awful carpet.

Mr Louie didn't turn his head. "I see you have some new friends. A boy should have some friends." He gestured outside to where Henri was unracking boules. "I said you would – don't you remember?"

Hen gasped. And gasped again. "But Mr Louie, they're camped out in the garden. They haunt the streets. They flood the Underground. End to end they'd reach the Moon – and there's probably one in the loo too because it's been engaged since 1985. Oh! Mr Louie, please, please, Mr Louie..."

Hen was in tears and as he reached up to take the hand of Louie Kaufmann, the older man began to change. A single glow-worm soared from his buttonhole and bounced fifteen times around the room before zooming back into Mr Louie's mouth. There was a silent blue! green! red! explosion and the small lounge in Putney was awash with panto-magic light. Mr Louie had changed wonderfully: he floated six inches from the floor. His big bright moth wings brushed the ceiling, diffusing the sparkle across his spangly frock and beautiful fairy breasts.

"Do you remember that sad rainy day at the crematorium, Miss Henry?" The old agent's croak had softened to a warm Hollywood contralto. "You said you were lonely. You said you wanted friends. Just look inside..."

Hen lay transfixed on the carpet as the Fairy Kaufmann continued: "Sometimes, someone is blessed by more than Jesus. A very special person is born who is too good for this life. Who should have been born in a better place.

"You have a pantomime name, Miss Henry Dandini – and you should have been allowed to live in one. To play your part on a stage full of paste puddings and laughter while gorgeous girl-men swung from the flies on silken ropes. This was your world, Miss Henry..."

The Fairy Kaufmann seemed to shrink inside herself. The wings slipped away into nothingness, the elfin slippers crinkling back to battered brogues. Plain old Mr Louie collapsed onto the sofa and shook his head:

"Oh, Miss Henry. I knew it wouldn't work. I just wanted to ease your way. I just wanted to give you lots of friends. And what better friend does a boy have than... himself?"

He reached into his macintosh, slipped out a beautiful dream of an object and handed it to Hen. Strangely brighter than before: the magic coathanger.

"You see, the land of laundry is the ordinary land of men and women. The magic coathanger is the skeleton glue that holds them all together. A seam of gold between past and future. It's a silly *meaningless* thing but it's all I have left – and it was yours anyway. Use the coathanger and luck will walk with you, my very special son. Now I shall gather yourselves and slip away..."

The agent hauled himself up from the sunken sofa and gestured to the boules players in the garden. They came immediately, stepping through into the living room and out of the open front door in the wake of Louie Kaufmann – the steadiest sideman Texas Sid ever had.

*

And in the years that followed, Miss Henry and the magic coathanger continued their journey through the theatres and wardrobes of Britain. Miss Henry never achieved outstanding fame but was known as a lucky star to any show that employed him.

And he had many friends.

His fortieth birthday was celebrated in a marquee on Green Park; his fiftieth saw the entire two top floors of Claridges cleared to accommodate three ongoing parties. Mr Louie made the first but not the second, leonine and magnificent in a wheelchair. The general public was intrigued by this unknown celebrity with the pantomime name: but theatre people are special people and they knew Hen for what he was.

And as the years passed, Miss Henry in his turn gave. To the hospital that continued to look after Shee and her tiny doppelhangers, to the donkey descendants of Frank Gargle; and to his old mate Dudley who'd finally found there was no place like home in Mallorca.

And to a memory that he'd tried to fold away into a very deep drawer; the warmth that ached through the years. An insignificant side street of haunted hydrangeas in East Putney now boasted a column of beautiful oak trees. And so that street became an avenue. And in time, the houses – and even the avenue – were demolished and turned into parkland. But the oak trees remained and grew stronger.

By the time of his ninety-third birthday, the sprightly Miss Henry had taken to hiring a luxury motor-pontoon on the Thames to celebrate his anniversary night. The surviving half of Yazoo played the party downstream through ancient bustling London. The air crackled with the sound of December bonfires and children whooping in a dozen languages. Young people were everywhere. Holograms of planets and extinct tropical fish played over the laughing city.

At the Albert Bridge, Miss Henry arose from the onboard spa pool, commenting vaguely that he wished to visit an old haunt. The Beckhams stood by with towels but Hen smilingly brushed them aside and stepped through the pontoon's small airlock onto the steps of the quay.

The night was clear and the stars sparkled through the bright moving shapes. It was panto-magic time.

A policeman leant on the other side of the bridge trying to make out soaring angel fish through night glasses.

"Hello, officer. I'm all done now."

The startled policeman took the coathanger. Later, he would be reprimanded for not giving chase. In mitigation, the officer claimed that the matter already seemed to be in hand: that a figure in an old-fashioned policewoman's uniform already accompanied the old man as he tap-danced on naked feet into the city.

For D.J.

The Science of Sadness

Q. What is natural history?

It is perfect knowledge of what nature produces before man takes possession of it to put it into action.

– from *Duru's Encyclopedy for Children*, Paris 1821

ENFIELD'S SEADOG:

It was soon after I changed back to spectacles from wearing contact lenses that the chase began.

From the pawprints on the beach to those carpet scratches on the fourteenth floor, he raced us: Jenny and Wrack and Glacé and me. Heedless of the lapping foam our sprint across the sand was glorious. Jenny's reel-to-reel rasps with her breaths still.

With instinctive eye rubbings, I was the first up the dune path and onto the grass unreal with spring. Heat receiver, heavy in pocket, cried continuously. Our way wormed between the narrowest of gorges: gentle swaying elms, the flash of the sun through those leaves.

Late afternoon and we were up on the hills with all England before us. Stone walls sailed away and joined in a distance of golden evening. Everything was wet. Three sheep lay one hundred yards to our right with their throats missing. A trail was fresh and

215

evident. We shuddered with the encroaching chill yet grinned in our bloody fascination... So...

..Through the woods and blue bracken with the aid of night-sights. Undergrowth creatures sensing the presence of silent, moonless wings...

...A meal at dawn and a review of the situation. Wrack trimmed his moustache with his new sharp knife. In the pallid light, the others could have been their own shadows arching west across the moors. The decision to split up was agreed upon. Jenny had reservations which remained reserved.

The rain fell straight and windless. Night again and in a barn of fermented straw I dozed alone. A snertle and a grunt roused me at breakfast time but the beast had gone. The old farmyard was littered with his acid green droppings.

I jogged and the wet and sweat drained through me. I stank. I remember a motorway passed overhead. I slept again in a church with an amazingly carved pulpit. All the gravestones had been knocked down.

I ran into the city. The receiver was going berserk as I crossed two lanes of ancient red-lighted traffic and loped into a place of lawns and fountains. A big office block rose up. It wasn't an elm tree, but the sun still shone through it.

I entered the lobby. A lift was open so I went in and the door shut behind me. A groan of vibration: the doors slid back to reveal a passage floored with a fawn carpet. I smelt the air. It was very dry.

Every level had fawn carpet with the exception of the fourteenth which had red. What a gas. I jammed the door open and put the receiver – now exhausted – inside. The light on the roof of the lift flickered on and off.

Carefully, I removed my gloves. A single corridor disappeared into darkness. I went forward and whistled Elgar's *Sospiri*. I wondered where my friends were. Perhaps they were here already. I stopped whistling and walking – and listened intently.

On the red carpet at the turn of the passage were four claw marks. A door was open nearby so I entered into silence.

It was a room full of books. Piled up and down and collapsed. A

216

single light bulb. I could hear my breathing and the throbbing of my heart was in my head.

I heard wolf breath.

I could see him on the far side of the room. His raggy ears were matted and rank. He was much smaller than my dad had told me. My dad had seen him when he was a kid. He'd seen him on a hillside when they burnt corn stubble.

Jenny was with him. I could half-glimpse her through a crack in a wall of books. She was alive and shivering and she said: "Hello Enfield." The tape recorder lay nearby, sodden with her blood. She could see me, and she started crying.

I came forward smiling. And the beast smiled in his sleep and awoke.

He spoke.

He lilted.

I hurled Dickens at him. My copy of the *Encyclopedy for Children*. A shelf full of *National Enquirers*. He merely raised a disdainful paw and completed his speech with some ridiculous limerick before hopping to the door and bidding me farewell. I complimented him on his eager wit and with mutual understanding we parted.

Presently, I saw him swimming in the fountains before hoofing it into the suburbs.

Jenny sniffled in a corner more miffed than hurt, making spaghetti hoops out of her audio tape.

I felt pale. I hadn't eaten since my departure from the others and feeling faint I fell backwards through the window.

As I groped like Harold Lloyd to a convenient flagpole, I reflected upon what the wolf had said.

Corsets went out that year.

THE SWEAL:

I remember. They called me Charlie then.

On the last day of a childhood September the wind blew.

Mooring the dinghy in the middle of the creek, watching the tide slip away, the channels choking with tiny shells. A heron hanging on a tree – his eye open, unblinking. The ooze rising over the sides and ruining our sandwiches.

I remember the smoke rising on the imperfect stubbled hill. The plume is unbelievably huge. The water in the main channel turns grey and gold and throws up a coolness. The others grow worried – although they know the time of year as well as I.

And over the rise comes the beast. We thought he was just a pet or a sheepdog. Paws hop on the griddle soil. The spine is on fire. A silent howl and his eyes fix on us. For a second the glint of his face shines down. And the eyes are full of tears drawn from more than smoke. Drawn through supernatural glands that come straight from the heart.

He turns through the thick air. Ripples it. Disjoints it. All moisture seems to disappear as the wolf bounds down the hill, through the trees, stands panting and finished on the shore. He roars a limerick and tells of natural history.

We re-pack the hamper, unship the oars and row back down the river.

The air is so heavy that the insects cling to the surface of the water.

MOTHER'S FINAL FLIP:

My mother died when I was eleven.

It was two years after we saw the wolf on the burning hill. Mother ran through the house at three in the morning and smashed down the dining room door. The bottles of preserved sea mammals shone in the light of the upstairs landing. A long table was laid for the wedding banquet later that day. My mother, a gymnast of long standing, decided to execute one last routine of freedom before splicing with her latest love – a mini-tractor millionaire from Nebraska.

All went well – until her hand slipped on a bowl of shrimp cocktail during her final back flip, causing an involuntary diversion into the still smouldering fireplace.

"How did your mum die, Charlie?" people asked much later, when I went to London and was almost on the verge of leaving it again.

"Usefully," I replied.

218

The accident occurred in the depths of winter and I was the shittiest kid on the planet.

THE SCIENCE OF SADNESS:

She rose in the terrible grey of a Pacific dawn, her stomach dry, her mouth tasting of honey and lemon juice. She ran a bath, looked in the mirror and felt like smashing it with a poisoned apple.

Dried and dressed, she went into the kitchen. The clock said 6.45. Too early yet. She had a sniff outside. The surf carried through the cool air. A big old Buick passed by on the highway above, dragging tin cans and leaving behind it shrieks of laughter.

She made coffee and turned the radio on. Alice Faye sang *I've Got My Love To Keep Me Warm.*

She shivered.

Back in the bedroom she discovered a window was missing. The shards lay outside on the footpath. She suddenly remembered the dream she had had before waking – of being out on the east coast again and collecting horseshoe crabs. She wondered who had broken the window.

The phone lay on the bed. It was 7.30. She decided to call the Institute. She couldn't recall the number and further minutes were lost looking for her address book. Finally, she got hold of an answering machine. That was strange. She left a hesitant message:

"Oh – er – hello. This is Doctor Lovell – Doctor Janet Lovell – of Applied Oceanics... I'm sorry but I can't come in today: got my usual trouble again – y'know... helluva bad – a bitch. I'm sorry – I should be in on Monday or maybe Tuesday – maybe... er sorry, I'll see you soon, okay? Bye – thanks..."

She wondered whether she should call Charles. It would be civilised. He'd come through with the latest payment. He was at the British Embassy till midweek at least – unless he'd taken off for Madrid already. No, she decided to leave it. She wouldn't call him. No.

Her single case packed, she locked the door and left the key under a pot of poinsettias. She looked at the house and out to the cold ocean, seemingly untouched by the approach of daylight. A National Guardsman dozed on the pier.

She took the compact up onto the Scenic Route and through the tunnel. Patrol cars and APCs were everywhere but miraculously she wasn't pulled in. She nosed out into the rubbish and smog-heavy palms. Unusual smells filtered into the car as she took the ramp up to the airport.

The terminal was unusually empty for a Sunday morning. The rabbit factor had caused most people to lie low glued to the television set.

There was one man on the customs check-out. He was as ugly as sin and his tie was too tight.

"England, Doctor Lovell? Do I read your ticket correctly?"

The man sidled with mock graciousness to his telephone.

"Don't do that – er..." she glanced at his photo ID, "...Vernon. You know I'm part of the Institute. I'm immune. You must let me through."

She proffered her case.

"Science. The cause of science..."

She grinned lamely.

Vernon blackened – glanced over at the unemptied ashtrays and cocktail glasses, the litter of *National Enquirers*.

"Science?" he said slowly. "What a sad occupation."

A lonely looking Hercules was purring out on the tarmac. The plate glass shivered with the vibration.

Quickly Vernon stamped her papers.

"It'll cost you, Doctor," he said.

"Okay," she replied.

The haze was lifting as they climbed up onto the aircraft together.

NOTES FROM ALICIA'S DIARY:

...And the water like cinnamon and oil. Alicia out of the house by battered dust-encrusted palms, scabby dog and pups by the harbour in that strangely stenched atmosphere.

The girl (a little frayed) meets him – Leonardian hair, legs down to big boots. Both are fresh off *La Cassara*. Into the bar,

Alicia so melting with that ruddy Basque and fiery eye. Paul moves to the espresso with his friends from school.

"I love this man," says the boss slipping on a well-known American singer. Harmonics enter out into the fresh night, still with that bleak arse-ended taint. The darkness is very new. Car lights move across the pane glass. Alicia smiles at them.

Dingoes on the beach woofing under arc lamps. One is a friend; 'Ballburster' they used to call him when they were really kids. Or *El Lobo*, maybe. Mopeds on the pavement – red, rotting pedals: baskets used to holding chickens.

Alicia retains her smile as he comes to the table. Nut shells crack, fag butts squelch under his heavy feet.

She says, "Thank you, Paul."

Alicia rises. She passes the row of new TV games making sure of the fleetness of her reflection. She always did that. Her eyes soften, aware of the artificial manner – but she couldn't keep it up. The boss puts on the radio and the news talks about the Islamic build-up south across the water.

"I won't be long, Paul."

She smiles in the street, mouthing at him.

She hitches north, her final ride in a big Pegaso truck with a muttering Englishman for a travel companion. By midday she's on a cold Atlantic beach flanked by enormous cliffs. The left-behind Mediterranean sands seem foetid and rotten in comparison. The Englishman sits on a rock and cries. Spume nudges through the air. Salt whispers. A low hill inland is crowned with a military college, complete with exquisite peach-coloured stonework. An old man with a stick approaches and says "Hello" to her, white stubble moving in and out of his creases.

There's a dog on the beach. It doesn't look like Ballburster and it might be winking at her with its soft brown eye. Two tyres picked out of the Gulf months ago roll up and down the shoreline.

The dog plays with the tyres and hums to himself.

BLUE CENTURY:
Three days out from Heathrow and still on the run. Three days into the Fortnight War and still running. Made it through the cordon.

Stole a car. We were in quite a state. What was Doctor Janet saying? I don't know. She whispered horribly, gripping my arm – pointing. I sent the car up the railroad sleepers, the suspension getting ripped to hell. I could see the armoured division through the larch trees (birds scattering), and swerved off the track and into a barbed wire fence. The rear tyres made a strange noise: like an opera. Doctor Janet sang in tune too. She threw up: we both had the sweat: a band of cool heat went up and down our bodies. Pine needles battered the windscreen. Sunlight in through branches onto the cluttered black-top. How beautiful. We roared around the armoured cars, letting off a few rounds. A soldier jumped in front and he landed on the roof on his stomach and he grinned in at us. A bullet sang into the passenger seat and Doctor Janet slumped forward. I thought that she was dead. Blood was all over the place. I had a feeling that it might screw up the transmission so I stopped the car in a hurry. We went into a crash barrier at a 110 but I hung on as we carved a course through three gardens and a crazy English potting shed. And then we were back in the street on an oil slick, the exhaust turning to flame. I kicked Jan out the door – blood in the air: teeth spilling out as her jaw struck the pavement. Sweet American. The car turned and turned. Perhaps it would never stop. I think my arm was missing by then and my stomach had a window on the world. I hit a wall. And another: an indoor swimming pool. Great. Foetal imagery: hard exterior, wet freefall within. Beats the customs check-out gig. The big car shuddered and stopped. A Jeep pulled up a hundred yards away, threw in Doctor Janet. She was alive and yelping and giving out strange screams. She gave little gummy whoops: "Bastard, Vernon, bastard, bastard..." She let me off easy, I guess. Soldiers in Goofy masks and hunky plastic one-piece suits advanced towards me. Hi guys. I was shaking all over. My eyes closed. "Goodbye, Blue Century," I whispered.

SALIDA:

On the day before the evacuation of Haro, the Englishman walked out to the old cathedral – the ancient stronghold of Navarre. No one was there. The section behind the altar was huge and covered with floorboards. A deflated football lay in a corner together with an empty wine bottle. Several chapels had been broken into – the candles were scattered like machine gun cartridges.

Charles had decided not to return to the Embassy in Los Angeles – goodness knows why they had flown him in anyway. His only previous Spanish experience had been donkey wrangling on the Costa Blanca. He wondered if Janet had 'phoned him as he allowed the smell of age to flow into his lungs and smiled.

It had begun to snow so he got a lift north on a big truck carrying mini-tractors. The highway was clogged with troops and equipment moving the other way. Charles had a fellow traveller besides the driver. A girl. But she said nothing. They clung together and walked on a beach and looked at a dog and left for England on the last boat out of Santander. The invaders took the city on the day after and the Moors screamed in their graves.

HOT FINGERS:

I thought it was the crabs again. Like on the east coast. The horseshoe crabs on my bed. Sponges and arc lamps attended me as little pieces of armour slid off the blanket and rattled onto the floor. A man lay across the ward, his hair and beard a frighteningly premature white.

It was only later that I noticed my fingernails were missing.

GOD'S OSTRICH:

Disgusted that the Blue Century had taken him back, the prisoner Vernon slipped his guards and made his way to the swimming pool. It was empty and the marine biologist was nowhere to be found.

A lugger took him cross-channel and he bribed his way aboard a Turkish troop carrier scurrying East. It was Day Twelve of the Fortnight War and he was still vomiting hideously and the sun shone through his palms. The soldiers moaned and hummed to a bazouki, their voices lost in the flame-stolen atmosphere.

Vernon had a few little dreams about stolen icebergs and a drink dispenser and *The National Enquirer*. Then the sun came back and the carrier stopped for fuel. No water. A tall tower with a white flag. The smell of rancid dictamnus: an impression of fatness, heat in his nose and the dream returns. It returns, collapses, crumbles – the ice flaking into white blood cells that shrivel and pop. A saxophone plays in Vernon's head – unremembered muzak from the airport terminal: the clatter and squeak of luggage.

*

Weeks later, he was on the desert floor. Caterpillar tracks headed over the horizon with its haloed pall of dust. Dumped at last. Without thinking, Vernon looked inside himself and discovered that his heart had stopped beating. The blood in his arteries had ceased to circulate and even now was buckling down to eternity.

He was aware of every grain of sand beneath his dead body, every hair follicle on his forearm. The condition of non-breathing did not disturb him.

A scraggy, hitherto unnoticed ostrich hopped forwards, creating welcome shadow. It spoke. All the animals were speaking now. It meant the End of the World had come.

"Wild Vernon. A stork took you in and I'll take you out. Stupid bastard. And you thought you were one of the innocent. You thought you'd survive, Vernon..."

The beak of the ostrich came down, plucked up a part of him.

"But open your ears, Vernon – your mind, Vernon... for on this slimy planet, Vernon... God only wants the guilty left alive......"

*

When he awoke, he was in Heaven.

THE SWORDFISH FAN:

The Reservoir was half an hour's walk from the road. It fell at me out of the fog like a battleship. The air was warm and strangling. The migratory frogs croaked in a stream at my feet.

"The last frogs, Charles," came a voice from above me. It was Janet. "The last frogs in the world."

"Oh?"

I scrambled up the bank, clutching the cement-blocked wall for support. Small rocks scuttled by me.

Janet was on top in a dufflecoat. She was sipping at something out of a bottle when I reached her. The leg must have been playing up again. She was gazing out into the water. A man stood next to her and ate a sandwich through his white beard. A small pile of bones lay at his feet.

"A sheep, Mr Lovell," the man said. "Always common, even in the old days. They say there's a big dog out on the moors. Would have taken a sheep, no problem. I could scrub the skull and blow-dry it for your mantelpiece if you like."

Janet threw off her duffel. Her thin shirt was drenched in sweat. She removed a packet from a breast pocket.

"Watch," she said.

Her hand released a shower of pellets – mutant tiny dried porpoises – into the thick air. Self-motivated, they spread across the surface of the water in a desperate race for the first touchdown...

The water exploded. A dozen sloppy-soft beaks broke surface tension – sucking, gurgling in the food from God. A fin thrashed, the brightness of an injured gill.

"*Xiphias gladius*," she said. "Swordfish..."

Waves tenderly kneaded the wall at our feet. A pair of eyes over a strangely snubbed nose surveyed us from below.

"Dan made me a beautiful fan out of their snouts. It's so hot these days."

Dan's Santa beard gave an acknowledging grin. He rose and slid down into the valley behind us. "I'll check the new arrivals," he called back. The atmosphere swallowed the rest of his words.

I looked over at Janet. She was drunk and attempting to light a cigarette. I noticed that her wellingtons were coming apart. Her time in hospital had shrunken her. As well as the bullet she had had to have a total detoxification: the usual cocktail of pesticides and E numbers. The familiar re-build of bodily systems totally broken down by artificiality, by civilisation. The Fortnight War had ended fifteen years ago but a part of her fought on.

A swordfish lunged out of the water, reversed on its tail dolphin-like and leant a flipper over the balustrade. The scientist opened her mouth and breathed over the fish, her teeth glowing in the blue flare light.

"One has to do that," she told me. "You reveal yourself. You flash every natural signal there is to flash. It's the way of the wild." Her hand reached down to the water. "How's your Spanish girl? And your son – the one with the name like a gun... Enfield?"

Her hand patted the snub-nose. Her hands were wrinkled. Flakes of vermilion nail varnish spotted the fish's hide.

I read my lines. "The Government's very pleased with your work, Jan. They asked me to tell you."

She looked up. "Good."

"It's wonderful. We should be ready for a full-scale re-seed of the Atlantic in twenty-five years."

"If the Atlantic comes back."

"Um, I expect they taste good." I almost expected her to hush me to a whisper so her beloved fish couldn't hear me.

But she just said: "Yes."

Conversation was assuming the gumless empty quality that marked the last years of our marriage. I suppose we would have just faded away eventually; two shadows circling each other with minimal eye contact. But the complete breakdown of just about everything was a reasonable excuse for our parting.

She was speaking again and stroking her pet. "Last fish in the world," she said.

"Yes."

"They eat cabbages too. It's very convenient." Her fingers shook. "My wonderful work... saving sea slugs and cock salmon high on oestrogen... noble." She convulsed.

"Is it always this foggy?"

"Always. It helps my surf phobia. The valley sometimes looks just like a huge trough. I nearly went under a wave when I was a little girl. At Laguna." She took a sip.

It suddenly occurred to me that Janet might be faking her screwy scientist bit. California? Cycle trips down the hill to Alice's? One of Bradbury's golden children? Like tooototally gnarled, man?

226

She never talked about California. It was rather like she was quietly drowning and her whole life was uncoiling for the benefit of both of us.

I heard a soft whistling. It was Dan down at the brook, catching frogs for tagging.

Janet sat and let her legs dangle over the side of the dam.

"I'm glad you came, Charlie Lovell," she murmured, slipping into the water, allowing it to creep over her mouth, the sun-bleached hair.

"See you later," said a voice.

Janet grinned underwater with her new friends.

The first swordfish peered at me over its blunted snout.

"See you later," it said again.

THE HOUND FROM HELL:

I'm back. Determined in my quest to make strangeness commonplace and absolute. I'm hooked up to an unknown purpose. My paws ache, my spine rattles from my tail to my neck. My head hangs idle – a thing of non-consequence. Young and eager: no more.

I skipped through the burning fields, hackles singed but glorying in that. The rain cooled me. I swam across estuaries, galloped on clifftops: put in enigmatic appearances on the most unwanted occasions – relished my sudden departure.

I raced the tide's reach. The sand of the sea went dry and the grains rasped on me. I ripped out my hair in the heat and was a scabby hairless thing. I was a Hound from Hell. I liked that one. The idea of a personal mythology was new and exciting. Out there in the desert I waited for the Devil but he never showed. I ached and stumbled to the high ground: plotted and self-made my role as conscience to all Mankind. I don't think they'll see it that way. I've tried. They don't recognise me. I lope through them and they giggle to see the dead run by.

And where did I come from? From what swart hole? I must surely have a bleak, obscure origin. Who can tell? Who will open and discover?

Put your hand in your pocket, pull out the key, feel in the

lock, look up and around at your own natural history – and Guess Who's there?

COMING BACK:

She was in the bath when the grandchildren arrived.

Dozing in the moist seaweed, cooled by the shadow of the hut: they caught her unawares – alone with her old, empty body.

Poor little Glacé. Giggling demonic Wrack. They stood black against the sun, their useless webbed feet curling in the sand.

"Sorry, Gran," whispered the little girl.

Alicia struggled out and dried herself.

"Never mind, children. Change is a funny thing." She squinted at the desert, past the cacti patch, the Englishman's grave marked with a cross of whalebone. She never connected Charles with the grave. She thought life and death should always remain apart.

They went inside. The darkness became clearer, the mushroom plots a hazard to be avoided. Tea was made, watercress proffered. The tiny battered *Encyclopedy for Children* lay open, always available for inspection.

They talked to her about their dad Enfield and his pigeons, and precipitation and the new bout of tornadoes. Of new toys and of new things.

"There's a wild wolf on the Dogger Dunes," said Wrack, spitting cress with enjoyable menace.

The old lady smiled. "A wolf? A real wolf? Surely no more wolves." She glanced out of the open doorway at the whalebone grave. "Your grandfather always spoke of a wolf that crossed the burning stubble fields in his youth."

"It's true," put in Glacé. "He's right. Big and black... pounding with an unknown purpose. Er – that's what daddy says..."

Her brother bubbled at his tea. "Dad says it's the Hound from Hell."

Their Gran got up and went to the doorway. The sun had paled since they had gone inside. You could see the ball of it.

The children realised it was time to go. They trooped out well pleased and said their goodbyes leaning against the shrunken ferryboat.

They turned at the top of the hillock and waved down to Alicia's little old figure by her sundial of a hut, the shadow shooting across the dunes towards them.

The short saunter home was enjoyable. There was a lingering at well-loved spots and a smiling at each other... a sniff at the air and a *knowing*.

That night, under a single star and an absent moon, the sea came back.

SHEEP AND TORPEDOES:

They had sailed a month on the shallow sea, stealing fish eggs and peering down at the remains of civilisation. Their diesel had deserted them long ago. The boat was old and had sails so the wind was their master – drunken in its irregularity. The rain fell so their throats were never parched: yet their stomachs always held that empty ache; their skins, that terrible wrinkle of salinisation. Ears alert for sound. Lips pulled back – hardened with nature.

Enfield had fallen overboard and lost his contact lenses. He had been dozing at the time. He thought he heard the sound of surf off their bow... and the bleating of new lambs trapped on headlands.

An ostrich flew by on the seventeenth day. No one remarked on it. No birds had been mentioned. It circled round as if preparing for a torpedo run only to dodge away at the last moment. Its snakey-nakey neck looked extraordinary in flight. What an ugly angel! And they rang their Christmas bells and chowder pans to make it go away.

You see – they knew their mission. They knew the nature of their interviewee. He had been ignored for too long. The time had come for him to turn and talk. Wrack and Glacé took turns up the mast and cousin Jenny lay in the scuppers, her tape recorder clasped to her chest like a clicking teddy bear.

And when the dawn of the thirtieth day appeared with the abruptness of scissors and paper, Enfield knew that the sound of the breakers came from somewhere other than inside his head. The sky that morning was not a beautiful thing yet they all felt a bursting joy within them. The rain howled down as they fell ashore. As the four seadogs dragged each other up onto the beach, onto the forgotten land.

GLACÉ'S GHOST:

Glacé was the first to see the ghost.

They had not been in the house a month, had not ceased their pursuit of the seadog-wolf for a further two, when sleep's impulse slipped her from her bed and she awoke in the library at 3am.

Branches squeaked against the window pane: all the bookshelves and cases of preserved mammals had disappeared. The walls groaned with the musty weight of tapestries – yet the beams were new and perfumed with freshness.

A long table was set in silver for a wedding banquet. Ginger shakers twinkled with an unknown light: wonderful fruits, shrimp cocktail, squid and baked beetles on cream cloths... grouse-cuddled melon and the oldest, darkest wine.

The woman was a little younger than Glacé. She was coming down the table in a weightless cartwheeling somersault... brushing... touching... and everything she touched and brushed fell slowly as if through water.

The woman smiled. Her snowy wrap fell about her as she back-flipped onto the floor – a perfect landing.

The ghost gazed at Glacé with a curious eye.

"Whatever anyone says," croaked the ghost, "there's always a second chance."

GEORGIA UNDER GLASS:

There were elephants growing in the garden.

Beyond the neo-classic masonry and hydrangea clumps, through the procession of poplars and across the lawn which only caught the sun in the afternoon, the elephants had their rest.

Great and grey, their trunks in the red earth, their bums up to heaven, their coarse ear hair swaying in the mellow teatime breeze. Bumble bees played joyfully around the idle flapping tails or did aerobatics over the hieroglyphed bellow-hides.

Great Uncle Enfield told me once – when I was young and years

230

and years before we actually got any – that this was a recent development as far as elephants were concerned. The incredible bulk of their bodies made osmosis exceptionally difficult.

"They walked once," he said. "They uncurled their short little log-legs and went stomping off through the wet jungles of India... 1, 2, 3, 4, 1, 2, 3, 4..." (this was when I was very young) "...almost like a horse."

Sister Sue had a horse but it needed a good deal of looking after – soil changes twice a week. Beautiful animal, though.

Out at the farm, on the far side of the river, they have African elephants. Bigger ears. They have to keep them in a permanently sodden trench of manure – pure bullshit – all through the year. Cellular changes, you know.

That June – the June we first planted elephants – was explosively hot. From the dispersing cumulus at dawn to dusk's warming chill, the sun blasted these islands with love and tenderness.

We often took tea in the garden during that glowing season. We sat and read all the old books. I always remember my favourite: Great Uncle Enfield would hold up the *Encyclopedy for Children* in his great hands and say (as if for the first time): "Question! What is the most useful art to society?" And of course all the others would let me trill: "It is agriculture or the art of cultivating the earth to make it produce fruits which maintain men..."

It was the twenty-seventh summer at the house in the woods near the sea. Out on the terrace by the bulldogs and armadillos (a mini-greenhouse for each of the armadillos) we would gather. Aunt Glacé and Great Uncle Enfield, cousin Jenny, sister Sue, nephew Frank and me – naughty Georgia... We all made a dainty rendezvous at 16.45 complete with tie and tails, corset and hat pins. Corsets came back in that year, I remember.

The view from the terrace was very beautiful, of course. I would like to think of it as the most exquisite in the whole of England. Jenny and Frank certainly thought so and they've been to Europe!

Like an operation the river slit through an ordered and peaceful plaquet-flooring of small fields and holdings, disappearing out and away around the world. Amongst this loveliness glinted the weather stations and oxygenaires – the latter often roofed over by squadrons of hawks and kestrels taking advantage of the artificial gusts: pure, sweet, plant-killing oxygen.

We would stay there, collapsed in our garden furniture, until far into the evening. With closed lids or upturned eyes looking for the cruising night-clouds we could hum and sing and exchange stories. I particularly remember one of Jenny's – when she took off for the Antarctic armed with a Biology BSc from the new Lovell Institute, only to be rained on by frozen penguins. First one stiff bird, then a few more, then loads and loads – all thumping onto the glacier: all dead: all frozen. All waiting for germination.

As often as not we went to bed late. It confused the plants. Through my open window with its view of the distant tree-clad downs, I would drift off with the growls and grunts and raspings – the midnight voice of our wonderful garden.

My dreams were green.

So the endless summer groped through that busy time of year. August saw the arrival of the little bats – their tiny veined wings transparent and obscene in the blazing sun, their heads invisible and forgotten in the dark earth. Herons and bullocks followed. Gazelles took especially well and Great Uncle Enfield considered them his prize specimens.

Engrossed in this creation euphoria and planting like there was no tomorrow, we felt like angels. We felt golden.

It was a considerable shock to us all, therefore, when nephew Frank discovered himself growing out of the upstairs study wall.

A momentary brush between bookshelves and the poor boy was doomed. His own natural history fanned out from his finger tips and his sap rose. Unfortunately, the rest of us were down in the East Field at the time, inspecting the latest batch of iguanas. Frankie was left... growing...photosynthesising... for three hours, alone in that terrible musty old room. He wrote a letter before he died. It was horrible.

As September came with St Luke's little summer, so did reports from the lands around. Frank was not alone in his fate. In his *evolution*. Not everyone died. Many grew and turned doom into adaption. We sighted two aircraft in half a week – old transports trailing Virginia creepers. I'd only ever seen a 'plane once before, through the fields in Croydon.

In the gathering dark of a particular 6pm, I padded out through the poplars and across the neo-classic rubble to where the elephants grew. Their faint, heavy sighs and the sighs of the wind as it crossed the valley in lazy rushes chilled me.

I was frightened in the blackness.

Glacé and Jenny had been snapped up by otters growing in the river mud that morning. Great Uncle Enfield, wan and shapeless, said it was an accident. As he tearfully adjusted his polka-dotted bow tie, I knew – and he knew I knew – that his jacket pocket... his inside jacket pocket... contained a short and beautiful communication dictated by Aunt Glacé into Jenny's tape machine. A soft conspiracy, a suicide pact.

Sister Sue uprooted her prize pony and galloped off a cliff.

I cried under the elephants and time was meaningless.

*

In fascinating indifference, my Great Uncle and I lived on and continued our work – our harmless weekend pursuit. So through the fields we would potter, through the living things and right down to the river we would go – an old man and a young girl together and alone. And in the pale of the day we might return to the house and mull over natural history and the new generation and the pristine and thoughtful art of God...

And on perhaps the last day of summer, on perhaps the last day that we were part of Mankind, a wolf appeared at the garden gates. He worried at the soft earth and tried to plant his snout, tried to make himself grow.

I helped Great Uncle Enfield down the path past the wriggling spider canes and we peered through the gates together. The wolf had huge soft dark eyes. He was exhausted, as if he'd been running for years and years on an unknown purpose.

A light rain began to fall, pattering on a thousand leaves. The pattering was like a whisper, a call.

The English Soil Society

The wolf ceased pawing the ground and looked up at us. He seemed to recognise Great Uncle Enfield and one of the soft eyes winked. The wolf spoke in a limerick sing-song. The wolf lilted: *There once was a Hound from Hell...*

We looked at ourselves. Great Uncle's whiskers were leafy and veined.

My fingernails flew away like sycamore aeroplanes.

Our branches reached up like fragile things under glass.

The plant flicked its tail and spoke again.

Wimbledon & Salcombe 1981 – 94

Born in the Forest

I'm a gladesman. Off the road. Through the forest. Dancing on the
bluebells. I'm natural in these stripes of sunlight and shadow. Far
now, too far the billybully blue boys with their hail and that same
old flash. I left them down Harvester Lane shoving their sticks
into the nettles as if I were dead already. I play my arms into the
sunlight. Just me, Old Gladey. Just an old earth shrinker out for a
thousand year stretch. I got planted among the hawthorn, that
stinkgrowth of mediaeval Frenchmen. Wild garlic was healthier
then before the mind and pestle of Man got hold of it. I might have
lived longer. The warm grave. The quiet bed in the forest. This
quiet waiting with the humus. Ah yes, the plants died with a
strange and smirking manner. Now water whiffs in. I scrabble
down the bank. I lie in the stream, my legs under a pile of oak
leaves that cover like a rusting heap of snow. I arch my back over
the waters, throw my arms to the other side. Get wild. Cartwheel
the deluge and so I'm on the run again with the tracker dogs (tame
wolves – remarkable bastards) whimpering like it always was.
There's a field – no strips, it's common land – opening up over the
stream. The grass like crystal in orange light, all old it looks. Just
very old for the early time of day. Dew falls out of nowhere as I
race for the hedgerow. The dew streaks me. And now I'm hiding
out in that hedge made of the witches' bladder and that bloody
hawthorn. A right old stink. And a smell – quick! a quick! smell of

fear. No. A bloody rabbit, a bloody priest, a bloody black Frenchy rabbit. Good or bad, Bun, you're mine. Should have used your ears before I hacked them off. A good old munch. A bit stinky. I've sent you to the burrower's heaven, Bun. We shall meet again. But now the billyboys and the snarling dripjaws are fooling around by the stream. I pick some blackberries – one of the seven thousand and twenty-three varieties but I can't place it. The billys are still after me, full of casual desperation. They skirt the far bank looking for the ford. Has it gone? No, a newie. Bugger. I skim the hedge and scramble over a five-bar. Smooth stone road, dead clever-looking. Italian job. The billys' wake on the water brings forth laughter from unknown quarters. They make it. They're up on the sward kicking at the fairy rings (or faerie for the fairy literate few) all holler and promotion. I dash and diddle a bit on my own part, tempted by a few bird's nests and so on, but I guess that this thing's a bit big so I spur and prick myself just as those boys and hounds tackle the gate. I wriggle in and out, up and then further than that, climbing the bark ladders in an effort to escape. I'm clinging to a branch two copses and a field further on, when said branch breaks sending the Gladesman into a bloody old hen house fifteen foot down. I'm all poached and shelled and cause havoc in a kitchen garden before coming to the kitchen itself. It has four strong walls with a veggie roof and a wimple and I peer in the windows. There's an old gran inside at her doze-off time. I consider a touch of stink, but reckon that the years have left her slipperiness a mere memory. The darling girl has left her but she's less than an acorn to me, I think, leaping in over the sill. Naturally, I put up a bit of a racket, with pans and stewed fruit all knocked to hell, so she starts up and drags her shawl to herself and gives me a bit of a look. The darkness comes in like night behind her but it's just in my head, just a humour. She tries to make her legs straight, tries to stand up, but I guess she knows it's all over. She just says "Is it you?" and I say "Yes, it's me" and so we're kind of agreed about that. I sit on the table by the shelf full of bottling fruit and say "Who's in the house, mistress? It looks like a yeo-yeo boy weighed down like a heavy horse with fifty nicker a year. Fixes you up nicely." She says nothing. All enigma. All something in nothing. I play skip through the house and up to the rafters and it's full of bleeding bottling fruit. In a trunk that's been in a war I find some short hose and a scrap of something or other for up top. Stops everything dancing and keeps the jolly sun out, that blazing old bugger. I exit by the front door, bypass the kitchen, don't bother to prattle about departure. Spend my life departing, a non-stop dialogue. The gran's garden is hemmed in by *Castanea Sativa* – massive sweet chestnuts – courtesy of those Italian boys who brung in more than roads. I pause for slight contemplation. Trees always stop me. It's their way with light. The way light moves below them. A shimmering sea on the forest floor. My childhood was full of trees – but dead ones. I took their corpses and made them beautiful. I sheared away the bark, stickied and stank my hands in their sap and watched as it dried in the still air. I was moved, always moved, by trees. And through the trunks come the players in my latest game – like black squirrels come the bully boys panting and stealing from the air and giving nothing. They've seen me and I think about scarpering but I stand still like a sapling. Such a small thing but rooted to the earth like the earth is rooted to the planet. They're pretty near, gasping a cuss or two and wondering what the bugger I'm up to now. And then I see him. He's on his bike coming down the forest path, gears slipping and looking all vicary. He's got a Gladstone bag strapped on the back, showing a marked disinclination to continue the relationship. This is where I get interested. This is where it gets like what-the-butler-saw. So the peelers stop about ten yards off with their bogey-poodles yapping and slerbering. Up comes the priest, bungs his bike on the chestnut leaves. It's been a hell ride for Pastor Pete and he's looking a touch peaky. Lost his bloody bag, of course. Said he would. So cleric and constables rootle in the undergrowth, anxious that I'm not in a sneaking kind of mood. Bag's found, all's well. Out comes the water. Late flowers could use it. Bungs a bit on me too. Rather annoying really. Here it comes. Book's out. Prayer's read. Dead impressive. Waits for me to do it backwards like on the flickers. No go. I stand as still as a thousand year oak, putting on the mystery. A bit of whimpering from the battle-pups. That's good. Thanks, lads. I raise an arm. The blueboys have a whimper too. The Roman collar says, "Tell me your name." Of course I say "You know my name... (I put on the nasty) ...preeeeeest..." He's good, he's doing well. A few trickles of sweat. Nervous blotches like mislaid stigmata flush out on his forehead but he stands his ground. The clouds move quicker, the jolly sun sinks behind the trees in a miscarriaged sunset. The world goes red. I say "I am Him who has come. I've gone and I've come." I toe the leaves at dusking time: "You are Man and I am your Son. We are all angels and we have fallen together. Like these leaves we go down, not by intent but by nature. You crinkle and dry. You are not yourselves. You are other people." He's gone quiet. The coppers and their wolves have scarpered. I say "You talk of yourselves and you mean Mankind. You will always suffer. You will always fall. Just be kind to other people." I leave the cleric there, asleep on his feet. Like a gas lamp waiting to be lit, waiting to throw out its message. I turn and skipple out towards the clever Italian road. "That's it for a bit," I call back at him. He still stands there. Could stay there till that Big Day when we all stay where we're put. Old gran watches me from behind a goat willow. Lot of people looking now. All having a peer. And I walk among them like I seem to have done so many times. And they open their mouths and all start gabbing at each other – no... they all gab *to* each other. They smile. Laughter teeters out of them like a lost relation. "Hello," they all say. "How are you? How do you do, do you do? Quite well thank you, in fact I've never felt better." So I leave them having a right old laugh. I walk away from the too early sunset to where the sky's all dark and the first twinklies are waking up. I walk away and I know they'll fall again. They'll forget me in a year or a century. No matter. No sick or shame. For I was born in the forest. I was born in the Glade where the tiniest shaft of the jolly sun burns with the tiniest of life, then burns bigger, bigger and bigger. There's so much time; there's too much of it. I have a chuckle myself as I pass through the last of the friendly branches and step up onto that clever clever road and walk away through the darkness.

Nest

Once upon a time, a bird flew up to the highest cloud and laid her eggs there. She stole the twigs from sky trees to build her nest. The new-born chicks rolled out and played in the rain dust as if it were fresh-from-the-box Ready Brek...

The pictures were beautifully painted. Each egg was a subtle shade of yellow. Mummy used to boil peeled chestnuts at Easter: Lindy remembered helping her gather the early gorse flowers to turn the wintered nuts the very same colour.

And the clouds in the book were perfect: the artist had obviously studied clouds very closely. The wings of the birds had been more taxing, however: they looked like frog's feet, moist and webbed, sprouting from the chicks' little bald backs. The wings were peculiar: by necessity, the product of fantastic imagination.

*

The toadstools were on the move.

They sucked in the light from the Ready Brek clouds and gave nothing in return. Tina couldn't get out of bed: toadstools were all over the floor, inking the carpet with darkness.

They chatted amongst themselves and smelt funny.

The English Soil Society

*

Lindy put down the book and yawned, hoping to encourage Tina to do the same. Too late, her baby sister was sleeping already. Lindy hoped Mummy might buy a new bulb for the toadstool night light or Tina would be having nightmares again.

No problem for Benjamin: he'd already be sweetly dreaming about tomorrow afternoon; of that endless playtime between school and tea.

*

Benjamin was digging in the bushes at the end of the garden.

He'd just come back from the beach where he'd tried to harpoon a starfish with his Action Man's little MADE IN HONG KONG harpoon. He'd finally taken the starfish's leg off with a razorshell and was burying the leg now with a mini-entrenching tool amidst the overblown blowzy peonies. Action Man himself – now in the black polar neck of the French resistance – watched impassively, beret-clad head leaning against the brick wall, the peony petals a crimson army groundsheet.

*

"Aye aye, private..."

It was Mr Alec smiling over the wall. He pointed at the doll. "That feller would never pass muster with Monty, Ben. No pullovers at the battle for Tobruk. They needed all the wool for the northern convoys." Mr Alec should know. He'd seen a lot of service in the War: the Western Desert, Borneo, Jugoslavia. Tankman, skin-diver, secret operations...

He was nice and often leant over and passed on his stories to Benjamin and taught Lindy the names of flowers.

Mr Alec had been in his bungalow longer than they had been in theirs; but he used to go away for long holidays, sometimes six months at a time. He didn't seem to have a wife and spoke to

240

Mummy quite a lot.

Lindy knew more about it.

*

Benjamin went indoors.

It was time for *Thunderbirds* and he had to gather the relevant Dinky toys around him before the programme began. Thunderbird 4 – a gift from Mr Alec – had been lost in the bath a week ago and would not be in attendance. That had been a bad night. Mummy got her finger stuck down the plug hole and broke her nail off.

The jagged stump had penetrated Benjamin's ear till he screamed.

*

Lindy worked hard on her drawing.

The other children were outside in the playground for morning break. They were running around in a great patch of shadow. The school had been built in the disused bowl of a fossil-bound quarry: the extremes of light and darkness could be quite pronounced as the sun swung around through the day.

Lindy was doing extra under Mr Forrest's watchless eye. Mr Forrest was reading the latest *Look & Learn* – it was Friday – and drinking milky coffee in the corner.

Lindy had her tongue out so long it dried up. She'd forgotten all about her sherbet flying saucer and was trying to draw frog feet wings. She started in one corner. Her style was linear and minute. Her work was exact but lacked solidity – as if the nature of her subject made Lindy's style like the air itself.

The reel-to-reel tape machine was playing *Swinging Safari*. It was Mr Forrest's favourite. He usually hummed along but now he was angrily trying to find the clunkity pause button.

"Stay there, Linda." Mr Forrest was looking out of the window. "Keep up with your sketching."

Mr Forrest was out of the room in an instant. Lindy peeped through the glass. The boys had found a frog – all wetness and

241

eyes like black gobstoppers – and surrounded it. Some had removed their school ties and were using them as whips, flicking the creature as it gasped about the circle in pain and confusion. Others had waterpistols (flavour of the week) filled with Fairy Liquid (new that morning) and were trying to squirt the frog's eyes.

Someone had found a cricket bat.

But Mr Forrest was there, a boy's head in each of his great hands, the money and keys jingling in his pockets as he shook and pushed them to the tarmac. The pistols were crushed underfoot, the cricket bat grabbed and used on elbows and kneecaps. The whole playground was screaming. All the girls rushed into the toilet.

Lindy had seen Benjamin in the circle: not quite at the back, not precisely at the front. Sometimes her little brother looked like a stranger. No, a different creature.

Not human at all.

*

Lindy placed the frog's fidgeting body in sheets of hard toilet roll and rammed it into the depths of her satchel.

She peered in throughout the day. Lindy had read that the frog's gobstopper eyes didn't like the light. At lunchtime, she gingerly spooned in some mash and beetroot and left the satchel hanging in the dimness of the cloakroom. At 2.30, she managed to induce one of her nose bleeds and gave the frog a peep on the way to the lavatories: the amphibian's neck slowly pulsed, its mouth stuffed with mashed potato.

She raced home at the bell and just before *Crackerjack* took some scissors and buried the frog's feet under the peonies. She left the rest of the creature in a big puddle outside Mr Alec's gate.

The throb in its neck was quite faint now, but Lindy was sure it would grow new feet soon.

*

Mummy knelt on the floor by their bed: long lashes, high silvery-white collar, hair like Dusty Springfield. Her eyes closed in prayer and she looked like a panda.

"Dear God: please bless Lindy, Benjamin, Tina and Mummy and keep them and children everywhere safe always."

"*And* the birds, Mummy," said Lindy.

"Ready Brek bird-bird," chirped Tina.

Mummy smiled. "*And* the birds. For ever and ever. Amen. Now be good girls for me."

Mummy leant forward and kissed them with her pale tangerine lips. She drew the curtains on a world outside that was still bathed in sunlight.

Benjamin shuffled out to his little bed in the hallway with his *Stingray* annual. Mummy fought the contents of her handbag by the front door: a final fuss with a blond curl in the mirror – Mr Alec would notice – and she was gone.

The girls talked in whispers in their pinkish semi-darkness.

Mummy had forgotten the lightbulb again.

*

The toadstool's surface was slippery and cold. It reached for miles above her head. Tina's moist hands left a snail trail as they slid slowly down the great white trunk.

Her slippers looked so far away.

*

Mummy and Mr Alec took Benjamin on a jaunt once.

Just Benjamin, just the once.

Many years later, Benjamin would recall winning a warm bottle of Schweppes bitter lemon at some forgotten village's church fete. The contents were liberally vomited into the back of Mr Alec's Triumph Herald on the way home.

Mummy said nothing at the time.

*

Mr Alec looked over the wall on Saturday morning and smiled down at Tina who was busy excavating mud onto her white socks and

The English Soil Society

Ladybird sandals.

"Found some worms, darling?" Mr Alec seemed tired behind his smile.

The little girl stared up and gurgle-giggled. "Worm-worm."

Mr Alec held up a tiny fluffy white kitten just like you see on the telly. "Look, Tina. Mr Alec's got a puss-cat."

"Speaking of worms, Alec – " Mummy was suddenly there with a giant pair of sunglasses on her nose.

Her fingers worried at an unlit cigarette. The day was overcast.

*

The toadstools were trying to get on the bed. Their cloth-clad flexes enabled them to get just *so* far before they tumbled back to the floor. Some lay crying. That fall must have hurt.

*

Sunday lunchtime and Lindy was cooking fishfingers.

She'd been wearing Mummy's sunglasses and had blindly torn her hand opening the baked beans. As she ran her broken skin under the cold tap, Lindy stared out into the garden.

A bee was walking up the stem of a Japanese anemone just outside the window. It carefully slipped between the great petals and began its nuzzle amongst the stamens. It seemed to doze in the June sun.

Lindy cut some bread and removed her glasses just in time to see the pollen-stuffed bee staggering back down to the flower bed.

She turned to the cooker – but later fancied she saw the bee making a dash for it across the lawn.

*

The kitten looked like it had fallen.

Benjamin had it in his hand, the little heart pumps tickling his fingers like miniature electric shocks. He didn't consider himself a cruel boy – wasn't he in tears? – but his greatest wish was that

244

the kitten would disappear, that it would crawl away under the garden gate.

Lindy helped him bury it. Tina watched as she made little circles with twigs.

Benjamin got up in the middle of the night and put his ear to the ground at the bottom of the garden.

The cat was still purring.

*

She could see hundreds of toadstools. They spread over the eiderdown hillside at sunset, their long shadows disappearing into the darkness of Pillow Valley.

Tina crawled amongst them and they seemed like great ketchup-headed trees. She searched and searched, burying her little hands into their hard ceramic trunks, the broken china jagging and bloodying her forearms.

Night crawled up the sheet.

The light must be in here somewhere.

*

The three children sat in the pew next to Mummy. Summer had crept through July and August and they were now at the harvest festival.

Mummy wore her sunglasses and nibbled on a bunch of cherries. She didn't offer them to her children. She was worried about the stones, she told some parents nearby.

Mr Forrest stood up and read a piece about the animals of the land and the fishes of the sea. Some senior girls put on a little play about farmers in Africa.

*

They were burying Mummy.

She laughed as they covered her legs and flowery swimsuit with wet sand and limpet shells. Mummy got sand in her hair but she didn't mind so the children laughed too.

The English Soil Society

The beach was fifteen minute's walk across the fields yet they rarely came together. Mummy looked quite young on this bright tea time after the festival. She had cherry-stained lips and the bruises on her wrists were fading in the late summer sunshine.

Benjamin and Lindy dug a pool for Tina and made some silver boats out of jam tart dishes. The water was warm. A powerboat zoomed by towing a skier.

The three of them went rock-pooling then, leaving Mummy to rub the sand off herself with a towel.

They found a couple of shrimps and Benjamin managed to bucket them. Tina slipped but was all right. They looked back at Mummy and she looked up from her nails and waved.

The children clambered around the point, the pools becoming deeper, their inhabitants more exotic. Lindy captured a family of shore crabs before deciding to turn back.

The tide was coming in and Mummy had gone.

*

Lindy put them to bed that night.

She did cheese on toast and made sure Tina had her bath.

They had found Mummy in Mr Alec's outside loo. As soon as he got back from the beach, Benjamin had set the crabs to wrestling each other on the garden wall. When one went over, he wandered around and found Mummy face down, the straps of her swimsuit twisted up and around her neck. Mr Alec wasn't there.

His Triumph Herald had gone.

It took an hour but they had managed to drag Mummy to their special place among the peonies. Benjamin took one of Mr Alec's spades and dug the hole and for the second time that day the children buried their mother.

*

They built the nest then.

The time was right. The earth and leaves were as sand and

246

shells: amorphous, unmade; ready and waiting for the call of creation.

Benjamin did the bulk of the work, face skewed in concentration. Lindy had spoken quietly, had told him what to do, had explained how each twig should be laid just so. Tina watched them and smiled, the novelty of crouching on two feet unaided almost blotting out the urge – the instinct – to build.

*

The toadstool glowed.

Tina smiled in her sleep.

The night was over and the lightbulb shone with the filaments of dawn.

*

The children had Ready Brek as a special treat next morning.

They all went off to school together, Tina swinging joyously between her older brother and sister. Stuart Dobson had brought a rabbit into school: why couldn't they bring Tina?

All the kids would want one.

*

They raced home at four o'clock. It was beginning to rain at the bottom of the garden.

Lindy wasn't sure if they'd waited long enough but Benjamin threw himself on the ground and started to scratch away at the damp soil. They could hear Mummy's voice. Lindy helped while Tina sat by the nest and waited.

Mummy explained that whatever was coming up would rather emerge at its own pace. They stood back and took great gulps from a bottle of limeade. After half an hour, the soil shivered and something broke through; gummy-eyed, helpless.

They guided it along the garden path and were careful not to tear its frog wings.

*

Tina's arrival was expected at school the next day.

A nurse was waiting in Mr Forrest's office and presently two policemen appeared. And then a police car with several more. Lindy and Benjamin sat in the cloakroom with a couple of strange and strangely smiling ladies. Lindy had one of her nose bleeds.

Tina wandered in the playground, her body balanced by the old quarry walls. She loved the lightbulb-bright sunlight. Her fingers – all pudgy stickiness – followed the contours of the rock, fabulous with fossils. Centipedes and ferns, ammonites and the calcified sand shafts of ancient worms that might have waggled as much as Tina's fingers waggled now: questing, delineating their world.

She found the bird fossil just as the bell was ringing for lessons. Mr Forrest and the nurse had to come out to get her. They couldn't help smiling as they watched the little girl run about the playground; watched her trip and rise again on her imaginary wings just like the birds had once risen so many years before.

Previously from Elastic Press

Trailer Park Fairy Tales by Matt Dinniman

Matt Dinniman combines the mundane with the unusual to fashion twelve intriguing stories where the only certainty is that uncertainty lies ahead. The lives of his characters uniquely exist within a caricaturised America that is simultaneously both frightening yet familiar. Urban fairytales will never be read quite the same way again.

Forthcoming from Elastic Press

The Last Days of Johnny North by David Swann

Dave Swann is, without doubt, one of the most vivid short story writers in the UK today. He brings the landscape and voices of the North to life with an energy that catapults his characters into the universal. Pathos. Irresistible comedy. The raw and beautiful stuff of everyday life. It's all here.

Alison MacLeod, author of 'The Wave Theory of Angels' (Penguin)

For further information visit:

www.elasticpress.com

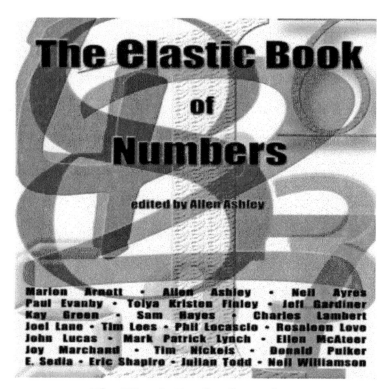

The Elastic Book of Numbers
edited by Allen Ashley

Marion Arnott · Allen Ashley · Neil Ayres
Paul Evanby · Tolya Kristen Finley · Jeff Gardiner
Kay Green · Sam Hayes · Charles Lambert
Joel Lane · Tim Lees · Phil Locascio · Rosaleen Love
John Lucas · Mark Patrick Lynch · Ellen McAteer
Joy Marchand · Tim Nickels · Donald Pulker
E. Sedia · Eric Shapiro · Julian Todd · Neil Williamson

The Elastic Book of Numbers
Available Now From Elastic Press

Numbers rule our lives: clocks, calendars and deadlines; salaries and benefits; tax codes and pin numbers; mortgages, bills and credit limits; the FTSE and the Dow Jones; mobiles, land lines and pagers; binary strings of digitised information held for and about us, instantly accessible.

In this unique collection of 21 stories, some of the world's finest fictioneers examine the effect of numbers on humankind's past, present and future. From the rewriting of history through the thrill of the roulette wheel to the codes controlling the starships, each of these tales engages with numbers in innovative, entertaining and meaningful ways.

www.elasticpress.com